A HAND TOUCHED HIS FOREHEAD, AND WORDS WERE SPOKEN IN A LANGUAGE HE DID NOT UNDERSTAND . . .

Memory vanished and there was only sleep.

When he awoke, there was a soft glow about him. Those ovals, which were not windows, held a light of their own, bathing the room, him—someone stirred and he turned his head slowly. Even that small movement required a vast amount of will and determination. The Lady Aiee smiled at him.

"They have told me of what you have done, and I have come that you may be tended by one of your own courtyard."

Ray's eyes closed despite his desire. "One of your own courtyard." But what had any Murian courtyard to do with him? This was not his world, nor his time, and he was the alien . . .

Fawcett Crest Books
by Andre Norton:

HUON OF THE HORN 24340 $1.95

THE JARGOON PARD 23615 $1.95

JUDGMENT ON JANUS 24214 $1.95

NO NIGHT WITHOUT STARS 23264 $1.75

OPERATION TIME SEARCH 24370 $2.25

SHADOW HAWK 24186 $1.95

SNOW SHADOW 23963 $1.95

STAR GATE 24276 $1.95

STAR RANGERS 24076 $1.95

VELVET SHADOWS 23135 $1.50

THE WHITE JADE FOX 24005 $1.95

OPERATION TIME SEARCH

Andre Norton

FAWCETT CREST • NEW YORK

OPERATION TIME SEARCH

THIS BOOK CONTAINS THE COMPLETE TEXT OF THE
ORIGINAL HARDCOVER EDITION.

Published by Fawcett Crest Books, a unit of CBS Publications,
the Consumer Publishing Division of CBS Inc., by arrange-
ment with Harcourt Brace Jovanovich, Inc.

ISBN: 0-449-24370-2

Printed in the United States of America

First Fawcett Crest printing: February 1981

10 9 8 7 6 5 4 3 2 1

OPERATION TIME
SEARCH

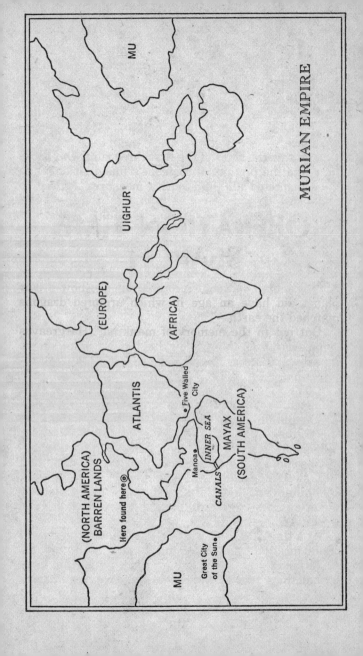

1

"ATLANTIS? A fairy tale!" The man by the window half turned. "You can't be serious—" He began that protest confidently, but that confidence ebbed when there was no change in the expression on his companion's face.

"You saw the films of the first three runs. Did those look like the product of someone's imagination? You have inspected all the security measures devised to make sure they were not. A fairy tale, you say." The quiet gray-haired man leaned a little farther back in his seat. "I wonder what *does* lie buried at the roots of some of our traditional tales. Norse sagas, once dismissed as fiction, have long since been proven to be chronicles of historic voyages. Much of our folklore is distorted clan, tribal, or national record. Dragons—now— Our planet did have an age in which armored dragons marched the earth—"

"But not in the memory of mankind!" Hargreaves came away from the window, his hands resting on his hips, his chin outthrust as if he welcomed battle, verbal at least.

"Don't you ever wonder why certain tales have persisted, why they continue to linger over centuries, told again and again? The man-devouring dragon—"

Hargreaves smiled. "I always heard it that the proper dragon preferred a diet of tender young maidens— until some doughty knight changed his mind for him with sword or lance."

Fordham laughed. "But dragons, in spite of their dietary habits, are firmly fixed in folklore around the world. And their like did once roam the earth—"

"At a time, I repeat, which far antedated the arrival of our most primitive ancestor."

"As far as we know," Fordham corrected. "What I say is that there is a persistence of certain types of fairy

7

stories. When we set up this project—and you know the reason for it—we had to have a starting point. Atlantis is one of the most lasting of our legends. It has become so much a part of our heritage that I think it is generally accepted as fact—"

"And all founded on a few sentences that were used by Plato to hang some of his arguments on—"

"But suppose that Atlantis did once exist." Fordham picked up a pencil, turned it end to end on the pad before him, but made no markings. "Not in this world—"

"Where then? On Mars—? They blew themselves up, I suppose, and left that pocking of desert craters—"

"Oddly enough, according to legend the Atlanteans did eventually blow themselves up, or the equivalent. No, right here on this planet. You have heard of the alternate history theory—that from each major historical decision two alternate worlds come into being."

"Fantastic—" Hargreaves interrupted.

"Is it? Suppose that it is fact, that on one of those alternate time lines Atlantis did exist, just as on another dragons overlapped mankind."

"Even if that were so, how would we know about it?"

"True. We could be separated from those lines by whole networks of major choices and decisions. Yet, suppose when we were close together, there was a kind of seepage—perhaps individuals even crossed. We have well-authenticated stories of strange and unexplainable disappearances from our own world, and one or two odd people have turned up here under very peculiar circumstances. And Atlantis is so vivid a story, has so seized upon the imagination of generations, that we used it for our checkpoint."

"Just how?"

"We fed into the Ibby every known scrap of material on the subject that is known by the modern world—from the reports of geologists sounding the sea bottoms for possible ridges of a sunken continent to 'revelations' of cultists. And Ibby gave us an equation in return."

"You mean you set up the probe-beam on *that*?"

"Exactly. And you have seen the resulting test films. Those came from Ibby's calculations. And you'll admit they bear no resemblance to the here and now."

"Yes, I'll say that much. And they were taken?"

"Right out there, over the landscape you've been viewing. We're set today for a ten-minute run, the longest we have dared to try. We use the mound for a checkpoint."

"Still having trouble over that?"

Fordham frowned. "We gave out the story that we are clearing to build an addition to the labs. This Wilson who is making all the fuss is chronically opposed to government authority. He's built up this 'Save our historic mound' crusade mainly to get himself space in the city papers and to harass the project. Started a rumor last year that we were dabbling in some weird new experiment that would blow the whole county off the map. He was warmed then by the security people. But he believes this mound thing is safe. However, 'Save our historic mound' isn't as good for arousing interest as 'Look out, the eggheads are going to blow us up.' His campaign is already running down.

"However, the mound makes a good checkpoint because it is older than any other surviving man-made landmark hereabouts."

"What if you turn up mound builders instead of Atlanteans?"

"Well, then we'd have a better set of films than those we already possess to rivet attention on the project, though those we do have are more to our real purpose."

"Yes," agreed Hargreaves. "And if this does work—if we can get through ourselves—"

"We can tap natural resources, riches such as we cannot imagine in this era. We've plundered and wasted and used up most of the living treasures of our world. So now we have to try to pillage somewhere else. Well, shall we go to see—Atlantis?"

Hargreaves laughed. "Seeing is believing; one picture is worth a volume of words. Give me a good film to take back to Washington, and I may be able to up your

9

current appropriation. All right—show me Atlantis."

The weather for early December was suprisingly mild. Ray Osborne opened the collar of his leather jacket. His ex-paratrooper boots flattened ragged clumps of last season's grass. The shadow of the Indian mound enclosed him now. Early Sunday morning—Wilson had been right in his suggestion about the time. The fence had had a gap just as he had promised. There was only one building in sight, the tower part of the hush-hush installation. And on this side of the mound, he was safely out of sight, even if anyone was on duty there.

What were they planning to build anyway—clearing it flat with bulldozers? What would people do when there was no more open country at all? Ray turned to face the mound, readying his camera for the shots he had been sent to take. His finger pressed—

And, as if that had thumbed the red switch of final doom, the world went mad. Ray staggered back, aware only of intolerable pain in his head, pain associated with violet flashes that blinded him. Silence— He rubbed at his watering eyes. Mist faded, and he stood, swaying drunkenly, staring about him in stunned disbelief.

The raw wound of the clearing, the distant earth-moving machinery, and even the mound were gone! He was in the shadow, not of mounded earth, but of a towering giant tree, with another and another beyond!

Ray put out a shaking hand. He could feel rough bark—it was real! Then he began to run down a moss-carpeted corridor between trees whose girth was that of monsters. "Get back!" shouted something inside his head. "Back?" asked another part of his dazed mind. Where was *back?*

Minutes later he burst from the dimness of that incredible forest into a grass-grown plain. A withered root protruded from the earth to send him sprawling, and he lay drawing air into his lungs with panting gasps. Soon he became aware that a hot sun beat down upon him, far too warm for winter. He pulled up to his knees to look about him.

Ahead no break in that plain, behind him the forest—nothing he had ever seen before. Where—where was he? Shivering, though the earth under him was warm, Ray forced himself to sit quietly. He was Ray Osborne. He had gone out to the project on Sunday morning as a favor to Les Wilson, to take some good shots of the mound to go with the article Les was writing. Shots—his hands were empty! The camera? He must have lost it back there when it happened— What *had* happened?

Ray dropped his head between his hands. He fought a battle with primitive panic and tried to think logically. But how can one think logically about something such as this? One minute standing in a sane, ordinary world—the next being here. And where was *here?*

Slowly he got to his feet, thrusting his twitching hands into the pockets of his jacket. Go back. He half turned to face that silent density of forest and knew that he could not go in there again, not yet. His heart began to thump heavily when he thought of it. Somehow this open land seemed the lesser of two evils. So he trudged on, to find a little later a break in the plain. Below was a narrow gully that housed a stream, and around that grew tall brush and saplings.

As he sought a path down the steep side, there was a crashing in the brush below. Out of that green thicket, straight at the almost perpendicular slope, hurtled a dark shape. Sharp hoofs pawed frantically at the wall, bringing down soil and stones. Then, appearing to realize there was no climbing it, the creature, with a toss of its antlered head, turned to face its hunters.

Ray clutched at the grass of the verge to keep from sliding over. The hunted animal was directly below him, head low, breathing in labored snorts. But he could not believe it was real. Elk, if this huge monster could be an elk, did not run wild in southern Ohio. It had an antler spread of more than six feet and was far

11

taller than Ray—as out of proportion as the forest trees.

From the brush leaped shaggy-coated wolfish beasts. Avoiding the reaching scoop of the elk's antlers, the first lunged for the animal's foreleg, clearly no novice at this wicked game. They made a running fight, dashing in to slash and then speeding away before the larger animal could well defend itself.

Ray was roused from his absorption in the battle by a shout. The hail drew one of the hounds momentarily out of the fight. It answered with a sharp bark. In a moment two-footed hunters appeared. They carried nothing Ray could identify as a weapon, though one of them had a short rod of metal. This he aimed at the throat of the cornered elk, and from its tip shot a ray of red light. Bellowing, the elk reared, to crash forward, nearly striking one of the hounds. The dogs rushed in to tear at the still quivering body, but the hunters pulled them back from the kill, sending them howling with well-aimed kicks and cuffs.

Drawing a dagger from a belt sheath, one of the men set about butchering the fallen animal. Another fastened leashes to the metal-studded collars of the hounds, while the third wrapped the fire rod in cloth and stowed it down the front of his jerkin.

All three were of medium height, but the broadness of their shoulders and the heaviness of their upper arms gave them a dwarfish look. Their coarse black hair, shoulder length, was sleeked smooth with grease and held by leather thongs. Their skin was between copper and olive in shade. Broad mouths with thick lips parting over strong yellow teeth, dark eyes, and hooked noses comprised their features.

They wore tunics of grayish leather, tanned to the flexibility of cloth, garments that reached from shoulder to mid-thigh. Over these were sleeveless metal-enforced jerkins. High thick-soled buskins covered feet and legs to the knees, but their arms were bare, save for bands of metal set with dull stones. Their wide belts supported sheathed daggers.

12

Ray crouched there, no longer attempting to reconcile anything he saw with reality. A dream—it must be a dream. In time he was going to wake up—

Then one of the dogs discovered him. Its red eyes found the source of the strange scent that had tickled its nostrils. With a howl it flung itself to the limit of its leash. The strand of hide halted its spring. In an instant it tried again. This time the thong parted. But, like the elk before it, it could gain no foothold on the gully wall. It continued to paw futilely at the gravel, giving tongue like a mad thing.

Bewildered, Ray was easy prey. With a shout one of the hunters pointed to him. The leader whipped out the rod and aimed. Ray had turned to him. The leader whipped out the rod and aimed. Ray had turned to run, but he was never to reach that safety a foot or so more of soil might have given him. Something within him stiffened; he could not move.

Unable to stir so much as a finger, he stood impotently waiting the arrival of his captors. With the aid of their single strange weapon, they blasted a series of steps up the side of the gully. He had not died at once as had the elk; that was all he knew.

They approached him in a body, and Ray stared steadily back at them. The immobility of their heavy features and the lack of readable emotion in their opaque eyes was disquieting. Masks, Ray thought, subtly evil masks. With an icy qualm he realized he was confronting something alien, beyond the boundaries of his old sane world.

Now they circled him warily, studying their capture. The weapon-bearing leader broke the silence with an interrogation in a guttural, hissing tongue. When Ray did not reply, the man's brutal jaw thrust forward pugnaciously.

Again he questioned, but this time in a murmur, almost sing-song. Another language, Ray guessed. His continued silence appeared to disconcert his captors a little.

At last the leader snapped an order. From his belt

13

one of the others freed a thong of hide and stepped behind Ray, to whip his powerless wrists together and lash them tight. Still under the influence of the strange weapon, Ray was forced to submit. He was shaken with a sudden loathing at the touch of the hunter.

Once he was bound, the leader raised the rod. No beam from its tip followed, but Ray was unfrozen again. Without a backward glance, the rod bearer walked away. The hunter who had bound Ray flicked him across the shoulders with the end of that thong, pointing after. Ray's loathing heated into anger, not only at his captors, but also somehow at the whole disaster that had befallen him. He might not know where he was or why, but the feeling that he would learn and exact payment after that learning steadied him. He found strength in his anger, and he clung to it as a drowning man might cling to a rock in the midst of a raging river.

They followed the lip of the gully for about half a mile before there was a break in the steepness of the wall. Ray, bound as he was, could not have descended their stair, and even now he hesitated over the scramble. The guard rapped him across the ribs with the flat of his long dagger to start him. But at the fourth step, Ray lost his shaky balance and tumbled forward, to slide down in a cloud of dust and gravel, ending with a knock against the trunk of a sapling, his skinned face lower than his long legs.

Surely, he thought grimly, if this was a dream, that ought to have awakened him. There was a dull ache at the base of his skull. Helpless, unable to gain his feet, he lay awaiting the pleasure of his captors.

They were leisurely in their own descent. One of them came to prod Ray up with a well-aimed kick. When he could not stand in answer to that encouragement, two of them heaved him erect. With a vicious push, which almost sent him sprawling once more, they started him on.

Blood oozed out from gravel cuts on his lips and chin, drawing the attention of small stinging flies he could do nothing to dislodge, since jerking his head about made him dizzy. When they reached the elk, he was made fast to a tree, while the hunters continued their butchery. After hacking portions of meat free, they fed some to the dogs and packed others in green hide. Then one, taking some entrails, dragged them along the ground, leaving a red trail.

A short distance away, he came to a black hole in the slope with a sand mound below it. Dropping the scraps of offals there, he broke off a twig, thrust it into the hole, and turned it around and around. Then he leaped away as a wave of large ants curled up and out.

The others had freed both Ray and the snarling hounds, and taking up the meat, they started downstream. Ray glanced back at the kill. It was buried under a heaving dark blanket.

He estimated later that they must have traveled almost an hour before the gully widened into a regular valley. The brush, which had torn his unprotected skin and left red scratches on the hunters' bare arms, became thickets of trees and patches of waist-high grass.

Ray's discomfort increased with almost every step he was herded into taking. His face, scraped raw, bitten, and stung, was puffed and swollen. His eyes had narrowed into slits in the tortured flesh. The steady ache at the base of his skull spread across his shoulders and down his back. He had lost all sense of feeling in his cramped arms. Yet in a way, he welcomed all these torments; they kept him from his thoughts. Where was he? What had happened? That this was a dream he could no longer believe, no matter how he held desparingly to such a hope.

The end to the need to keep staggering came at last. Abruptly the valley came to shoreland, and the stream flowed on to form a miniature delta on the lip of a rolling sea. Sea?

Keen salt air roused Ray to something again approaching coherent thought. Sea? In the midst of a continent? He looked upon the pale crescent of sand with a kind of dull horror.

15

There could be no sea here. But then *here* was not his own world! He was firmly caught in a nightmare.

A hail from the beach urged his captors to a swifter pace, and they dragged him with them, one on either side to jerk him along. Down at the edge of that incredible water, smoke, thin and tenuous as morning mist, plumed up from a driftwood fire, and several dark figures stood to greet the huntsmen.

"Still say fairy tale?" Fordham did not raise his eyes from the viewscreen.

When Hargreaves did not answer, he glanced around. There was a frown drawing the other's features into a pattern of angry belligerence. Fordham had witnessed that reaction before. This time he welcomed the sign of doubt battered by evidence.

"All right. I see something—trees—like those on your other films."

"Trees?" Fordham pushed. "Do they resemble any you have seen before?"

"No—" Hargreaves' admission came reluctantly. Fordham continued to press.

"Trees such as those," he pointed out, "have probably not been seen in this part of the world for several hundred years. The early settlers are reported to have had their problems when they cleared this land. Sometimes it took years to remove virgin forest, stump and root."

"All right! I'll admit you have something, that we see a section of country through that beam which certainly is not out there now and may not have been for a long time. But time travel—Atlantis—I have to have more proof before I send in any recommendation—"

"You have the films to take back with you. I only spoke of Atlantis as a possibility—I didn't promise it. You may merely see pre-Columbian or just pre-Revolutionary Ohio but there. We have no way yet of proving or disproving Ibby's equation. But you'll have to admit it is an impressive beginning—"

"I want to see the film of what we've just watched,"

16

Hargreaves said. "I want to see if I can spot the change when the beam went on."

"Take a little time to set it up—"

Hargreaves' scowl grew deeper. "I've got plenty—for this. And I want to see what I'm taking back. There'll be a lot of questions to answer."

"There—" Fordham settled down in the projection room. "Here we go, Now—here's the cutting as is."

Raw earth under the weak sunlight of winter, a bulldozer to the left throwing a shadow, the rise of the disputed mound—

"I'll admit I saw a change. I only hope that the film shows it!"

Fordham laughed. "Hypnotism? That's what you think I'm doing? What would be the point? Unless you think I've ridden a hobby completely out of sane bounds. This is the first time we've held a beam so long—so we should have more detailed evidence."

Hargreaves stared at the screen. "When can you—" he hesitated.

"Go over the line ourselves? So far we can only look. We don't know about the going. We'll have to build up a lot more power—"

"That growth of timber—" Hargreaves watched the great forest, or that portion of it the beam and film had trapped for them. "Might be a lot of other resources to be tapped. Looks like an empty world—"

"Yes, be practical. Suppose we can open a door into wherever that is, draw upon the resources there. Now—what sort of reaction do you believe you would get to a presentation before the committee if you stress that?"

"They would want to be sure it had a fifty-fifty chance of working. How soon before you will be able to make a real experiment?"

"Send someone through, you mean? I don't know. It has taken us two years to get this far."

Hargreaves shook his head. "Get your films; let me

17

show them. We may be able to grant you at least half of what you asked for."

"Generous. But I suppose to be expected." Fordham's words were not as grudging as they might have been. He was inwardly satisfied with his half-convert.

They watched the run-through, Hargreaves well forward in his chair. There was the scar of the cutting, the mound, then a flicker, and the trees. But a sharp exclamation from Fordham broke the hum of the projector.

"Langston," he called to the operator, "backtrack. Hold it slow just before the switch—"

"What—?" Hargreaves' protest stopped as he looked at his companion. Fordham's satisfaction of moments earlier had disappeared.

The scar about the mound again came into view.

"To the left of the mound—right there—look!"

Hargreaves looked. A figure, difficult to distinguish, but surely a human figure, stepped within the path of the beam. That which had shown as a flicker when the film was run at normal speed now became a flash that made him blink. Then there were the trees and, surely, beside one of them still that human figure.

"Come on!" Fordham was making for the door in a surprising burst of speed for one of his age and habits. They were actually running as they passed down a hallway and into a small outside parking area. Fordham jerked at the door of his car and scrambled into the driver's seat. And Hargreaves had just time to make it in beside him and slam the door before they skidded across the concrete, heading for the gate.

The guard saw them coming and must have had his wits about him, for he threw the automatic switch just in time. Hargreaves released his breath in a faint whistle of relief. At least Fordham had not plowed into that barrier as it looked he might do.

Luckily the road was deserted beyond, for they entered it at a prohibited speed. Caution must have caught up with Fordham somewhere along that stretch, for he slowed to turn into the lower cutting, where they bumped and skidded along the rough road of the earth movers.

Then once more the director was out and running for the mound. His fear or excitement kept him several paces ahead of Hargreaves, but when the latter rounded the end of the mound, he came upon Fordham at a dead halt. The director held a camera in his hands. But of the figure they had seen on the film, there was no sign at all.

"He's gone!" Hargreaves stated the obvious.

Fordham looked up from the camera, his face bleak. "He's gone, yes—out there—" He looked over his shoulder to where they had seen those rows of trees. And Hargreaves shivered, knowing how that other had gone but not where.

2

"WHERE?" Hargreaves heard himself putting that thought into words.

Fordham's answer came in a voice hardly above a whisper. "Atlantis—perhaps."

"But—you said that the forest could be pre-Columbian —or even later," Hargreaves protested.

"Sure. It could be that—or anything. You saw it, and the film—and you see this now—" Fordham waved the camera. "That poor fool went in, or back, or out— whichever way you want to express it—and we sent him."

"Can you get him back?" Hargreaves pushed aside speculation, reaching as ever for hard fact.

"It will take at least four days, maybe more, to build up the power in the beam again. These things have to be timed. Why do you suppose we selected this particular date and hour to try it this time? It isn't just a matter of pressing a button to open a door. There has to be a careful working from code. Four days—" He stared around him. "And we have no way of telling how fast time passes over there. He won't be just sitting there for four days—he has no idea that we'll try to get him back. He may be miles away when we are ready."

Hargreaves turned away from the mound to look out over the raw cutting. "But it will have to be done. And the sooner we get to work doing it—"

"Of course." But Fordham sounded as if he knew already they faced a hopeless task. Hargreaves still gazed at the cut.

"Atlantis—no!" And there was determined refusal in his voice.

Ray stumbled, to sprawl face down in sand near a fireplace rudely built out of rocks. Exhausted, he was content to lie there, paying small attention to the

20

hunters and those others who awaited them in this camp, but he was not left undisturbed.

Legs, slightly bowed, encased in boots of stiff hide to which patches of thick hair still clung, moved into his restricted line of vision. Then one of those boots was thrust under him, and he was rolled over, face up to the sky. The newcomer wore the same leather tunic as the hunters, but a kilt fashioned of metal strips clashed together as he moved. Instead of a metal-reinforced jerkin, he wore breast and back plates cast in single pieces to fit his barrel chest and wide shoulders snugly. His left arm from wrist to elbow was sheathed in a metal cuff guard, but his right was bare save for two jeweled bracelets.

He was bareheaded, and the long black strings of his hair were whipped about his face by a rising wind. But he carried in the crook of one arm a helmet with two batlike wings set in a center ridge. A sword swung at his belt. Taller than the hunters, less swarthy of skin, he seemed of a different caste. But the same emotionless mask covered his features.

After a long survey he barked an order, and one of the hunters came to slit the bonds about Ray's wrists and pull the American to his feet. The officer asked questions and the hunter replied, with a pantomime, as well as words, explaining the capture. When he had done, the officer proceeded to interrogate his prisoner by gestures—a wide sweep of hand to the west and then one word:

"Mu?"

Ray shook his head. And the officer seemed disturbed at his reply. He frowned and pointed east with another question Ray did not hear very well. Suddenly the American understood—they wanted to know where he came from; that must be it.

He pointed back to where that grim forest must stand. For any more than that, they knew as much as he did about it. He was unprepared for their reaction to his answer.

The officer's eyes narrowed as might a cat's. His

thick lips drew apart in a snarl, displaying purplish gums and yellow teeth. Then he exploded in a cackle of derisive laughter, his disbelief very plain.

Rounding on his followers, the officer made another of the hunters repeat the story of Ray's capture. It was given as before. Then the hunter pointed to Ray's bare head, to his wind-ruffled short brown hair, and reached out a hand still unwashed after the elk butchery to tug at the leather jacket their prisoner wore, directing the officer's attention to it. He promptly signed for Ray to take it off. The hunter rifled its pockets, producing a handkerchief, a notebook, and a spare film pack.

In a few minutes the prisoner stood shivering in the wind, his clothing all spread out on the sand. But his captors still searched the pockets as if they were convinced he must carry some important object. One of the hunters appropriated his pocket knife; another turned his wrist watch around and around until ordered sharply by the officer to hand it over. Shaking out the handkerchief, the leader piled therein the contents of Ray's pockets, tying it all into a bag, placing that in a wicker basket.

Ray stooped to reach for his clothing, but the officer's hand shot out with a backhanded slap that sent him sprawling. A hunter tossed a package of hide to the captive. Hot with anger, Ray pulled on a meager garment that was rather like a kilt and utterly inadequate as protection in the growing chill of the wind. He wondered what would happen if he tried to jump the officer.

Even as his imagination supplied a few details satisfactory to him, steel fingers closed upon him again, spinning him half around as his right arm was whipped away from his body. On the pale skin of his right forearm was a small bluish circle, radiating lines, a juvenile attempt at tattooing that the years had not erased. The officer sneered as he inspected it. Then he flung Ray's arm from him and spat.

"Mu." Not a question now but statement.

So night came in the new world. Apparently they

had some future use for him, for he was given a portion of roasted elk. Then his arms were tied again—and his ankles as well—and one of the men flung a skin coverlet over him as he tried to burrow into the sand for warmth.

Where was he? Suddenly that mattered more than how he had come here. The historic mound, then the trees, now here. Indians? But even if time travel was possible outside of fiction, these were not Indians. And the sea did not run into Ohio and—and— Ray fought the panic again rising in him, which wanted to set him running, screaming—

All right, he did not know how he got here, nor where *here* was. But his immediate problem was the hunters and what they planned to do with him. After a while his tired brain was as benumbed as his shivering body, and he slept, exhausted.

The shrill cry of a bird awoke him in the early dawn. Under a makeshift tent of cloaks, the officer snored and twitched, and a sentry nodded by a dying fire. So the dream continued. Ray attempted to sit up, but his bonds bit cruelly into his flesh. By digging his heels into the sand, he edged along until his shoulders scraped one of the boulders about the camp site. Cautiously he worked himself up to a sitting position.

In the east a faint pink deepened. A gray bird dived to seek breakfast in the waves. With a sharp nod the sentry roused, yawned, and spat noisily into the fire. Then he got to his feet, looking at Ray with an evil grin.

Opening proceedings by planting the toe of a boot in the prisoner's ribs, he twitched Ray forward to inspect the security of his bonds before slamming him back with a jolt against the rock. Having carried out one duty, he went to stir the fire into life.

Ray shook his head. Dried blood and dust encrusted his face. A pulse throbbed heavily in throat and temple. If he could only get his hands free—

The officer rolled out of his tent and unbuckled the clasp that fastened his undertunic. Dropping the garment by the armor he had shed the night before, he ran out into the waves. As he splashed there, he suddenly shouted, and the rest of them came to their feet, calling and pointing to the open sea, where a black shadow cut through the blue-green.

Returning, the officer dried his body and dressed, loosing a volley of orders that sent his men into scurrying activity. One of them unfastened Ray's ankles and hauled him to his feet.

A ship was coming, but it was unlike any vessel Ray had ever seen pictured. Perhaps half a mile off shore it halted its rush, oars flashed from its narrow sides, and it scuttled on in like a water beetle.

Ray had seen illustrations of Roman galleys, but those had also masts and sails. This only possessed bow and stern superstructures, crowned with roofs, which were also upper decks. The waist was lower, and there the rowers labored in open pits. The bow came to a sharp point set with a brightly painted figurehead. From a slender pole on the afterdeck whipped a blood-red flag.

There was a look of power to this slim, cruel vessel, an air of grim efficiency. Whoever Ray's captors might be, they were evidently well able to care for themselves in this strange world.

The ship came to anchor, and a few moments later a long boat swung overside to hit the water. With a rhythmical sweep of oars, it made for the shore where the hunting party waited, their bundles ready, the fire smothered in sand.

Now the officer cut the cord about Ray's wrists. He rested his hand on the hilt of the sword in a way to be understood. To suit his captor's convenience, the prisoner must be freed, but he would be foolish to try an escape.

Six men and an officer made up the boat crew. They shouted questions at the hunters as they splashed overboard to drag in their carft. The commander of the shore party pulled Ray forward, showing him off. It would appear that his capture was a noteworthy exploit on the part of the hunters and that the officer in the boat was openly envious. Then the hunter-officer pointed inland and asked a question to which the other nodded assent.

Unloosing their dogs, three hunters padded away while the others made for the boat. Ray climbed in clumsily, his legs and arms still stiff from his bonds, and was shoved down between two seats. They headed back to the vessel.

Nearing the flank of the ship, they warded off their boat with shortened oars until a rope ladder dropped. Two of the shore party went up, and then the ladder was thrust into Ray's hold. He climbed awkwardly, giddy from the swing, chill with the fear of losing hold and falling, to be caught between boat and ship. The officer from the camp came behind, impatiently prodding him on.

The prisoner dropped down into the crowded waist, and behind him the officer flung up an arm to salute a red-cloaked individual. The red cloak, so like a smoldering coal, drew the eye. It was not really a cloak, Ray saw, but a long crimson robe, the color of new-shed blood, which covered a tall, very spare man from throat to heels.

Beneath the rounded dome of a closely shaven skull, large black eyes peered from either side of a jutting, beaklike nose. The mouth below was sunken, the lips puckered, and the chin had a sharp upward hook. With one earth-brown hand the man caressed the bony line of his jaw, staring not at the officer making the report but at Ray.

And under the probing of those lusterless black eyes, the prisoner suddenly felt unclean, as if something foul with slime had crept across his flesh. The hunters and their officer were brutal, but, Ray realized, this man was something he did not, could not understand, wholly alien to his own world. He experienced a shrinking inner horror under that gaze, a need to range himself against the wearer of the red robe and all he stood for.

And so strong was this surge of revulsion that it frightened him.

"So—Murian—"

Ray quivered. He could not have understood those words, yet he did. Or was it only with his mind that he "heard"?

"So, Murian, like all your kind, you would stand against the Dark One? Puny follower of a dying flame, think you that we cannot link your will to ours in the end? Remember, the Bull One can trample out flame. Who can withstand his will?"

Ray shook his head, not in denial of the other's words but in an effort to clear away the giddiness that the realization he *did* understand carried with it. Who was the Dark One? Murian—what was Murian?

A faint shadow of some emotion crossed the Red Robe's mummy face. "Seek not to evade with such feeble tricks. You understand well what is said to you. Get you down with your fellow and learn humility."

Thought reading? Well, it could be a part of the rest of this wild dream. Ray did not resist when three of the warriors standing near on him and bore him further along the waist. At the far end they spread-eagled him against the wall and made him fast by bands of iron set in the planking.

When they had left, he turned his head and saw that he had a companion in restraint. Fettered as was he, so close by that the fingers of their hands almost touched, was another captive. He drooped limply in the irons, his head fallen forward on his breast, so his long hair veiled his face. But by the rest of his appearance, he was of a different breed from the ship's company.

His skin was no darker than Ray's, and he was as tall. The long locks of hair were the color of polished bronze, snarled and matted and, in one place, bloodstained. A tunic of yellow, mid-thigh in length, hung in tatters from one shoulder. Its rags were confined at the stranger's waist by a broad gem-studded belt. But there was only an empty sheath to show he had once been armed with a sword. Like the hunters, he wore

26

high boots, but infinitely superior in workmanship.

Ray wondered if the other captive was unconscious. At least they were in the same trouble and perhaps could make common cause. He hissed softly, hoping for an answer. A groan as faint as a sigh answered him. Ray hissed again, and the other stirred, turning his head with painful slowness.

The perfection of the stranger's features, marred now by cuts and greenish bruises, was remotely like that of some Greek statue, Ray thought. But no son of Argos had ever possessed such high, wide cheekbones, nor the heavy, drooping lids that half concealed blue eyes. He stared at Ray, amazed, and then his battered lips worked. In the soft speech the hunters had once used, the stranger asked a question. When Ray shook his head, the other was visibly startled.

"Who are you who have not the tongue of the motherland?"

Mind-touch again! Ray tried not to flinch. At least this time such contact had not brought with it the suggestion of foul invasion.

"Ray—Ray Osborne—a prisoner—" he answered slowly, in English the other seemed to understand.

"From whence come you? Remember—think slowly that I may read from your memory, see with your eyes—"

Obediently Ray retraced his bewildering journey, from his visit to the mound to the unexplained forest, the plain, the meeting with the hunters. And panic must be battled anew. What had happened? Where was he? On what sea? In what world?

"So that is the way of it—a slip-through. But I do not recognize your time."

"My time?" Ray repeated.

"Yes, you are from the far future—or the past. It is known to the Naacals that perhaps man can travel so. Though those who have tried, by our records, never return. But for you it came by chance, which is indeed a strange thing, since only adepts of the first rank

27

think upon such things—then only after much training and study."

Ray swallowed. Without surprise, this stranger apparently accepted such insanity as possible, knew that it had been done before. A slip-through—through what—into where? Where—if he only knew that, perhaps he could fasten on something that did make sense. He asked the first question he could sort out of a bewildering whirl of thought.

"Who are these men—in this ship?"

And the reply was ready enough. "We are prisoners of the Atlanteans—the children of the Dark One. Look you to their sign—"

With his chin the other indicated the red banner on the deck above.

But that was impossible! Atlantis had never really existed—it was only a legend of a continent supposed to have vanished in catastrophic disaster before the first stone of the Great Pyramid had been laid. It was the fable that had given a name to one of the great oceans of his own world, but it was only fantasy.

"Why do you think captivity has twisted my wits?" the other asked calmly. "I speak the truth. We are prisoners of the sons of Ba-Al, the Dark One of the Great Shadow. And five days hence this ship will sight the cliffs of the Red Land itself—"

"But that can't be true!" Ray protested. "Atlantis is a myth, a Greek myth—"

"Of Greek, I know nothing. But I say to you, Atlantis is real, too real, as you shall see when we dock at the Five Walled City. It is as real as these hoops forged in the fires of its smithies, which now hold us in bondage, as the hate of that son of Ba-Al who commands the obedience of the captain of this vessel, as the stripes they have laid upon our bodies. The Red Ones now rule the wind and wave of the western sea. Shame be to us of the Flame that it is so. Atlantis waxes. So strong does she think herself that she moves now to stand alone against the world."

Ravings, of course—

28

"Why do you strive to close your mind to the truth? You are awake, you are alive. Do you not feel, taste, breathe, see, even as I? Accept the evidences of your sense—that you have passed from your time and world into ours. It must be, as the adepts say, that men without preparation cannot face such journeys, for it seems that you cannot now allow yourself to believe the truth."

"I dare not," Ray whispered. His mouth was dry, parched, and he shivered with a chill not born of the wind against his half-bare body.

"Are you then a nothing one who has no control upon his thoughts, no reins upon his fears?" demanded the other sharply and with some scorn.

"Madness—it is madness—" Yet Ray reacted to that scorn with a small spring of anger that gave him strength.

"No. It has happened to others. I tell you, the adepts have done it—"

"And none returned—" Ray pointed out.

"True. Yet perhaps they did not meet with disaster either. Tell me is it not true that you still live? And while a man lives, all else is possible. Could you reach the city of the Sun, there would be those there to show you the true paths of time. Are the men of your age so ignorant that they do not know time is the great serpent, that it turns and coils upon itself so that one time may almost touche upon another? One can then, perchance, slip through. While those who have gone on such quests have not returned, our seekers have seen through into other times and places. They have looked upon the fields of Hyperborea, which has gone from us a thousand, thousand years and is only a legend now. Do not fear what is past; look to the future, for these black hounds of the Great Shadow are about us, to be grappled with in the here and now. And that is a peril worse than any you have yet faced!" His words were now cold and hard in Ray's brain. "I will swear Flame oath to you on that!"

If he *had* passed into another time, then he was

utterly, nakedly alone, incredibly lost. Again the American fought panic.

"They have named you Murian; better that you be Murian. If they guess you are otherwise, then the priests will have you. And those of the Great Shadow—"

"What is Murian?" Ray interrupted.

"A son of the great motherland, as am I. For I am Cho of the house of the Sun in the motherland. Those of my courtyard are swordsmen to the Re Mu himself."

"The motherland?" Learn, learn what he could. Hold to the fact that if this *was* the truth, all the knowledge he could gain would be weapons, tools, or defense.

"The land in the far west, where life began again from a few seeds, legend tells us, after Hyperborea was swept away. Mu mothered the earth, and from her shores came forth men to people Mayax, Uighur, and Atlantis. Re Mu rules the world, or did until the fish ones of Atlantis dabbled in forbidden learning and fell under the Shadow—or marched under it by their own wills!

"Their first Poseidon—their leader—was a son of the house of the Sun in the motherland. But in time his line died out, and the people chose their own ruler. He was strong in will and in desire for power, and he turned from the path to life to assail the wall between the Shadow and our earth: that wall nurtured by the Flame to protect man from all that crawls in the outer dark. He drank power as the herders of the hills drink strange dreams from the juices of the tracmon.

"And he did not want to stand again in the Hall of the Hundred Kings to receive the word of the Ru Mu but to go his own way—"

Listening, Ray forgot fear, fastening on the need for getting a picture of this new world, erecting thus a barrier against dangerous thoughts.

"Thus began the rule of Ba-Al, the father of evil, hate, lust, all those thoughts and desires within a man that do him harm. It began secretly, underground, in caves, then more openly. It was a corrosive within the ranks of warriors, the companies of the people, the

30

seamen. Only the Sun-born remained true to the Flame. Then, on a last day, the Sun-born were put to the sword and thereafter has Atlnatis stood alone."

"There is a war going on?"

Cho shook his head. "Not yet. The motherland has been dangerously drained of her old strength, having given so generously to her children that she is nearly a hollow shell. Her best men and materials have been spread among the colonies. But now the Poseidon, grandson of that first devil worshiper, is ready to rend the veil of peace. He mouths his defiance—which is one reason why I stand here—"

"You were captured in a fight?"

"No, I had not that much satisfaction. I was sent hither to the Barren Lands to search out any secret forts or strongholds of the Atlanteans, places where their vessels may hide between raids. We were on a scouting expedition ashore when we were ambushed by pirates. Learning my rank, they did not slaughter me out of hand but sold me instead to this Red Robe for three swords of Chalybian forging and four emeralds. More perhaps than I would bring in the open market of Sanpar, the accursed, where the Witch Queen rules the scum of all nations. That was at dawn this morning."

"What will they do with you?"

"Should I escape the altar of Ba-Al, it will be to rot in their dungeons—or so they reckon. Three ships of ours have vanished during one moon, and none of their crews escaped. But if the Flame will favor me—" He stopped abruptly.

3

SOMEONE was descending the ladder into the rowing pit. Ray heard the clink of armor and the thud of more than one pair of boots. Two of the hunters passed before him carrying a polished bone-clean skull with huge antlers—the elk's? They lowered their burden to the deck and went away. But the officer behind them remained, stooping to cover the skull with a cloth. A hurried thought message reached Ray.

"Stand ready, comrade! If you are freed, make for the corner of the deck in the shadow of the ladder. If I cannot join you, dive for the sea. It will be far better than aught this ship offers—"

Cho had not asked if he could swim, thought Ray. But the Murian's gaze was on the officer, and under that steady regard, though the Atlantean did not lift his eyes to meet it or seem aware he was so watched, his movements grew less certain. He fumbled a little, and then he did look at the prisoners. As his eyes at last met Cho's, he arose slowly. He might have been moving under compulsion.

Held by the Murian's stare, he came to them, one slow step at a time. Stopping before Ray, he plucked at the iron ring holding the American's right wrist. Then, after the arms were free, the Atlantean went down on one knee to unfasten the ankle rings. But all this time the officer worked by touch alone, his eyes held by Cho's. Ray stood free. He hesitated only a moment before he sped to the shadow the Murian had indicated. Then he turned. The Atlantean was now loosing Cho.

Suddenly the officer jerked upright. He shook his head and raised his hands uncertainly to his forehead. Ray shifted from foot to foot, hands on the rail. It was apparent that whatever had made the Atlantean obey Cho's wishes was failing. Could the Murian reassert mastery? Maybe. The officer was stooping again to the ring.

Then he swayed. Recovering balance, he smashed his fist into the Murian's face. A second vicious blow split Cho's lips. Ray leaped, but not for the sea.

"Go! The guard comes—"

The American lost the rest of that order as he attacked. His arm crooked about the officer's throat; he dragged him back and struck sharply against the base of his skull. As the Atlantean fell, Ray clutched at the sword in his belt, bringing its heavy pommel down against the owner's head.

"Go—" ordered Cho again.

Ray made no answer. He pulled at the rings and used the sword blade to lever them open.

"Come on!"

Together they ran for the corner by the ladder. Cho struck open a port.

"This is for a flame thrower. Let us hope it is also wide enough for us. Through with you! Can you swim?"

"A fine time to ask. But yes, I can."

"In with you then. And try to stay under the surface for as along as you can."

Ray wriggled through, a tight fit, scraping his bare shoulders. Then he was in the water, and automatically his arms and legs moved.

"Follow me!" He caught sight of a white body.

Blood pounded in his head. He must breathe, he must! There was an arc of pain banding his ribs. Just when he thought he could no longer stand it, he came up into light and air. Before him a smooth shoulder cut waves, and he took that as his guide. The muscles of his back ached; the water stung in his face and in the scrapes on his shoulders. He had swallowed some, and it made him sick. But he swam on, though his strokes were uneven now. The shore—the ship—he could sight neither, only sometimes the swimmer ahead.

Doggedly Ray fought to keep moving, his head above water, limiting time to the next stroke. If only he could rest! Little thrills of pain shot along his legs; heavy

33

weights seemed suddenly to have been attached to his arms.

His knees bumped painfully on a harsh surface—rock. Gritty sand puffed up between his feet. Exerting all his remaining energy, he threw himself forward, to be seized and pounded on by the surf. With his mouth and eyes filled with sand, coughing and retching, Ray crawled out of the clutch of the waves and lay face down on a beach.

Presently he stirred. The stinging salt in the cuts on his face and body were an irritant that brought back a measure of consciousness. Sun seared him as he blindly pulled himself up to look about.

A little to his left Cho lay, partly in a rock shadow, his head pillowed on his arm. Ray sat up straighter and began feebly to brush the coating of sand from his body. Then he crawled to the Murian, took him by the shoulder, and tried to rouse him.

"Come on—we'd better get away—" Ray croaked. "They'll send a boat, pick us up again." It was a little hard to believe they had had any success, even this far.

"There is no need." Cho had yielded to his urging hand and was sitting up to look seaward. "The sons of Ba-Al go—"

Ray shaded his eyes with his hand against the glare of sun on the water. Oars flashed along the sides of the vessel. Incredible as it seemed, with their escaped captives almost within reaching distance, the Alanteans were making no attempt to come after them but were heading out.

"Why—?"

"Because the hunter comes—"

Ray's gaze followed the Murian's pointing finger. Far out, just sliding over the horizon, was a needle-like shadow.

"From the fleet. And these scavengers would avoid direct battle with such. Mark how they change course to flee."

The Atlantean vessel was veering sharply to the east. If the newcomer continued on its present course,

34

there would be a wide space between them, increasing all the time.

"Will the Murians go after them?"

"No. To initiate attack is forbidden. We can defend if they strike first; that is all. But they cannot be sure of that, so they flee an enemy equal to themselves as rats do when the farmer sets torch to field weeds." Cho laughed but with little amusement.

"But the Murian ship—why?"

"It comes for us."

"How do they know?"

Cho spread his hands in a gesture of bafflement. "How can one explain? Are men of your time so ignorant of ordinary powers? Is it possible to live so crippled? Yet, it seems that you do. I have been calling with the mind ever since I was taken. At last my men heard; now they come."

"Calling with the mind?".

"As I speak to you now without words. You must learn our tongue, though, for it wearies one too quickly to draw ever on the inner power for ordinary matters. It is so we can call—to those who know us, are seeking us in return." He sighed and then asked a question. "Why did you not do as I bid and leave when my control over the Atlantean failed?"

Ray flushed. "What did you think I would do? Just cut and run?"

Cho eyed him intently, but what he thought he did not broadcast. When he spoke again, it was of a different matter.

"See, the dwellers in the Shadow have placed their receiver on the highest notch. They are not minded to be overhauled but run like beasts before hounds."

Oars no longer fringed the sides of the vessel; yet that sharp-prowed ship was disappearing eastward with what seemed to Ray an amazing burst of speed. The Murian cruiser did not alter course to intercept the enemy. Still it stood in for the shore, high enough out of the water now that an orange flag could be seen.

"Now they must take to the oars," Cho murmured.

Scarlet-painted blades ran out, dipped, sending the vessel on at a slower rate of progress. In color the ship was a clear silver-gray, and it cut the waves into foam with majestic pride—though to Ray's eyes it had a curious half-finished look without masts. When it reached the former anchorage of the Atlantean vessel, it heaved to, and a boat was lowered. It was quickly manned and headed for the shore.

A last powerful swing of oars sent the small craft through the surf, the two men jumped waist-deep to guide it in. Ray studied the newcomers with keen curiosity. It was plain these tall young men were of a different race than his late captors. Their skin, beneath the golden wash of suntan, was fair, and their long hair shaded from white-blond to mahogany.

Tunics of leather covered them, and each wore a sword. Jewels glistened and flashed from armlets and broad collars. And they moved with a kind of light grace that Ray mentally associated with practiced Judo fighters he had known in his own time.

But they cast aside all dignity as they surged forward to Cho, laying hold on him as if he were something precious they had lost and feared never to see again. After greeting them all, he turned to Ray.

Keeping his eyes on the American, he reached an empty hand out and made some request. Instantly the leader of the boat party drew his sword and laid its hilt in Cho's hand. The Murian planted the point of the blade deep in a patch of sand between the American and himself. Then he caught Ray's right hand in his, drawing it to rest with his on the hilt of the upstanding sword.

Still gazing intently at the American, he chanted a sentence that was taken up by the men behind him. Then the leader stepped forward, a short dagger in his hand. He pricked the wrists of both men so that two small trickles of blood mingled on the sword hilt.

"Thus do I claim you sword brother and shieldmate, new son of my mother's courtyard, one blood with my house henceforth—"

The words of the oath burned clearly in Ray's mind. He knew an instant of hesitation, the feeling that if he accepted such kinship, he was stepping through another door. But even as that warning doubt pricked at him, another portion of his mind denied it and reached almost greedily for what might be security of sorts in an alien world. Was any acknowledgment expected of him? He could see this was some formal rite, which might carry—that inner warning shrilled—more responsibility than he could guess. But he answered aloud:

"Yes." And he knew Cho understood.

For the second time Ray was in a ship's long boat. But this time Cho was beside him. And he was no prisoner—or was he? Had he really any choice? Against that wariness warred a feeling of expectancy, which continued as he followed Cho up the ladder, over a deck crowded with men who cheered the appearance of the Murian, and down into a large cabin. And the cabin then claimed his full attention.

By the standards of his own age, Ray suspected, it might be considered barbaric because of the lavish use of precious metals and bright colors. Yet it was not Oriental, nor did it follow any "native" style of art he had ever seen. And he did know a little about art through his photography.

Around the walls were panels of a dead-black wood, which were inlaid with intricate designs, combining gem stones with bright paint or enamelwork. Between these hung long curtains of brilliant fabrics. A table of the same wood as the panels occupied the opposite end of the cabin, with long benches on either side and a high-backed chair at its head.

From beams overhead swung two balls of rosy light, encased in filigree globes. The chains from which the pendants hung swayed with the motion of the ship, so that the light appeared to wax and wane.

As Ray halted to stare about him, Cho went to the table. He poured liquid from a flagon into a stemmed goblet, listening meanwhile to a young officer he had

37

introduced to Ray as Han. Suddenly the Murian put down the flagon with a click and uttered a sound of protest. Then he glanced back at Ray.

"We have been recalled. This northern sea and that of the east are closed, which means—"

"War?" Hazarded the American. One world or another, one time or another, he thought dully, war seemed to be ever-present.

Cho nodded. "If and when the Re Mu wills. But now we go home." He turned to Han, apparently asking more questions.

Ray felt a steady vibration creeping through the walls and the deck of the cabin. He steadied himself with one hand against an inlaid panel, suddenly not sure of his balance. He was eying one of the benches as a more secure base when there was a sharp movement from Han. The young officer flung up his arm as if to ward off a blow; his mouth twisted in pain. Then, with only an inclination of his head to Cho, he turned and left them. Cho soberly watched him go.

"Lanor was his sword brother, and Lanor fell beside me with a pirate dagger in his throat. Han eats sorrow this day. But that debt will not go unpaid. We shall remember it when we stand sword to sword with those of Ba-Al, and the accounting then shall be a just one. Now, do you eat and drink. Then we shall sleep—for no man can do well empty and weary."

They drank, a wine Ray thought, from finely wrought goblets. And they ate from plates that were works of art, though once he saw what they held, Ray was more interested in contents than containers. It was only when he was satisfied that he raised his eyes to the wall of the cabin behind Cho's head and saw that the panels there were three in width and the design on them was not a decorative pattern but had meaning—a map!

Ray leaned forward, his breath coming faster as his eyes followed shorelines on that unbelievable map. Some of it—but how little—was familiar. There were two continents, one north and one south, but bearing only a vague resemblance to those he had known. The

38

Mississippi, the Ohio, most of the north-eastern and southern portions of the North American continent were now under sea, while Alaska was linked firmly to Siberia. The heartland of Brazil, to the south, was a landlocked ocean. To balance the drowning of lands he knew, there were two new continents—one east, one west—so that the map was now roughly diamond-shaped, a land mass at each corner.

More than anything he had seen during the past two days, that map drove home the sharp lesson of the change.

"What is it?" Cho set down his goblet and put out his hand. What the Murian read on his face, Ray did not know, but in some measure his shock must have been mirrored there.

"That—that map!"

The Murian looked over his shoulder. "More decorative than useful, I fear," was his comment.

"Then—then that is *not* this world?" The American breathed more freely.

"It is, except that it is not a chart by which to set any ship's course. In mass it is right enough. See"—Cho went to the wall—"here are the Barren Lands." With a fingertip he traced the remaining part of the Ohio Valley north. "Hunters come here, outlaws, but there are no regular settlements. It is too harsh a hand to attract many, only those who have need for a wilderness in which to hide or those who have a desire to explore a little. Now, we are about here—" His finger moved down into the sea. "We head south—to cross the Inner Sea—" Swiftly his finger moved to Brazil. "This is Mayax, loyal to the motherland, strong and rich. Then we go through the western canals to the western ocean and thence to Mu—" His goal was the land mass to the west.

"And Atlantis lies to the east," Ray stated rather than questioned.

"True. Is this so different from the lands of your own time that you find it fearful to look upon? Why should that be so?"

39

"Because"—Ray hunted for words—"because it is hard to believe that a man may walk about his ordinary business in a land he knows well one moment and the next be—elsewhere, where all is different. All that shows as sea here"—it was his turn to approach the map—"is land for me. And it is densely populated with many growing cities—too many. Men are finding that expanding population a threat. And here, this is also land—" He set his palm over the sea of Brazil. "But there is no Atlantis, no Mu—only ocean and scattered islands—"

He heard a small gasp from Cho. "How long, how very great a time must separate our worlds, brother! Such changes on the face of a planet do not come easily. You have spoken of Atlantis as a tale in your world. Do they then have an ending for it? Or do they speak of Mu, the motherland?"

"There are stories of Atlantis, supposed to be tales only, with no fact. It is said to have vanished beneath the seas in tidal waves and earthquakes because of the wickedness of its people. This ocean in my own time is named the Atlantic because of the persistence of an old belief that Atlantis lies somewhere beneath it. Of Mu I never heard."

"What did you do in this northern land of yours, brother? Were you a warrior? When you brought down the Atlantean, you used a strange blow such as I have not seen before."

"For a while I was a warrior. Then there was family trouble, and I was needed at home—"

"Needed at home— But now—when you cannot go home—?"

Ray shook his head. "That need is past." He did not want to think about that. "I was about to return to the army when this happened to me. New buildings were being put up on a government project." He did not know how much of this Cho would understand but felt a need to put it all into words. "When they started to clear the land, there was trouble because of an old Indian mound. People protested against its being leveled before it

40

could be properly investigated. Les Wilson—a man I know—was trying to get them to wait. He was writing articles about it, and he wanted some good photo shots of the mound. I promised to take them. And I was doing just that when—when I found myself in a forest of the biggest trees I'd ever seen. That's the whole story. And I still don't know what happened or why."

Cho looked puzzled. "Shots of an Indian mound," he repeated slowly, as if completely bewildered.

"A machine—a camera of our time" Ray explained. "You use it to take pictures of objects, a very popular way of keeping visual records. And the Indians—they were native of this north continent whom my people found in possession of the country when they came from the east to colonize it about four centuries ago, four hundred years. Some of the early tribes, who had already vanished before the first settlers of my blood arrived, had built great mounds of earth that still remain, and we study them, trying to learn more about the people who made them."

"If the world is so much older in your time," commented Cho slowly, "there must be the remains of many, many vanished peoples from which you can learn."

"Yes, in many places there are ruins and old tombs of long-forgotten races. Some races we know of only by a few scattered stones, which say that man once built something there. That and no more—"

"You have a liking for this pursuit of those gone before?"

Ray shrugged. "I'm no archaeologist, but there is a kind of treasure-hunt lure to such searching. And I have read much about it. I had a lot of time for reading a while back." Once more he pushed away the sharpness of memory.

"Brother, I might try to say many words to you"—the Murian regarded him soberly—"but words cannot banish thoughts, no mater how well they are intended. You fight now upon a field where no sword brother, however well meaning, can stand at your right hand or

41

your left, for the battle is yours alone. But to each day its own evils. Forget this for a space if you can"—he spread out his hand upon the map—"and let us sleep."

Ray followed him behind one of the curtains to a small side cabin, where there were two bunks. Cho was already stripping off the remaining rags of his water-soaked tunic.

" 'Rest while one can' might well be the slogan of all during these troubled days. What man can say what a new morning will bring?"

Reluctantly Ray crawled into a warm nest of soft covers. His eyes closed, but there was no rest for his thoughts.

"Well, what do you have?" Hargreaves slumped in the chair. A dark sprouting of beard accentuated the shadows under his eyes, and he blinked slowly, as if the effort to keep them open and focused properly was almost beyond him.

"We know the man now. He's Ray Osborne. Wilson put him up to coming out to take some pictures of the mound. He's an acquaintance of Wilson's, does part-time photography for the local newspaper."

"Newspaper!" Hargreaves burst out hoarsely. "Just our luck to have a newspaper mixed up in this. We need that about as much as an N-bomb!" He fumbled with a cigarette pack and threw it from him savagely when he discovered it empty. "I suppose Osborne's disappearance is already burning up the wire services east and west."

"Not yet. We have that one small piece of luck, or edge. Osborne wouldn't have turned in his shots until this morning. I notified Wilson that we've confiscated them and Osborne is under arrest for trespassing," Fordham returned.

"In the name of Judas, why? That'll bring the whole pack down on us, yapping about freedom of the press and all the rest they cry about!"

The director shook his head. "No. They've all accepted the idea that this installation is top secret. Our story is that Wilson sent Osborne in, knowing it was closed territory—that he tried to pry. That buys us time, as Wilson has been warned about breaking security before. Luckily Osborne was a loner—"

"How much of a loner? Let Wilson get his family stirred up properly, and some lawyer will be out here in an hour, baying at the gates."

"This much of a loner." Fordham picked up a slip of paper from the desk and began to read:

"Ray Osborne, son of Langley and Janet Osborne, old family here in the valley, but no relatives now closer than second cousins. Born in 1960, which makes him around twenty now. Had one year of college, then drafted. Served overseas six months. Specialist in unarmed combat and scouting, interested in photography. Ten months ago his parents were in a traffic crack-up, his father killed, his mother badly injured. The Red Cross got him a hardship discharge, as there was no one else to take care of her. He came back here, took a part-time job, and looked after his mother who was an invalid. A month ago she died. He told the editor at the paper that he intended to go back into the service. He has no close friends; his army service and the circumstances of his mother's illness broke off most of his past relationships. Was a quiet sort of chap, did a lot of reading, hiked about the country taking pictures. Sold some of those. No trouble, well accepted, but nothing strong for or against him in town."

Hargreaves sat up a little straighter. "Well, if we had to send a man out wherever this one went, we're in luck that it was Osborne. No family, no friends, to make trouble. I wonder—"

He stared at a wall it was obvious he did not see.

"Yes?" prompted Fordham after a long pause.

"You say he told people he planned to re-enter the service. I think it can be set up that he did. So now, let the papers go through and he's our man; then we can hold the whole story under wraps while we move in to get him. Because the brains really want him—and badly. With what he'll have to tell us, he's worth more

43

than twelve space platforms and one moon station. We've got to get him back and pump him, pump him down to the last breath of air he took out of wherever he is!"

"If we can—"

"We have to; that's orders. Don't worry. They'll send you every man, every bit of material you need to put it through. We have to get him back. Do you realize that we're on the trail now in a direction the Eastern powers have never prospected? This is ours alone!"

"And if he's dead?"

"Then we have to get his body anyway—"

"We can probably get the beam on again soon. But that merely opens a very limited area. What if he's traveled miles away? There'll be no way of tracing him—"

Hargreaves loosened his tie a little more so it lay in a stringy loop on his rumpled shirt.

"They're working on that now in another way. You get the door open, and maybe they'll have figured out how to find our man by that time. But Lady Luck had better ride with us on this one!"

4

A DREAM of trees, of running along a long moss-grown aisle between their huge boles, pursued ever by what he could not see— Ray awoke. Outside the narrow porthole that gave on the sea, it was night. The other bunk was empty, his cabinmate gone. Yet this time he had awakened with all senses alert, knowing just where he was, as if, beneath that disturbing dream from which he carried only a wisp of memory, some acceptance had been at work. This was the present, and it was as real as the fabric under his hands as he raised himself on the bunk.

He reached for the kilt he had thrown aside when he had lain down but found other clothing. Fumbling with unfamiliar buckles and fastenings, he dressed. The sandals were light on his feet as he knotted their thongs clumsily about his ankles. Then he went into the outer cabin.

The rosy light was stronger with the coming of darkness. There was no one there. Should he go on deck or wait? His momentary hesitation made him aware of the polished surface of a mirror, and on impulse he went to face it.

A stranger, thin, with a sun-reddened skin and unruly brown hair, stared back at him. The scant gray tunic revealed a body that, for all its leanness, promised endurance. Buckles of silver, thickset with small green stones, glittered on his shoulders, and a belt patterned with the same gems encircled his waist. But he was suddenly shy and ill-at-ease. This was not Ray Osborne. And the confidence with which he had awakened began to fade. As he turned abruptly from the mirror, someone entered the cabin.

Ray's eyes widened. This was certainly Cho, but the Murian was now no bedraggled fellow prisoner. A red-gold tunic clung to his body. Jeweled armlets

45

encircled both wrists and upper arms. His sword belt and the hilt of the weapon that swung from it glittered icily. The long hair was swept back and held by a metal band from a face where there was still the imprint of bruises. Like the cabin and its furnishings, his splendor held something of that exuberance of color and ornament that Ray's time deemed barbaric.

The Murian laughed. "So—you look astounded, brother. Does dress do so much for a man? This is what is due my rank. Nor"—he surveyed Ray critically—"does our garb suit you ill. True Murian you look, or will when your hair grows. It is over-short for a free-born warrior. And now—food!"

Cho clapped his hands, and a man in a plain tunic entered with a tray. The Murian waved Ray to the table, where covered dishes and goblets were being set out. It was difficult, if not impossible, for Ray to identify the contents of those dishes. He had eaten earlier in a daze of hunger and weariness, knowing only that it was food. But now he was more attentive. There was a stew and a platter of roasted meat already cut into bite-size portions. Small cakes were dipped into individual bowls of thin jam. And with it all, a tart wine.

The Murian sighed when they had finished. "We lack only fresh fruit. But that is not for a ship's board these many days out of port. You rested well?"

"I dreamed—" Ray did not know why he said that, and he was startled at the sharpness of Cho's response.

"Dreamed of what, brother?" There was such a note of command in that that Ray answered readily.

"Of trees, such a forest as I found when I came into this time. Of running between them and behind—"

"Behind?" The Murian was still peremptory. "Behind what?" he asked again as Ray did not reply at once.

The American shrugged. "I do not know what, except that I ran from it. No matter, it was only a dream—" He was surprised the other seemed to take it so seriously.

" 'Only a dream'—why say you that, brother? Dreams are spirit guides for any man. They forewarn; they show the feelings our waking minds do not know. Do not the men of your time think any upon the meaning of dreams?"

"Not like that. Anyway, it was perfectly natural for me to dream of running from some mysterious danger in that forest, seeing as how all this began for me there."

"Perhaps you are right." But, Ray thought, Cho did not look convinced. "Shall we go on deck?" the Murian said.

He held out a cloak and then took up another for himself. The moon hung round and full above the ship, its clear light cut now and then by a drift of clouds. The oars were inboard, yet the ship drove on, though no sail was set. Ray realized that the ever-present vibration of the fabric of the ship must come from some motorized form of propuls. Cho had gone to stand by the steersman, and now Ray joined him.

"What drives the ship now that your oars are in?"

"This—" Cho answered readily, leading the way down to the waist. On the aisle between the rowing benches was a half-open hatch, and Ray looked down into a small metal-walled cabin. Apu, Cho's second-in-command, adjusted levers on a box that hummed and droned with life and from which spread that vibration.

"Our energy receiver. Waves of energy are broadcast from land stations and picked up by ships. It cannot be used close to shore or in harbor, and in some of the older ships not even in the Inner Sea. Oars serve them there. Each vessel is assigned a certain wave length from which to draw, and then only at stated times, unless there is an emergency—"

Han came along the deck with a message. Ray began to find his ignorance of the spoken language irksome as Cho translated for him.

"There is a ship to the west. But it cannot be one of ours, for the recall went out long ago. It may be a pirate—or Atlantean. We shall not try to speak it, lest we provoke attack—"

He was interrupted by a cry from Han. Far out in the

47

black of the sea, an orange light curved up from the surface of the waves. Cho shouted an order, and an instant later an answering green glare sped from the bow of their own vessel. The light out on the sea dimmed and then glowed red.

Cho was calling orders. Ray moved back out of the way of the men, who were running to different stations. Now their own green beam became pearl-white, turning the night ahead of the ship into day but leaving the ship itself in the dark. That glow across the water turned white in answer.

A little of the tense rigidity left Cho. "It is one of ours. Atlantean ships cannot counterfeit that signal. We must learn its mission and why it lingers here after recall."

Their beam of light became a series of flashes. When the other replied in kind, Cho read it for Ray. "Ship of the fleet, *Fire Snake,* disabled in storm. Can move by oar power only. Who are you?"

"Signal them aid," the Murian said to Han. And this time Ray, to his surprise, understood his words.

Again that distant light flashed.

"Ship badly disabled. We cannot make the Inner Sea. The Sun-born Ayna says farewell—"

Once more Cho gave orders. Their own ship changed course to the west, centering on that beam.

"We shall take the crew on board and then sink her," Cho said. "There can be no lingering to nurse a cripple with the wolves of the Red Land out! Little fortune for the Lady Ayna to so lose her first command—"

"A woman commands a ship?" demanded Ray.

"But of course. All the Sun-born have a duty to the Re Mu. Perhaps a lady will one day be sent as his mouthpiece to some colony. How then may she order the fleet for such an undertaking unless she has already commanded a ship?" Cho asked in surprise. "Is it not so with your people, brother?"

"No. At least not in my nation."

"Many must be our differences. Some day we shall compare them. This Lady Ayna is of the house of the

48

Sun in Uighur. I have never met her but have heard of her wisdom and courage. And she will destroy her ship with her own hand, if that must be done."

They sped on, that guiding light ever brightening. Han still shot flashes from their own ray, answered at intervals from over the waves. Suddenly Cho shouted to Apu tending the receiver. Then he said to Ray, "They have been sighted by a raider. It will be a race as to which of us will reach her first."

Waves boiled from the knife-edge bow in milky foam. On deck men stood to battle stations with tall shields, swords loose in scabbards, and some busied themselves about squat machines.

Now they could see the *Fire Snake* bathed in the light of her own signal ray. She lay low in the water, her waist deck almost awash. And out in the dark somewhere must be the raider creeping in for the kill.

Cho's commands passed along from officers to men. Ray could make out figures on the doomed vessel, shadows flitting across her slanting deck. Her small boats were being slung into the water. Then all but one pushed off, heading for Cho's ship. Cho pointed to the one remaining.

"That waits for the Lady Ayna—she must destroy her ship."

Over the deck, now awash, darted a slight figure, to leap to the waiting boat. With mighty strokes the rowers sent the small skiff surging from the side of the sinking vessel. There was a moment of silence while, by the aid of the light still on the deserted deck, they could see the boats racing toward them. Then a column of purple flame flowered upwards, filling sky and lapping sea with angry brilliance. With a roar it and the *Fire Snake* disappeared.

The first survivors were already climbing over the rail of Cho's ship, and the commander went to welcome them. At his coming the strangers cried about some slogan and raised their arms in salute. Then came an officer. He reached back to aid one who followed, and the Sun-born Lady Ayna stepped upon deck.

49

She was slight, no great beauty, but she carried herself as might an Empress of Ray's imagination. Her dark hair was bare of helmet. A band of pearls about her forehead, the ends twisted in her braids, proclaimed her rank. She wore a knee-length tunic and over it armor for breast and back.

"Hail, Lord Cho!" she said clearly. Her voice was low, but it carried well. "Since the *Fire Snake* sails no more, I crave your favor for these, my men."

Again, to his astonishment, the speech was clear for Ray, though he was sure she was not mind-beaming it to him.

Cho raised fingers to forehead in return. "The Lady Ayna, Sun-born of Uighur, need only make known her wishes. This ship, its men, are at her command."

The girl laughed and lost some of her defensive dignity. "Let us then be gone, Lord Cho, lest even worse befall. One of the Red Ones noses in, lured by our signals."

Cho nodded and gave an order. The Lady Ayna beckoned forward her officers. "This is Hek, this Romaha."

In turn, Cho introduced his men. Last of all the Murian's hand fell on Ray's shoulder, and he drew the American closer. "My sword brother—Ray—"

The Lady Ayna smiled. "Happy am I to greet you, my lords, though I could wish mightily that we met at a more fortunate time and for a better reason. Atlantis comes to war openly it seems—"

"The recall would bring that to mind, yes. Will you grace our cabin?"

With the sure step of one at home on shipboard, she went down into the great cabin, where Cho led her to the high chair and called for wine.

"Can it be true—that they dared to take the *White Bird* in an open attack?" She sipped at the goblet Cho had offered.

"That is the reason given for the recall. If so, they must at last bring upon themselves the full wrath of the Re Mu."

She frowned, turning the goblet around in her fingers. "The dwellers in the Shadow will discover that, though the mother has long been patient, there comes an end to forbearance. They will not soon forget—those who survive it—the punishment to follow. Is it true, Lord Cho, that you were prisoner of the Red Ones? Such a message reached us."

In answer, the Murian held out his hands. Still to be seen about his wrists were the marks of bonds. "Ten days did a pirate have me, then I was sold to the Atlanteans—"

She gasped. "So it is true! They dared to lay hands upon one of the Sun-born, using him as if he were an outlaw, a man of no house! How did you then win free?"

"With the aid of the Flame, working upon their dark minds—"

Her eyes shone. "Yes! That they have no answer for, much as they have tried to find one. The Ba-Al himself is powerless against it. So you escaped—"

"Also by the aid of my brother." Again he touched Ray's shoulder. "For I was near drained with weariness, and at the end I could not hold the power. But he had me free in spite of that."

"After you had first freed me," Ray corrected.

At his words the Lady Ayna started to give him her full attention. "Who are you who speaks no tongue of any land of ours? From what ship came you, Lord Ray?"

"From no ship—"

"Then whence? I know of no colony in the Barren Lands—"

"Through time, from the far future, I think. I know it sounds impossible, but it must be true. There is no other explanation. I was in my own time, then suddenly I was in a forest, and then I was captured by Atlantean hunters. They took me to their ship—where Cho already was."

She continued to eye him narrowly, as if she could read his mind, weigh and assess his every thought. "This is truth. I have heard the Naacals speak of such

51

journeys in the temple schools. But none who have ventured forth to test it have yet returned to us. And you are not like unto us— So you have come a long way, and you have ill-chosen your time, or chance has ill-chosen it for you."

Ray wondered at her calm acceptance of what he considered still a most improbable explanation. What sort of reception would a Murian suffering the same fate have received in his own world? He flinched away from imagining it. Maybe he was lucky.

The Lady Ayna arose. "My thanks for your aid this night, Lord Cho. Now I must report to the motherland. Have you a cabin for my body rest?"

Cho parted the wall curtains and showed her a waiting bunk. She entered and stood for a moment, one hand ready to draw the drapery behind her. "Good fortune to us all, from this hour forward." Then she allowed the tapestry to fall into place.

An hour later Ray crouched shoulder to shoulder with Cho at the bow of the *Wind Ruler*. Their heavy cloaks were damp with spray. The moon was hidden by gathering clouds. But they knew, though they could not see it, that somewhere in the dark a raider was attempting to cut across their course.

"Dare we carry that attack to them, tooth and claw, they would slink away like the cowardly carrion eaters of the plains. But to fight, while we are alone in a sea they now claim, would be deadly folly. For all we know, they but scout for a pack, a fleet that would be down on us as the condors of Mayax gather to a puma's kill."

"What if they attack?"

The Murian laughed shortly. "Let them but try that."

All the crew had stood to arms when they had sought the *Fire Snake*. Even though the *Wind Ruler* was now back on its former course, the shield wall stood, the machines were in the open, and men kept their battle stations. Now, at another order, there was a faint ringing, and on the sides of the rowers' benches screens arose level with the planking of the upper decks. Next to Ray was a long tube projecting from a box, and three

52

sailors stood to duty there. An officer, one of the Lady Ayna's, came to report.

"Yes, all is in readiness," the Murian said. "The men of the *Fire Snake* did not join us empty-handed but brought their own flame throwers. They mount these beside ours. We need only send up the battle flare. Then the raider will blunt its teeth upon death!"

Cho went from bow to stern, Ray behind him. As he progressed, the Murian inspected the preparations, but when he reached the afterdeck, he paced back and forth, twisting the border of his cloak until the fabric split in a long tear. Ray tried to see through the dark.

"If they would only come in," he muttered. Long ago, or so now it seemed, and very far away in space (he could think of this world better as divided from his own in space), he had been trained for war. Not this kind, but battle did not greatly differ. And even as he spoke those words, he knew the answer—waiting was an age-old weapon used by many men in many places during the centuries.

"That is just what they will not do," Cho continued. "Well do they know the value of forcing waiting upon their enemies—waiting until the first sharp vigilance relaxes ever so little. Then comes the attack. We must keep an untiring watch. If I ever cross the five walls those sons of Ba-Al use as their shields and meet them face to face with their backs to those same walls and no hole for them to bolt through—then shall all waiting be done and every moment of this night paid for. But those clouds across the moon—Sun forbid we have mist and fog in the morning!"

Ray glanced at the lowering clouds. "Those mean bad weather?"

"Perhaps. We can only hope the Sun will not forsake us. Come—let us see to the foredeck again."

Planking had been laid across the rowing benches in the waist, making a new deck, which seemed firm enough. This space was filled with an orderly complement of men, quiet now for the most part. On the bow deck three of the tube and box machines were now in

53

place, their crews beside them. And there was a soft light.

"No sight as yet, Sun-born," reported a lookout.

Once more Ray was puzzled by his ability to understand. But this was no time for questions.

"Nothing—" Cho repeated as if to himself. "Fog at daybreak, think you?"

Han held his head high, seeming to sniff the wind, studying the clouds across the sky, then glancing at the waters.

"Mist for sure, Sun-born, rain perhaps. I fear we must sail by director alone."

Cho struck the rail with his fist. "A cover under which that raider can creep unseen!"

"Yes, Sun-born. But for us also a cover—if fortune favors us."

Cho turned briskly. "Just so it must be. They may draw their net to find it empty. But never must we underrate them, nor think that fortune smiles wholly upon us. And I believe that none of us will breathe easier until the shores of the Inner Sea close about us."

"Truth in your words, Sun-born. The Atlanteans know all the tricks of the father of all Shadows, and evils are thought-spawned from him."

"Be it so." Cho's tone was stark and cold. "Even if fortune chooses to fail us and we be taken, the last and mightiest trick lies still in our hands, to be used at our bidding alone. The Sun-born Ayna pointed the way for us this very night."

"You mean—blow up the ship?" asked Ray.

"So would we go Sunward in all honor, taking many of the enemy with us to a final judgment. No ship of the motherland must fall into their hands while one of the true blood lives. And such an end would give us cleaner, swifter passage from this world than any Atlantis would grant a prisoner, as well we know."

The Lady Ayna came to join them. "You stand to arms, Lord Cho?"

"To await the raider. It will come." He nodded to the sea, certainty in his voice. "You have made your report?"

"I have told of the loss of the *Fire Snake,* and the Great One was approving of what I have done. The Re Mu sends greetings and bids you haste, for no aid can be sent if we are attacked." She hesitated. "But something then happened, Lord Cho, and this gave me fear—"

Her voice was lower, and Ray saw she clutched her cloak about her with hands on which the knuckles had whitened with the fury of her grasp.

"I—I was cut off!"

Cho swung around, his expression one of amazement. "What do you mean?"

"My contact with the motherland was broken—and not by the Re Mu. Never before has such a thing happened."

"How broken?"

She shivered as if the warmth of the cloak was gone and the wind chilled her to the bone. "It was as if a black curtain was drawn. When I thought a question—there was no answer. I waited for twice around the silver rim of the timekeeper and tried again. There was no response, not even from a shore watcher in one of the Mayax temples!"

When Cho remained silent, she added, almost pleadingly, "What can it mean?"

The Murian's face was closed still, as if he were thinking so deeply that he did not see her or any of his surroundings. She put out a hand to touch his arm, and he started under that contact, light as it was.

"What—what is it?" she asked again.

"It may mean that those of Atlantis have tampered with the Sacred Mysteries to discover the secret of the Sun-born—" he said.

She shrank away from him as if he had spoken some monstrous thing. Han exclaimed aloud. But Cho's eyes were blazing.

"Those soon-to-be-dwellers-in-the-outer-dark-and-cold! That they should so dare! But the Re Mu will have been warned when it happened. This means that the door of the inner power is closed to us. If we must fight,

55

we will not dare to call on anything save the might of our own arms and weapons, lest we open to them what we would die to protect."

The Lady Ayna regained a measure of her former serenity, or perhaps it was control. "What man may argue with fortune? But we can be worthy of that intrusted to us. And one does not speak of defeat before the battle is joined." Now she smiled at Cho as if she did not wish him to take her words as a rebuke. "Let me try once again—but if the raider comes, I ask you to summon me." She left them.

Cho looked to Ray. "It seems that you have truly been drawn into a net. This quarrel means nothing to you. And safer by far would be the empty plains of the Barren Lands than these waters when the Red wolves are out!"

He was very right—this was no quarrel of his, Ray thought. It was settled, it must have been, eons before his birth. Yet, there was something else— At the time it had been only words, a ritual of another race. Now it was a thing Ray remembered and held to.

"You said to me, when our blood was mingled on the sword hilt, that we were brothers—"

"That is so!"

"Then does it not follow that we share battles also? It seems that though I come not here of my own will, yet now I do have a choice—and I make it thus— Having no country any longer, I stand by friends. I think I have those—"

"There is no need to ask that!" Cho returned.

"And I have also enemies—out there—" Ray gestured to the sea. "So I choose—"

Cho nodded. "May you never regret it, brother."

"Amen," Ray thought, but he did not say that aloud.

5

"SO they have blacked out your radio," Ray hazarded, putting his own interpretation on what he had just heard from the Lady Ayna.

"Blackout—radio?" Cho returned.

"Yes, your communication system."

"You think of a machine to do this?" Cho smiled. "I had forgotten how little you know of us. We need no machine to communicate with the Re Mu, we of the Sun-born. In times of stress even certain of his higher officers are trained by the Naacals to accept thoughts, just as my mind can now touch yours. This was the manner in which the Lady Ayna reported the loss of the *Fire Snake*. Only those born with such powers, or those trained in them, can do this."

"Then how can the Atlanteans interfere with telepathy?" Ray asked. He could believe part of this after his own experiences.

"That we must discover. None but those trained in the thought-send could do so, and of that number all were known. Or so we believed until tonight. We knew that the Red Robes had something like unto it, but we thought they could not interfere with the true sendings. But now—they can! The Re Mu and the motherland will never know our fate here in the north unless we win through to Mayax. In all our history such a thing has never happened, nor did we believe that it could!"

Slowly the sky was lightening in the east, but only to a leaden gray, and a cold drizzle came, piercing the warmth of their cloaks, to make them shiver.

"Mist and rain as Han foresaw," Cho observed. "Let us hope the sons of Ba-Al find it as difficult to sight us as we shall to see them. Come, let us break our fast."

Below deck they found the Lady Ayna huddled in the seat at the end of the table. Her face under the rosy light was haggard. She forced a wan smile and then shook her head in answer to Cho's unvoiced question.

"Their wall remains, my lords. If we fight, it will be alone."

Cho dropped heavily on the nearest bench. "So be it. But perhaps it will not come to that. The Flame willing. Let us have food—" He clapped his hands for the serving man, and the Lady Ayna sat up straighter.

"The ships of the motherland are famed for their provisions. Uighur cannot serve forth the dainties of Mu. Or so I have been told by our officers who have returned from tours of duty there," she commented.

"Where is Uighur?" Ray asked.

She turned her head to stare wide-eyed at him. Cho went to the map set in the cabin wall. He pressed his fingers to a spot in its frame, and part of it moved to the right, hiding a portion of Atlantis. This revealed at the left the rest of Mu in the Pacific and, beyond, the coastline of the Asian mainland, but one very different from that Ray had known. Again the sea swept far into what would be China, and a portion of the Gobi Desert, and the highlands of future Tibet formed a new shore. This Cho indicated.

"Uighur."

But the Lady Ayna continued to stare at Ray. "How is it that you know not Uighur?"

"For the same reason that two days ago I did not know Mu either. I am from another time, remember? We had no memories of Uighur there."

"But of Atlantis—" Cho said slowly. "Why should the Red Land carry as a legend into the far future when all the rest is gone? What did they do, those followers of the Shadow, which set so great a fire blazing in their time that its warmth and smoke went on down untold centuries?"

The Lady Ayna's eyes were bleak. "I can think of one kind of disaster. What *did* your people know of the Red Land, Lord Ray?"

"That it lay in the ocean as a continent, an ocean in our time unbroken save for a scattering of small islands to the far east and west. That it sank in a combined earthquake and tidal wave as the result of some evil doing on the part of its inhabitants."

"A lost land. And did they ever seek it in your own time—strive to find remnants of it?"

"They tried so hard that they proved scientifically it had never existed at all. It was supposed to be purely a legend."

The serving man brought in a tray, and they began to eat, with need dictated by hunger. But Ray glanced up often at that map and wondered. Why was it that remnants of such a civilization as this *had* not existed somewhere to bear out the truth of legend? True enough, the world he saw on that chart was greatly altered geographically from that of his own time. But certain portions remained the same. And all—every fragment— of a high civilization could not have vanished so completely.

"The raider is in sight!" Han stood in the doorway.

Ray's spoon fell back into the bowl before him, splashing the contents. Cho crossed the cabin in almost one leap, but the American was close on his heels as they reached the outer deck.

"There!" Han pointed to a black shape in the mist.

"To stations!" Cho shouted.

Someone joined Ray at the rail—the Lady Ayna. She ought to stay below, he thought, and then remembered that she had commanded a similar fighting ship, knew more about such matters than he.

But the raider appeared not to have sighted them in turn, for it stayed on course, slipping back into the fog. Even after its going, the tension on the *Wind Ruler* did not lift.

"She will be back," promised Cho. "Now she tries to scent us as might a hunting panther sniff a trail. See—she returns!"

He was right. Again the sharp bow of the other ship cut the curling mist. She had come part way around, and the *Wind Ruler* was closer. He found it hard, Ray discovered, to think of that sinister dark wedge across the water as another ship, bearing men such as those now standing silently about him. There was no sound of voice, only the swish of foaming waves from their own bow as the *Wind Ruler* held to her course.

Then, as if she had known where they were all the time and had been playing at cat-and-mouse with them, the raider changed course a fraction more and made straight for the Murian vessel.

Calmly Cho gave his orders. "Apu, keep us on course, full speed ahead, no matter what chances. We must make a running fight of it. Use flame throwers, Han, only if we come close enough to be sure they will hit. Hold all fire until the command."

Officers scattered to their posts, Hek and Romaha from the Lady Ayna's command taking their place in the waist. The soldier-servant came from the cabin with three shields of reddish metal and long cuffs of the same. Cho slipped the cuff over Ray's left forearm and showed him how to clip the shield fast to that.

"These are a defense against flame throwers," the Murian explained. "Should you see one of those black tubes, such as our men wear now at their belts, in use, keep up the shield. I do not believe this raider carries death-breathers; raiders seldom do. We shall hope not, for against those there is little defense."

Wearing his own shield, Cho went to the wheel. "A night and a day will see us into the Inner Sea—and freedom from all pursuit."

The Lady Ayna shrugged like one tossing off a burden. "Then," she answered almost gaily, "what have we to fear? Surely we of the true blood can keep the followers of the Shadow off that long. See, even now they waver as if fearing to attack, though they have come into position to do so—"

Indeed the dark ship appeared to hesitate, though the mist was so distorting, half revealing, half concealing, that this might only be illusion. But it seemed to Ray that the bow of the raider did swing a little to one side as the *Wind Ruler* continued on course. The Lady Ayna was right, the headlong advance of the enemy checked, swinging farther away. They passed it, now near hidden in the fog, unchallenged.

"They fear us! They dare not test the might of the motherland in open battle!" exulted the girl.

Cho shook his head, plainly ill at ease. "I do not like it. By all the rules they should have attacked then. But they turned aside—"

"What can any raider hope to do against a ship of the fleet ready and willing for battle?" she returned. "It is merely that the captain over there is a man of sense. They may skulk about, seeing if their Ba-Al will give them some small advantage, but they will not risk fronting our bared teeth—"

During the next two hours, it seemed as if she were right in her reading of the situation, that the hovering ship feared to press the Murian vessel openly. The raider stayed just within the curtain of the mist, in sight, keeping pace with them, but did no more.

Han, however, shared Cho's mistrust of that slinking menace. Now and again he looked up from the wheel, glancing almost apprehensively at their unsought companion. And so it continued until high noon loosed a watery sunlight through the clouds.

Cho ordered food served to the men on deck. And they, too, ate where they stood, ever on guard.

"It may be that they wait for night and the dark to favor them." Cho brushed crumbs from his fingers.

"Let us also yearn for that, Sun-born," replied Han. "Engaging at night is a chancy thing. Escape may be ours—"

Cho flung back his cloak. "Not so! She is coming up!"

The raider was moving in with a darting speed. Ray drew the sword Cho had given him and looked curiously at the burnished blade. This was no weapon to fit his hand. He held it awkwardly and ran his finger down one of the keen edges. His mouth was dry, and he found himself swallowing too often. At last he slammed that weapon back in its sheath. His bare hands and knowledge of infighting might serve him far better now. But in spite of his training in his own time and place, this was the first real war he had ever faced.

Around him the crew made preparations with quiet efficiency, adjusting their weapons. He envied them their knowledge and the skill that gave them both occupation during this wait and a defense when the test came.

"Remember, the shield is for protection," Cho cautioned.

Ray nodded grimly.

Then, as sudden as a squall in the tropics, came the attack. From the bow of the raider shot a green ray, bright even in the sun, striking the side of the *Wind Ruler*. Ray caught the scent of burning.

"Too low!" cried the Lady Ayna.

Inch by inch that green light crept up to where the Murians waited. Cho's fingers dug into Ray's arm. "Your shield—behind it!"

Ray swung the shield across his body, crouching a little behind that barrier which suddenly seemed very light and useless. The beam slanted across the deck where they stood.

One of the men stationed by a death-breather screamed horribly. Convulsively he flung out his right arm. On the bare skin, writhing as might some loathsome reptile, was a patch of vivid green. The sailor screamed again, flinging himself back from the machine he served, falling to the deck close to Ray. Instinctively the American started forward, hand half out, but Cho's grip jerked him back and away.

"No! We can do nothing. He is already dead, and it will attack any other living flesh."

The man shrieked once more and then lay still, the others edging away from his crumpled body.

"See—it seeks now other victims, having fed once," Cho hissed.

That splotch of green, no longer seeming part of a beam of light, but something far more tangible, with an evil life of its own, wriggled from the arm of the dead man, fell upon the planking, lengthened into a snake, and began to inch along. Han leaned over the wheel. In his hand was a pear-shaped crystal. As he held it out, a spark of fire shot from it to strike directly upon the serpent light. There was a shrill hum that hurt the ears and the green thing was gone, leaving a blackened smear on the deck, from which arose a tiny curl of smoke.

"That—that was alive!" breathed Ray.

"Not as we know life," Cho returned. "That is one of the favorite weapons. They will try again—"

Once more the parent beam came from the raider, this time aimed much higher. It struck upon Han's shield, to cling there, as if it struggled to find a way through from behind that metal barrier. Baffled, it withdrew, only to strike at the rest, one by one.

When it reached Ray, it was a weight pressing him back, so that he retreated a step or two in surprise, before standing up to what was really no great force of pressure. The rim of the shield was in close contact with his body, and behind it he braced against something that writhed, turned up and down, and tried to find some crack in the metal through which to reach him. Then it was gone, and the beam swept along the metal screen protecting the waist and came to the foredeck. But nowhere did it find a second victim.

As yet the *Wind Ruler* made no counterattack, which led Ray to wonder. Nor did it deviate from the course or slacken the speed Cho had ordered. The raider had fallen a little behind now, as if the need for launching that beam had slowed it. But with the failure of its first blow, it plowed ahead to launch a second, which came in a rainlike patter.

Ray looked down. Inches from his feet two small slivers of metal stood point down, still quivering. Han cried out; another such sliver hung from his shoulder. Cho leaped to take the wheel.

"Loose the death-breathers!" he ordered.

One of the sailors near Ray steadied the tube on the box, while his companion inserted therein a ball of an unhealthy yellow color. One of the men bore down on a small lever.

63

The yellow ball rose almost lazily into the air, swung up and out to the raider, and crashed upon her bow deck. There was a puff of saffron smoke. The raider swung quickly, but the smoke crept back along her deck, a cloud thicker than the fog that had veiled her earlier. It hid all but a small portion just above the waterline.

Cho passed the wheel to one of the sailors. "That—that was against all orders, except for dire necessity. How is it with you, Han?"

The officer leaned limply against Ray, who had moved in to his support. His face had a sickly greenish tinge beneath sea tan. The metal sliver must have carried some deadly poison.

"Another must take duty, Sun-born—I—"

His full weight slumped against Ray, and the American shed his shield to ease him to the deck. Cho took him into his arms, supporting his head.

"Grieve not for me—I go to the Sun. Light a candle from the Flame—for—"

His head rolled against Cho's chest, and the Murian touched his sweat-beaded forehead gently. Then he looked to the raider, dipping and rising in the waves as if there was now no sure hand on its wheel.

"You have paid, followers of the Shadow—but the payment will be asked again, and yet again! This do I swear by the Flame! Han's true and lasting blood-price shall be collected in the Five Walled City itself! It may not be this year—but it will come!"

Ray helped him wrap the dead officer in his cloak. When they arose, the sailors were gingerly picking the metal darts from the deck, gathering them with careful attention not to touch their discolored points. But for the sailor who had died of the green fire and for Han, the fight might never have taken place.

"Sun-born! Look to the raider!"

They had drawn away from the other ship, leaving it wallowing in the waves apparently without direction. But now it was answering to some competent hand again, creeping forward, though not with its former speed, to follow them still.

"How can this be?" cried the Lady Ayna. "The death-breather—it should have killed all on board!"

"They must possess defenses of which we know naught," Cho replied. "But it appears they are crippled. Give us until late tomorrow and we are free. But if they bring by signal another of their kind—"

"Yes," the Lady Ayna echoed him, "there remains that. See, they creep it is true, but they do not leave us."

The *Wind Ruler* had drawn a length ahead of the dark raider. Still now that ship fell in behind, keeping the same course. A crippled hound, plainly, yet one that had not given up the hunt. And there was something uncanny in that determination.

Night came early under a cloud-filled sky. And still the silent Atlantean vessel pursued them, nosing along sullenly with perhaps not the will nor the power to draw level with the *Wind Ruler* again. The Murians hoisted a white running light, but there was no answer from across the water. However, their own illumination spread across the waves, making sure an enemy boarding party could not come upon them unaware.

Ray rubbed his smarting eyes, strained from too much watching astern. Like those about him, he had not discarded the tall shield, and its weight cut more and more heavily into his arm muscles.

Sometime late tomorrow, Cho had said, they would be at the entrance to the Inner Sea and could expect aid, if they must have it, from the forts at the inlet.

That black shadow by the wheel was Han and the sailor, sewn into their battle cloaks, ready for daybreak burial. And still the dark and silent enemy plowed in their wake.

The Lady Ayna had gone below, but Cho had taken the wheel and Ray elected to wait as long as the Murian kept duty. He had never been so tired before—or so it seemed. Nor, he had to reluctantly admit to himself, so afraid. Hand-to-hand combat, even steel to steel, a man could brace himself to face. But the crawling green fire that had something akin to life and a rain of poisoned metal thorns had no equal in his past training. His fingers curled as if about a rifle—a weapon eons away. That, grenades—mentally he made a list of what he wanted now in place of the useless sword weighting his hip.

At last Cho relinquished his post to a crewman and spoke. "Rest now."

In the cabin there was no sign of the Lady Ayna. Ray put aside the shield and pulled off his sodden cloak. He saw Cho stumble to the nearest bench and half collapse against the table, leaning forward, his head on his arm.

His own head back against the wall, Ray closed his eyes. A moment earlier he had wanted nothing but sleep, to close his eyes and forget everything. But now, against the dark of his lids, he saw—trees! Rank after rank of them, towering into the sky with limbs beginning many feet above his head. Between them were shadows that flowed to and fro like the wash of restless waves. And deep inside him a faint uneasiness stirred weakly. He knew a small, faded desire to walk under those roof-high branches, deep, deeper into the shade of the trees. Somewhere within them was the gate, the rent in the fabric of time, and if he could find it, he would return—

The trees grew darker and darker until trunks, branches, and restless shadows were all one and the same. And in Ray the wish to return to the gate was stilled. He slept at last.

There were five men now in the director's office instead of two. But one of the five held the attention of all.

"I can promise you nothing, gentlemen. Psychophysics is as much of an experimental program as this 'Operation Atlantis' of yours."

Fordham put down his pipe. "I know there're a hundred different experimental programs in existence—"

66

"Put that in the thousands, and you'll be closer to the truth," said the first speaker.

"All right, thousands then, Dr. Burton. And, tell me this: does *anyone* know what's being done—the all-over picture?"

"They have the reports—"

Fordham smiled wearily. "Who reads them? Probably several different committees. But does anyone ever try to coordinate the whole picture any more?"

"Probably not, until something such as this happens and there is a state of emergency," the other agreed.

"Now, do I understand you right, Dr. Burton? You believe that you might have a way to influence our man to return to the point of recall—through some mental process? Always supposing Fordham does get his door—or whatever you want to call it—open again?" the man in the general's uniform leaned forward to demand impatiently.

"Stress that word 'might,' General Colfax," returned Burton. "We've had a few results that have amazed us, but it depends upon the man tested and the circumstances. There is this in our favor—this Osborne was suddenly thrust into a situation for which he was totally unprepared, which would put him under immediate strain. According to his record"—he picked up the sheet of paper before him but did not glance at it, rather looked from man to man in the room—"he has had no contact at all with our type of training. However, he is said to be a 'loner,' which means he may be self-sufficient to a point, enough not to panic immediately. What he will, or did, make of his transition from here to there is anyone's guess. We can only try to compare him with the controls we have studied.

"He may have lingered about his point of entrance, seeking a return—if he can possibly have figured out what did happen. If so, our problem is relatively easy. If he was frightened enough to run—panic-stricken— then we can try the brain call. I have hopes of that because he will be unique in that time era. Therefore, always providing he had not gone too far, we can hope

67

that a call pattern attuned as closely to the type we think he may be as we can set it will bring him back."

"A lot of 'ifs' in all this," commented General Colfax. "I say we would be on the safer side sending in a squad—"

"Just suppose you marched your squad through, General," Fordham cut in, "into a wilderness such as the North American continent was perhaps four thousand years ago. Hunting one man across such country would not be easy. If Dr. Burton can call him back—"

"*If* again! What makes you think the country would be so different?"

"You saw the film," Fordham replied simply. "Did that look like downstate Ohio to you? Trees such as those—"

"—take centuries to grow, I know," Colfax replied. "And if the doctor's gadget does not work?"

"Face it!" Hargreaves blinked bloodshot eyes. "We may never see Osborne again. He could have been dead an instant after that film was shot. We aren't sure anyone could survive such a trip. But even if we don't find him, we'll have to send explorers through sooner or later. Maybe the doctor's think-beam can help on the next try, if it doesn't succeed with Osborne."

"When will you be ready?" Fordham asked Burton.

"We haven't gotten anything down to a walkie-talkie size. No, we'll have to dismantle, transport, assemble again. I can't honestly give you any estimate. We'll work round the clock and cut all the corners we can. But it will be several weeks at least—"

"Several weeks," General Colfax repeated. "I wonder what will happen to Osborne meanwhile. If he is still alive!"

6

RAY awoke and lay blinking for a moment or two, trying to hold onto something carried out of the dreams—something of importance. But already it was gone. Cho stood above him, only partly visible in the gray light that was not clear day.

"It is dawn," said the Murian, as if that statement had some inner and important meaning.

The American arose, wincing at cramped muscles, to follow Cho to the upper deck. Fog and clouds were gone. Around them lay the sea as smooth as those restless waves might ever be. In the east the sky was rose and pale gold. But on deck lay two bundles sewn into cloaks.

Cho paused. "Han—my friend—" Then he walked to the rail. Others raised the planks on which those bundles lay. All of the crew were there, to Ray's reckoning, standing at attention as if for review. The banner, which crackled in the wind from the ship's mast, was now halfway down the staff.

"Sea"—Cho's voice grew stronger with each word—"our heritage from ancient days, open now for these, your sons. Having performed with honor their duty, they are now at rest. Shelter their bodies while their spirits abide safe in the halls of the Sun—"

The boards tilted. Ray heard a catch of breath from the Lady Ayna. Then the rising sun turned the waves into a golden glory as the *Wind Ruler* sped on.

Night, or the gloom of the day before, had been in keeping with the black shadow of the raider. Ray did not know why he had expected to find it gone with this new bright morning, nor even why his surprise at seeing it still behind, just within eye limit, was so disturbing. It came no closer; perhaps it could not overtake them. But the crew of the Murian vessel continued to stand to arms and keep a wary lookout.

Their conversation was broken at times by long pauses as they watched their own wake.

"It is all wrong!" Cho set both hands on the rail as he stared at that distant pursuer. "They are dead; they must be. That ship is manned by the dead!"

The Lady Ayna caught her lower lip between her teeth, as if by that pressure alone she could keep from words she would rather not utter. But Ray answered,

"You may be right; you know the powers you control. But as long as it comes no closer—" Only he felt it, too, the gnawing of nerves caused by that ever-present shadow on the sea that did not move in or give one the chance to strike back, remaining always a hovering threat, the worse for what it aroused in one's imagination.

"Yes, as long as it does not come close—" the Lady Ayna echoed him. "And we must be near the sea gates of Mayax. Do you know, Lord Cho, I have never seen the motherland. Even as Lord Ray, I shall visit a strange country when we harbor at the City of the Sun. Is it like unto Uighur?" She was almost chattering, trying to use words to cloak her thoughts.

Cho gallantly seconded her. He turned purposefully away from his stern watch. "It is very different. Uighur is made up of mountains and narrow valleys, but in the motherland wide fields border broad rivers. The city lies at the mouth of one such river. Sometimes at nightfall the dwellers in the courtyards take small craft and go out upon the water for their pleasure. They sing together, and the harpers play—"

The Lady Ayna sighed. "Thus, in times of peace. Yes, different from our windswept land where the horse herds run free and wild to the outposts, beyond which outlaws struggle with beast-men and devils of the Dark to keep life within their bodies—"

"Do devils of the Dark then still exist?" asked Cho.

"The skin and long fangs of one were delivered in a packet of tribute hides the month before the *Fire Snake* sailed. Sometimes the youth of the courtyards hunt them. I have a dagger with the tooth of a devil forming

70

its hilt. But that devil was slain in my father's youth. They take to the heights and are solitary things, coming out only when they have a bad year and famine drives them to new hunting country."

"So. Yet it is told in Mu that all devils were slain long ago, being now only in stories to frighten children. The devils, Ray, are like—in part—to man, shaggy with heavy hair, yet walking erect. Their fangs are long and curved thus—the upper ones, that is. And always they live in high, wild places. They hunt in the darkness of the middle night. And they leave great, strange tracks in the mountain snow—"

"Snowmen," memory supplied Ray.

"You had them in your time?" the Lady Ayna questioned eagerly.

"Another legend—still in the country that you call Uighur, which in my day contains the highest mountain lands of the world. Your devils have been reported, their tracks seen, but none have been killed or captured—"

"How odd that this is so," the girl said slowly. "The devils known in your time, yet a land such as Mu forgot. how much else remains?"

"Say rather," Cho broke in, "why do some linger while others are forgot? Devils of the Dark—Atlantis— why these?"

The day wore on, cloudless, full of light. It was warmer, so they put aside their cloaks. And now there were birds above the waves, which were more of a blue-green. Trails of dark weed laced the surface of the sea, and once a fish broke water, rearing its head as if to gaze intelligently at the passing *Wind Ruler*.

"Dolphin!"

The Lady Ayna followed Ray's pointing finger. "Sea dancer," she corrected. "So these, too, you know, Lord Ray?"

"In my time they have growing importance. We have learned that they are highly intelligent. We are seeking to communicate with them."

71

She looked from the American to the dolphin and back again.

"It is known that the sea dancers are friendly, that they have been known to aid swimmers in difficulty, and they are under the protection of the Sun. No man dares raise a hand to hurt them. But they are of the sea, and while we go upon its surface in ships, swim in it a little, it is a world closed to us."

"No, you wouldn't have subs"—Ray nodded—"or scuba masks or the new water lungs—"

Cho was listening intently. "Is it then that your people have found a way to make the depths of the sea open to man? How?"

Ray described submarine activity as best he could. How men in his era not only traveled in the depths, but how, equipped with water-breathers, they could roam at will, more nearly part of the sea than man had been since the first amphibian had crawled from the waves to begin land-nourished life.

"But—how wonderful!" cried the Lady Ayna. "Ah, to travel in the sea! Truly you live in a time of wonders, a time when man must have the whole of the world open to him! We have been taught that once war is conquered, this would be so—"

"War is still with us," Ray replied. "Many of the things we have learned have come because of the necessity of defense or attack in war. No, my age is far from golden—"

"Golden?" She repeated inquiringly.

"Mankind looks back to a golden age when there was no war and all was peace and happiness—"

Cho smiled wryly. "When was that age then, brother? In our time, which is a legend to you? No—you see for yourself how much peace abides with us. In the days of Hyperborea? We have our own legends, and those speak only of death and disaster struck from the spark of man's greed and lust. If there was a golden age—where would one seek it? In the past—no! We have been taught to look to the future."

"Which to my time is dark," Ray replied.

"Lord—the signal!"

They turned to look southwest at the foreman's call. Against an afternoon sky a white trail mounted up and up, making a line across the blue.

"The signal tower of the outer gates," Cho said.

"It would seem that we have won our race after all," the Lady Ayna commented.

Ray looked astern. The raider was there, but only just visible, as if it had stopped.

It was that, Ray thought, which had kept them uneasy, the waiting for some last attack from that sinister black blot.

The Lady Ayna drew a deep breath. "The air is cleaner for its going. Look ahead now, not behind. The future still awaits us."

There was a bustle about them. The metal walls that had shielded the waist dropped back. The machines of war were being covered by their crews. Ahead, on a narrow tongue of land pushing into the sea and ending in a fringe of rock teeth, was a tall tower.

Cho was giving orders and moving about the deck.

"We will go straight in," he said when he returned. "I shall not stop at Manoa but head directly for the canals. See, they acknowledge us with banner salute."

There were puffs of white from the tower's head; then a flag dipped and rose again. The wind pulled it straight for an instant, and Ray saw its insignia, a rising rayed sun on a green field.

They rounded the reefs, altered course to the west, and shortly saw another cape to the south. On this stood a squat, earth-hugging building that had the look of a fort. Cho smiled. Some of the strain had gone from his face.

"We are in now. Let us eat and drink in comfort."

It was still day when they returned to the upper deck. Cho strode up and down restlessly, paying little attention to the others.

"Now we no longer sail alone," pointed out the Lady Ayna. "That is a grain carrier and, beyond, a merchant

73

ship from the motherland, and next is a ship of the northern fleet.

"Some of these have been recalled to lie idle here until the North Sea is safe again. Others do business in these waters. But the Inner Sea is always safe—the storms of the north and the whims of the southern gales are unknown here."

"Why are those turning?" Ray asked. Two ships ahead were altering course, opening a lane for the *Wind Ruler*.

"Because we fly that." Cho came up to them. He pointed to their own flag, its full sun proudly emblazoned on a crimson field. "They know we bear urgent news, and so the word has been passed to give us open water."

When dark came, a light was trained upon that banner, continuing to proclaim their need for swift passage. And it was accorded them the next day also, even though they were in the crowded shipping lanes about Manoa's harbor. This capital of an imperial province Ray saw only from the sea. But its soaring white towers and pyramids gave the impression of a long-established civilization.

He discovered during these days that the tongue of the motherland was becoming his. At least he could understand easily, though when he replied, his own tongue still twisted over its clicking consonants and slurred vowels. He practiced all he could, while Cho also gave him a grounding in the Atlantean language.

They met with their first delay at the canals to the western sea. Ray could detect no resemblance here to the continent of his own time. This backbone of southern America must ruse in the future to form the sharp spine of the Andes, but now the only heights visible from the deck of the *Wind Ruler* were gentle rolling hills behind the canal port city.

There was confusion on board, a coming and going of officials. But finally they were passed through, and the keel of the *Wind Ruler* slid into the waves of another sea.

"Thanks to the Sun, we are free at last!" Cho returned

from seeing the last port officer overboard. "After what has happened, I do not like delays, nor do I find port gossip of high interest."

"The Re Mu—" began the Lady Ayna.

"Yes, to him we must give truth, not words to hide it, lest alarms spread. And what truth we have is not pleasant. The Re Mu—perhaps he will see ways in which we might have done better. His is the wisdom we cannot aspire to. And this was my first command—"

"Ah, but you return with your ship," broke in the Lady Ayna.

"Which I might not have done had fortune frowned upon me as she did upon you. There is no disgrace, my lady, in failure if one has acted to the best of one's ability—and tries again."

"How blue the sea," she said abruptly, as if she would turn her thoughts outward. "It is gray along the shores of Uighur, and too dark in the north where it washes the Barren Lands—"

"Why do you call them the Barren Lands?" Ray asked. "There is wilderness, yes, but they are not barren. There are forests—" He paused, thinking of trees dark and tall, yet alive.

"Perhaps because no colony has been set there," replied Cho. "To us of the motherland, they seem forbidding, as if hiding secrets not for the eye of man."

"Yet it is not so in your time, is it?" the Lady Ayna said. "Tell us about them then."

He told them of the crowded and crowding cities, of the ever-pushing population that covered the earth with more and more dwellings, of superhighways, of airfields, of the thrusts into space—

"You seek to rule the moon, perhaps land ships on other worlds!" marveled Cho. "Man does so much, yet you say that all this is still flawed."

"Yes. The more devices man makes, the more death comes from them. Machines take to the skies, they fall, and those in them are killed. Or else they sow death as they fly, and women and children are killed in their homes. Men talk around the world, but they break

75

every law they have made. Some of them have greater wealth than they can reckon; others die for want of bread. So it is—"

"As it always has been," mused the Lady Ayna. "Yet you are still men, some good, some evil. Have you ever ridden in the sky?"

"Yes."

"What was it like?" Cho demanded.

"Like swimming, a little. One can see the world below or be caught in the clouds—"

"That I would like," said the Lady Ayna. "It would have been good had you brought such a bird with you—"

Ray laughed. "There are many things I could have brought that would have been highly useful, but I never thought of a plane."

He told other tales of his own time as they sailed across the western ocean. But the Lady Ayna never tired of hearing of the planes that took men through the clouds.

"The Naacals should be able to make such," she observed. "It should be suggested that they seek such knowledge."

Cho was startled. "But one does not suggest matters to the Naacals; it is for them to decide the paths of wisdom to be opened to our feet."

"When they hear the words of the Lord Ray, they should be moved into *that* path," she insisted. "It would be pleasant to look down upon the clouds, to travel as a bird—"

Her insistence apparently disturbed Cho. "Ray shall talk to the Naacals, yes. That is only what will follow when they hear of this coming. But we cannot make suggestions—"

"Who are the Naacals?" Ray asked quickly when it appeared that the Lady Ayna was prepared to argue.

"The priests of the Flame who are the guardians of ancient wisdom and the seekers after new—to teach mankind. They journey between colony and colony spreading knowledge, increasing as ever they can our stores of learning. Many things they tell only to the Re Mu, and perhaps a few of the Sun-born who are discreet and have the proper care for wisdom. My mother was so honored when she became a daughter of the temple after my father's death."

"I shall enter the temple when my sea duty is done," said the Lady Ayna.

Cho smiled. "Say you so now, my lady. But I will wager that within the year you will summon some warrior to your right hand. Then we shall hear no more of temples—"

Her eyes sparkled, and there was a curve to her lips. "Do you have the power to read the future as a Naacal or one who has passed the Nine Mysteries?" Then she swung away from them and was gone to the inner cabin. Ray looked to Cho for enlightenment.

The Murian still smiled. "So say all women sometimes—that they would have naught of us and prefer temple powers. It is quickly forgotten when the time comes for the marriage bracelets—"

"We are not too far from Mu now?"

"We should harbor before nightfall and sleep this night in my mother's courtyard. I do not believe we shall be summoned for audience before the morrow, though the Lady Ayna may go this night."

Within the hour came the welcome call of "Land!" Then the oars were put out, and the rowers took their places. One of the officers beat stroke time on a small drum, and they pulled together with practiced ease.

"Harbor police." Cho indicated a light craft skimming toward them.

"What ship?" They were hailed from the police boat.

"*Wind Ruler* of the northern fleet, the Sun-born Cho commanding, with urgent news for the Re Mu."

"Pass free." The police cutter was already on its way to meet a lumbering merchantman.

The oval harbor was full of shipping. Heavy merchantmen, stately passenger vessels, ships of the fleet, barges, and fishing smacks swung at anchor. And the docks hummed with throngs of laborers.

Beyond, the city rose terrace by terrace, such a one as might have come out of a dream. White flashing metal, rainbow hues, it built by wall and tower up and up. The houses and palaces Ray had seen from afar at Manoa were the rough dwellings of an outpost village compared to this.

"There lies the heart of our world. What think you of it, brother?" asked Cho. "Does it equal the cities of your age?"

"I do not think my time holds its equal. In size, yes, but not in beauty."

They docked, and Cho handed over his command to his second officer. There was an honor guard drawn up to salute them with swords as they disembarked. Its officer spoke to Cho.

"You have made a quick voyage, Sun-born."

"Three days from the Inner Sea," Cho answered with some pride.

"Fair time indeed, my lord. There is a litter waiting for the Lady Ayna. And you, my lords, are you for the Lady Aiee's courtyard?"

"Yes—" Cho sounded impatient.

The Lady Ayna stepped forward. "It seems our ways part here, my lords. Surely friends and battle comrades need no farewells of ceremony. Till we meet again may the Flame guard you."

She raised her hand in salute and was gone with her escort, swiftly swallowed up in the crowd. But the officer had remained behind.

"Your commands, Sun-born?"

"Let us go as swiftly as we may—"

He opened a passage for them. Ray would have gone more slowly, trying to see what he could, but Cho hurried him on. Two or three turns from one crowded street to another brought them away from much of the press of traffic. There were still carts, horses, camels, but many pedestrians. And the range of garments, the brightness of color, and the difference in races Ray glimpsed were hard to assess when he was constantly urged on. It would seem that he walked the streets of a city wherein most of a world was stirred into one rare mixture. And he longed to be able to sort out sounds, sights, and impressions at greater leisure.

Cho turned into a narrow, quiet lane, outstripping their officer escort. He stopped before a scarlet door set in the left-hand wall.

"Many thanks for your company and aid, my lord," he said, the door already swinging under his sharp push. Ray hesitated for a moment, and the officer smiled.

"All of us know of the Lord Cho. He is a good son to the Lady Aiee. May you rest in the light of the Flame, lord." With a salute he was gone.

Ray entered a large garden, closing behind him the door Cho had left ajar. There were palm trees and flowers, and a pool rimmed with mossy marble. Ferns grew there, reflected in the quiet water. Cho stood by it, and now he looked to Ray.

"She is coming—"

The woman who crossed a lawn of closely mown grass did not look up but seemed intent upon her own thoughts. She was as tall as Cho, her skin almost as fair as the pearls about her throat and the robe she wore. Her hair was yellow and hung in thick pearl-twisted braids to her waist. But the calm beauty of her face was all Ray saw.

Memory stirred in him, and he could not help what he did then. He turned on his heel and went back to the red door in the white wall. He went blindly, seeing not what was there but what was in his mind. The door did not yield to his push, however, as it had to Cho's eager hand. And he beat on it with force enough to bruise his fist.

"My son—"

No words—only in his mind, as it had been with Cho when they first met. And—somehow—healing flooded in with those words, pushing away memory. But he would not turn; he dared not. For the last time his fist struck against the stubborn panels of the door. He did not want—he could not turn and face—

79

"Ray."

His own name, not as he had feared to hear it in re-awakened bitter pain, but in another voice. His hand dropped to his side.

"Ray—"

That was such a call to obedience as he could not push away. Reluctantly, how reluctantly, he turned—and faced eyes—eyes that were all encompassing. They saw into him, not just as he stood now but as it had been for him in the months past. Those eyes reached across the barrier between this world and his own, and knew— He was sure that they knew—

"Ray—" for the third time. This was not a demand for attention now but a welcome. And there was a hand on his. He was as aware of that as of those all-knowing, all-seeing eyes. The hand drew him back into the garden, and somehow it also drew him in the same instant over or through another door, unseen but sensed. For a space Ray was free of the world of his birth.

7

"AWAKEN!"

Ray opened his eyes. He was shaking with cold, an iciness that struck far into him; yet he was not lying on a frigid bank of snow. But neither was he on the couch where he had gone to sleep.

Bright bars of moonlight, so bright that they dazzled his blinking eyes, lay across the floor before him. And under his bare feet that floor was chill. How had he come into this hall and why did he stand there, one hand resting on a door latch? He had no idea; he felt only complete bewilderment.

"Awaken!" Again that low-voiced command came from behind.

He turned to face a robed and cowled figure, half in the shadow, half in that shattering moonlight. Now a hand raised to toss back the cowl. Ray confronted the Lady Aiee. She held up her other hand between them, and on the outstretched palm a small ball glowed into life, with a clear white light that for the moment hurt his eyes.

"Come—" Her voice was soft, hardly above a whisper. She turned as if she knew she would be obeyed, moving soundlessly along that moon-striped corridor to a partly open door.

Within, she placed her ball of light upon a small tripod, and immediately it sprang to heightened glow, making plain the room with its chairs, its couch, and a table heaped with linen book rolls.

"Hither!" She waved him onto a chair by that table, and Ray sat down. Still he shivered with the cold that was not so much a part of the air about him as of some inner chill.

The Lady Aiee poured wine into a white flower-shaped cup. And into the liquid she measured drops from a finger-long vial. "Drink!" She put the cup into his hands.

Again Ray obeyed. The liquid was warm in his throat, warmer still as he swallowed. As he set aside the emptied cup, she came to him, setting her hands one on each shoulder, drawing his eyes to meet hers.

It was—it was like being whirled away by a force of power one could neither understand nor control. Ray's feeble, instinctive resistance was swept aside instantly. What she wanted of him, he did not know. But she was willing some answer from him.

At last she broke the contact, the pressure of her fingers leaving his shoulders. And only when it was released was Ray conscious of how determined that hold had been.

"What—?" For the first time he dared a question and then was not quite sure of what he wished to ask. How had he come into that hall? What did she want of him?

"You were walking while asleep," she told him, "moved by some force not of your waking mind. I had to learn the nature of this force, from whence it came—"

"Walking in my sleep! But—"

"You will say you have not done this before," the Lady Aiee replied. "That is the truth as you know it. Listen, my son. You have heard that I am of the temple. As such, I have had training. Your own time depends much upon material things, upon knowledge where there is proof that a man can see, hear, taste, or feel. We have other learning, which is not so easily made manifest. It deals with the unseen, the unheard, that which can be sensed obliquely but not held out into the clear light of day.

"But you are not of our blood or of the shaping of this world, and much that lies within you is new to us. You may have powers we do not know, experienced as we are in such matters. Forces we do not understand you can bend to your will. With one of my people, sleepwalking is the sign that they are under control. It can be an evil thing, and the victim must undergo cleansing in the temple—"

82

"Under control?"

"Moved by the will of another. And this is a thing the sons of the Shadow do."

Ray shook his head. "I am no Atlantean. I have told Cho—you—the truth."

The Lady Aiee nodded. "That I know. To one of the temple, the touch of the Shadow is like fire soot on a man's face. And had you been possessed against your will, then I would have learned it when I 'read' you a moment ago. But something stirred you to walk while one part of your mind was at rest. And that is important to learn. It may be that your own time still has ties upon your spirit and would reclaim you. Or it may be—"

"What?" It all sounded plausible when she spoke, though his training and background made him question it as having no more validity than the moonlight in the hall had substance.

"That something else strives to use you. When you were taken by the Atlanteans, one of their Red Robes looked upon you, did he not? And those who took you gave to him the possessions you carried when they made you prisoner. Thus he has a mental picture of you and, in his hands, things that you have worn close to your body. From so much a strong quest-mind can build even more. But if that is the case, then you are safe for a while. The draft you have just taken will make you no longer a target for such a searching and invasion. And those in the temple will work for you."

"But—that's witchcraft! It doesn't really happen! Like sticking pins in a doll and imagining your enemy is going to suffer—"

There was such a sharp intake of breath from her that Ray looked up. "What know you of pins and dolls and ill-wishing?"

The warmth had gone out of her voice, leaving it remote and unfriendly.

"Stories of my time in which men of sense do not believe."

"No? Then they are fools and not men of sense. The

old powers must be nearly forgotten. But certain forces do come to the call of an ill-doer. Do not disdain old stories, man out of time, for in them lies a core of fact. There is light and there is dark in the world, and to each certain men incline. If they are willing to pay the price—for each demands a price—then certain knowledge and the power to use it becomes theirs, by degrees of hard learning. Those who have not the learning see a few material objects and believe that is the whole of the matter, not knowing they should cringe and flee from what lies behind those playthings. And in this time those are not playthings. Listen and believe. Scoffing might cost you your life!"

Ray was impressed in spite of himself. She believed so implicitly in what she said that he must accept it as a part of this life.

"You think that perhaps that Atlantean priest was trying to get at me some way? But why?"

"For such reasons as you yourself can list if you think. You are far from stupid. First, you are a new element that has been tossed into an old quarrel at a time of crisis. And such are ever to be treated warily—"

"But I'm just one man with no particular skills—"

She lost some of her remote withdrawal. "One man before this has upset the balance, turned the tides of history into a new way. What you carry in your mind may be of service to those with whom you choose to stand. That is one reason to lay mind-control upon you—though to try to do so in the very citadel of the Sun shows audacity beyond belief. On the other hand, you are among us, accepted and secure. Thus could you be eyes and ears for them. No"—she must have read his expression aright—"do not be angry. It would be to their advantage to have this so without your conscious knowledge. Perhaps"—she frowned now—"in my concern I did ill. It might have been better to have watched and waited—"

"To see where I would have gone?" He caught her thought. "If I try it again—"

The Lady Aiee shook her head. "You will not now, at

84

least for a space of days. Did I not say that the draft cut you free from influence? But those in the temple will know more than I. Now"—once more her hands were on his shoulders, this time drawing him to his feet—"do you return to your bed, where you will sleep well, and in the morning you will awake refreshed with a mind at peace."

Had that meeting been a dream, he wondered, when he rolled over on the couch and felt the warmth of the sun strike across his head and shoulders? Yet it clung to his mind in sharp detail as dreams do not do, almost as if it were a warning.

"Ho!" Cho came in. "Rise, brother. Not only food but a fair morning awaits!"

They swam in a pool with silver sand at its bottom and an array of fantastic, leering monsters carved about its rim. Then they dressed in silk tunics.

"Your hair grows," Cho observed. "That is well. A free-born warrior does not go cropped as a debt-server." He combed his own long locks and fastened them with gemmed clips at the nape of his neck.

The Lady Aiee was already seated at the table on the terrace above the garden when they joined her. She crumbled small grain cakes in her hands and threw the bounty to a flock of brilliant birds on a stone walk below, laughing at their greediness. To Ray as well as Cho, she offered one of her hands after brushing off the crumbs, and the American tried to copy the Murian's grace in kissing it.

"A fair morning, my sons. But it cannot be spent as one wishes—"

"A summons?" Cho asked quickly.

"Just so—to the palace. Mayhap afterwards we can show Ray something of the city." But it seemed to the American that she watched him gravely, as if her thoughts were serious. Did she still think that he might be a threat to all this, an unconscious spy in their midst? Ray lost the small exultation he had felt since waking. There might be no cloud across the sun, but a ghost of last night's chill crept up his spine.

Cho began a quick coaching of what must be done according to court etiquette, and Ray forced himself to concentrate upon the other's words. It would seem that the Murian Emperor did not live in such state that semiprivate meetings such as they were now summoned to attend were ordeals, yet there were forms to follow.

The Lady Aiee interrupted her son after a moment or two. "Ray, the Re Mu is like unto no other man of our world, nor, I believe, of yours. He is truly one set apart, the selected of the Sun-born, having undergone during his training such ordeals as no ordinary man can face. Our rule does not pass from father to son, as is sometimes true in the lesser kingdoms, but to the best man of the next generation, after careful selection, of all the Sun-born blood. He who sits on the Sun throne is indeed the one of us who had proved his right to hold all power in his two hands. Be not uneasy before him. He sees much deeper into truth and falsehood than other men, and the honest man of good heart is fearless in his presence."

Was that again more than reassurance—a warning? Ray could not tell. But there was no retreat now, and, as far as he knew, he was honest. Ray was startled at his own thought. Why should he question his honesty? Warnings—witchery—push them out of one's mind, concentrate only on what *had* happened. He had a straight story, and every word of it was the truth.

They went in curtained litters, not a mode of transportation Ray fancied, but one that was dictated by custom. And there was an escort from the palace to clear a path and see their trip was made as quickly as possible. When their bearers at last put down the litters, Ray emerged in a courtyard where a fountain played. Before them was a flight of stairs up which the Lady Aiee led them, Ray falling in a step or two behind at her left, as Cho walked to her right. To the sentry at the top, she gave their names, and he stood aside before the entrance to a hall.

At its far end hung an ivory-colored curtain and beside it a gong of beaten silver, with a mallet of the same metal. The Lady Aiee struck the gong twice, and before the murmuring echoes had died away, a voice from beyond the curtain spoke.

"Enter, Aiee, my daughter, with the son of my brother's son and the stranger from beyond."

They came into a larger chamber where there was no use of jewels or metal to break the ivory walls and flooring. Above them the roof was a dome, its center open to the sky, and directly below that opening were four men. Instead of the brilliant silks Ray had seen before, three of them wore long white robes, such as he had seen on the Lady Aiee the night before, the cowls thrown back as capes. And they were aged, stooped, their hair as white as their robes.

The fourth man sat a little apart. His tunic was yellow, his belt of that reddish metal of the shields that had protected them in battle. On his head was a crown in the form of a sun disk surmounted by a nine-headed serpent.

The Lady Aiee went to one knee before him; Cho and Ray, less agile, followed her example.

"Greetings, Aiee. And to you, Cho." The dark blue eyes of the man who ruled most of the world were now turned on Ray. "And to you, also, stranger, who has come so far a journey. Come you hither—" He arose from his chair and led them to the other end of the room, where benches of ivory were cushioned with silk. There he waved them to be seated facing him.

"The Lady Ayna had much to tell us—" he began.

Ray could not help staring at the Emperor. Those dark eyes—like the Lady Aiee's, they seemed to see not what was directly before them but what lay behind outward appearances. They were old, very old, with wisdom, such wisdom as the American had never encountered in his own time and place. Yet the man could not be of more than middle years.

The Emperor was looking at Cho. "You felt that this raider was a strange ship?"

"After two of my crew were slain, we released the death-breather. Though it enveloped the ship, yet still it followed us. It was as if those aboard were not dead."

One of the Naacals had drawn nearer, and now he spoke. "In our knowledge that weapon has no defense. They must now possess wisdom we have not."

"If so, I fear they have paid such a price for it as will lie heavily on them in days to come," the Re Mu replied. "They are to be pitied—" He paused and then smiled faintly. "You have done as was right, Cho. And now—" Once more those eyes were turned on Ray.

"I think you have already done us some service, man from the future, when you freed Cho from the Atlanteans. Perhaps you have powers beyond our knowledge, strengths strange to us. But why do you throw in your lot with Mu?"

"My own world is gone. As for aiding Cho, first he aided me. Otherwise—I do not know." Then after a moment Ray added, "Is it possible for me to return to my own time?"

The Re Mu turned to the priest, and the Naacal answered in a high, thin voice:

"Had the youth come to us by dream, even as we ourselves visit other times in spirit, perhaps this would be so. But to go in body, that is a different matter. None of us who have ventured to do this have ever returned."

"I believe that this truth you must accept," The Re Mu said. But his eyes probed deeper, deeper, for a long moment before he added, "Your given name is Ray, which is like unto our word for the Sun power, a potent sign. Tell me, what thought you of this Atlantean ship that should have been a dead hulk, yet still came after?"

"That it was evil."

"So agree all of you. I, too, believe that it contained evil. And to face new evil is a thing to think long on." He fell silent, and when he spoke again, his voice held a formal note.

"Let this youth be numbered among the Sun-born, even as a son of our house. The duties of that station shall be his, for I say unto you now, my son, among us duties far outweigh rights. And it may be you will

88

discover our world a harsh one. Learn of it what you can, even as it shall learn of you."

It seemed that their audience was concluded and they were free to go. Once more in the outer corridor, away from the actual presence of the Emperor, Ray tried to understand what had been the reason for the Re Mu's impact on him. It was not the Murian's physical bearing, fine though that was, nor any great wisdom in his words. It was rather what he did not do or say but what was ever behind him like a great, billowing cloak, which made him a figure of awe and veneration.

They returned to the litters and their waiting escort. The Lady Aiee was smiling.

"Since we are no longer on summons," she said, "I have asked that we be taken to the marketplace that Ray may see the busy heart of the city."

It appeared proper now to loop back the curtains of the litters, or so Ray assumed when Cho did so, and he could see more of the city. The streets were wide and well paved, with stone-rimmed beds of flowers and small trees ornamenting them at intervals. Then, at the edge of a circle, they came to a halt, and the Lady Aiee dismissed escort and litter bearers with her thanks.

Ray saw some in the crowds more plainly dressed than he and his companions. But there were none in rags, nor did any appear to be less than well fed.

"The flower sellers—" Lady Aiee indicated a side way that was a riot of color. Cho went to one of the booths and returned, after a moment or two of bargaining, with a small bouquet giving forth a sweet fragrance, which he presented to his mother. She sniffed it appreciatively.

"Now why does not the spring's breath ever grow in our garden? The Flame knows we have tried to raise it many times, tending and cosseting it. Yet always does it shrivel and die. One of the mysteries no Naacal can solve. Now"—she placed her hand on Cho's arm—"do I not owe homecoming gifts? What better time to choose them—"

"While we are still greatly welcome?" Cho laughed.

"Ah, yes, by all means, let us profit by that. Where to, my lady?"

"Krafiti's, I believe."

They went past the alley of the flower sellers and came to a side way, where the street was lined by open-fronted shops. Sun struck in here and there to raise rainbow arcs from wares spread on display trays. Ray had never seen such an open showing of gems, and he gaped, amazed, lingering behind the others. Many of the jewels were set in the red metal new to him, and he asked Cho what it was.

"Orichalcum. It has many properties and is a compound of gold, copper, and silver, but in what proportion of each is the guarded secret of the smiths."

One of the merchants arose to greet the Lady Aiee. "Indeed the Flame favors me this day, that the Sun-born lady and her lords find it their pleasure to visit my unworthy shop—"

"Indeed, Krafiti, if you will fashion masterpieces, then you must continue to tempt us past forbearance. I have heard much of a certain pearl headdress—"

"Let the Sun-born but be seated and it shall be brought for their inspection. A-Ham"—he spoke to his assistant—"bring forth the crown of one hundred and ten."

"Now we shall see true beauty," Cho told Ray in a whisper. "Krafiti is a master craftsman, and his agents bring him the finest stones from all over the world."

The assistant reappeared bearing a tray of ebony. On its black surface rested the life-sized bust of a woman, also of the same dark wood, and on the head was the crown.

A net of rose-shaded pearls was meant to confine the wearer's hair in the back, and over the forehead rose the nine-headed serpent constructed of the same gems, some as large as Ray's thumbnail. The Lady Aiee put forth a finger and stroked the head of the serpent before she spoke.

"Well do you design your temptations. Now that I have looked upon it, I cannot rest until it is mine."

"But, of course! Did I not fashion this thinking of the Sun-born? To none else would I offer it. If you do not wish it, then it shall be broken apart and the pearls used otherwise."

"It is mine. Let it be brought to the courtyard. Now show us armlets, for I owe homecoming gifts to the warriors who have seen duty in far places." She smiled at Ray. "It is the custom among us to present small treasures to those returning from difficult journeys. Choose you one of these and wear it with good fortune."

Ray looked down at a bewildering array of gemmed arm bands. Then he glanced up at her. "You choose for me; it is your gift."

Her smile deepened, and he knew she was pleased.

"This then—" She took up a band carved from jet in the form of nine-headed serpents, small diamonds making the reptilian eyes. "The serpents are for wisdom, which all men need. And it is unlike all others—"

"Save this one," Krafiti answered. He held out one of milky jade, made to the same design, but with ruby eyes.

"Then that is yours, Cho, if it pleases you."

"As it well does," he replied promptly.

"Upon the inner side you shall set names," the Lady Aiee ordered. "For the black 'Ray,' for the jade 'Cho,' and send them with the crown."

"It is done, Sun-born."

Ray looked at them lying together, black against white, and both the brighter seeming for that contrast. Serpents—they appear to revere snakes here, he thought, not to hold the prejudice of his own time against that species. The arm band was beautiful in its craftsmanship, a work of art, and it was a gift of friendship. Yet somehow— He did not know why he wished it would remain where it now was, to be worn by another. It was as if that black band held some dire promise.

He got to his feet quickly, suddenly conscious the others were waiting for him. And the Lady Aiee was watching him closely.

91

"What is it?" she asked a little sharply.

"Nothing. The contrast, black against white, makes them more arresting—"

She looked to the bands. "Yes, that is true. And that is all?"

"All," he replied firmly. He was going to have no more of forebodings born in the imagination—they seemed to be far too easily nurtured in this world.

8

THOUGH life in the courtyard of the Lady Aiee might have luxurious outer trappings, it was not, Ray discovered, an idle one for any of them. His own task seemed to be learning the Murian script for reading of the book rolls. And it was not easy. In the passing of time Ray began to note that there were portions of Murian life that were not as open to him as those rolls over which he pored.

The Lady Aiee vanished for hours, active in temple duties. That was the one major building in the city that he had not been invited to visit. It was, he gathered, the very heart of the land. Why had they neglected showing it to him?

Or was it neglect, Ray asked himself one morning when he had gone to the window to rest his eyes on the greenery without. He had caught a word or two between Cho and his mother that very day, enough to know that Cho was going to the temple for a special ceremony devoted to those lost at sea. Yet nothing had been said to Ray concerning this.

Was he—had he walked again by night in answer to what the Lady Aiee seemed sure was another's will? If he had, he did not know it. Did they still hold him in a certain supicion so they would not take him into any shrine they held in respect?

The Sun was the symbol of their supreme being. That had been easy enough to understand, and it was one of the oldest of all beliefs. But there was a Flame to which they alluded now and again, also a sign of religious power.

So far he had kept within the bounds he thought they had set for him, going only on such errands around the city as he had been invited to share, to the market, to the docks with Cho, and once on a pleasure party on the river, where the Lady Ayna and her hostess in the city had also been guests. What he had seen, Ray stored away, to mull over privately. But there was always an uneasy feeling, now growing ever stronger, that what he was shown were only surface things and that all that really mattered in this land was kept from him. In spite of the ease of manner and friendly attitude of those about him, he remained ever the stranger.

"My lord—"

So intent was he upon his own thoughts that he was startled by those words from the doorway. And in his surprise a small suspicion sprang to life. Perhaps he was never really left alone. He glanced back at the serving man.

"Yes, Tampro?"

"A messenger, lord, from the Great One."

"The Lady Aiee, Lord Cho, they are gone—"

"The messenger would speak with you, lord. He came in haste."

A royal messenger, for him?

"Admit him."

But Tampro had already gone, and a moment later a man in the uniform of the palace guard stood in his place.

"To the Sun-born, greeting. The Great One asks for your presence in the Hall of the Sky."

Ray nodded. His thoughts were jumbled, and he forgot the formal phrase that should answer that. He followed the other to a litter, noting that again the curtains were drawn after his entrance so that he could neither see nor be seen. Why? His imagination supplied a score of answers in almost as many moments, and each wilder than that which had preceded it. The bea rs moved at a jog trot, which suggested the need for speed.

He heard the challenge of sentries, a low-voiced reply from his escort. Then they were out of the bustle of a city street into comparative quiet. Finally the bearers came to a halt and set down their burden.

Ray emerged, but not in the same fountained court-

94

yard he had visited before. This was a narrow space between two high walls. No plants grew here to break the starkness of those white stone stretches, and there was a promise of grim purpose that awoke wariness. Directly before him was a door giving entrance to a tower.

The white surface of its sides was smooth except for the door. But, as Ray looked up, he saw symbols of gold set above. And for all his past patient study, these he could not read. The messenger-officer stood in the doorway motioning for Ray to join him.

"The Great One waits!" Impatience was in his tone. "Above—" He stood aside to wave Ray onto a stair that curved about the inner wall of the tower. And the American climbed that alone, the officer remaining below.

There was a curious simplicity to the inner portion of the tower, as if it had been deliberately designed to copy an older and ruder form of architecture from a day when men built in rough stone and learned skills even as they so built. The stair came through an open well into a room that occupied the whole of the tower's interior, an empty room. Again the stair curved up, leading higher, through a second empty room and a third.

Then he came to the topmost section. Awaiting him there were not only the Re Mu but also two of the Naacals. Behind them the circular expanse of the wall was broken at intervals by opaque ovals, certainly not meant as windows, for, though it was bright sunlight without, no light entered through them but came from globes resting on tripods near the three seats. The rest of the room was as bare as those below.

Ray knelt, feeling awkward and foolish, but following the ritual of the court. However, none of them made him greeting. Instead, he found himself the center of their probing gaze, and his distrust grew. This had the feeling of an inquisition, save that he had no crime to answer for—

95

"That is the truth. We do not summon you to any accounting."

It was the Re Mu who spoke. "No, not for anything in the past are you summoned here, but rather for an act to come—"

Ray was bewildered. "You believe that I mean you harm in some way?" Here it was, Lady Aiee's suspicion. So he did have a right to feel apprehensive.

"No—you may be able to work us well, not ill! Tell him, U-Cha."

"It is thus," one of the Naacals said. "Those of Atlantis have now truly closed the lanes of thought, an act never before committed since land and living things rose from the slime of the sea bottom after Hyperborea was dashed to the depths.

"Always have certain minds in the motherland been trained to communicate with like in the colonies. Thus does the Re Mu give his commands to the viceroys of the outer lands. Now we can so speak only to the frontier posts of Mayax, no farther. Those who have chosen of their will to march into the Shadow have set up a barrier none of us can pierce. And what foulness they plot behind that cloud—that we must learn for the sake of the motherland."

"It is thus." The Re Mu leaned forward a little, and again that overwhelming aura, which seemed as much a part of him as his cloak, engulfed Ray, whether by the Emperor's deliberate will or not, the American did not know. "We cannot break this barrier. But there is a small chance that you might be able to do so. You come from a time when different thoughts and powers are a part of its people. What bars us may be no hindrance to you. Would you be willing to aid us in trying to see what our enemies would do?"

"Do you mean—send me to Atlantis?" Ray asked slowly.

"Not in body, no, but in mind," replied the Naacal U-Cha.

"For such voyaging," the Re Mu added, "we have many safeguards. Ah—" He broke off, his eyes holding

Ray's. "I see that you know little of the mind and its powers. Your strength in your time is founded on other means. So, to you, this is a fearsome thing, for you would not loose what you neither understand nor can control. But do not suspect this so much. Have you not already talked mind to mind? Once you are taught, you will have use of the inner power as have all the Sun-born. But I respect your hesitation, since to you this is an unwalked willderness over which no trails run, an uncharted sea."

He was useful to them, Ray thought. They would be careful of a tool they needed. And it was true that he had communicated with Cho and the others, and no harm had come from it. Still—the Lady Aiee had warned him—he might already have been tested as a tool—by the other side.

"Not so!" Again the Re Mu read his thought. "Think you we would dare to use what we doubted? You shall see the proof of that here and now."

The second of the Naacals drew forth from beneath his cloak a crystal such as Ray had seen in the Lady Aiee's hand on the night he had walked in his sleep.

"Hold this within your two hands, touching first your heart and then your forehead."

The priest did not hand it over but tossed the crystal through the air, and Ray caught it. Obediently he closed his hands upon it, palm to palm. It was not cool as he had expected, but faintly warm. He brought his hands to his chest for a long moment, and then, at the Naacal's gesture, raised them to his forehead.

"Return it now—" The Naacal held out his hand, and Ray tossed the small sphere back even as it had come to him. It glowed faintly, but otherwise it was as it had been before. The three, looking upon it, nodded as one.

"None tainted with the Shadow could have done this," the Re Mu said. "Now, what is your choice? It must be freely made."

"How will I know what to look for—if I go?" Ray asked.

97

"You will be sent to the proper places," replied the Emperor.

"When?"

"Now. Delay is dangerous."

Ray ran his tongue over his lips. Yes or no? He did not doubt that they believed firmly in what they would do. But to him it was questionable. Still—let them try, if it meant so much.

"All right," he answered quickly, suddenly afraid his reluctance would win.

The Naacals took over. A stone in the wall turned at a touch, opening upon a basin of water that held in its depths a sparkling life. They stripped him and bathed him in that water, which left his flesh tingling. Then they wrapped him in a robe as white as theirs and set him down in the chair that had been the Re Mu's. The Emperor now stood behind Ray and cupped his hands in a blindfold over the American's eyes.

"See a dark curtain hanging before you," ordered the Murian ruler.

Suddenly it was there, black, thick, tangible, falling in heavy folds.

"Go through—forward!" rang the command in his ears.

Ray obeyed. Between his fingers he felt the smooth fabric of that curtain, its weight across his hand as he pushed at it to open a slit. Then he clung to it in agony, for flame washed about him, searing.

"Back!" Somewhere a voice shouted that, but very faintly.

Ray stumbled ahead. The slit was open and promised an escape from the fire he could not see. He plunged through it and was out, in the midst of light.

He stood at one end of a long, columned hall, the red walls of which were swallowed by shadows. On those walls in mute colors, but missing no details, were murals such as fiends out of hell might have devised and executed. Ray tried to turn his head, his eyes away, sickened. But the will he sensed in control of his actions made him stare at each horror as he went, as if assessing all their obscenity and cruelty.

As he came along the dusky side of those pillars, Ray discovered he was not alone in the hall, for beyond was a black stone altar and, about it, a group very intent on some action. There was a chant he did not understand, but he paused behind a pillar, knowing that this, too, was something that must be witnessed.

On the surface of the altar crouched a statue of gold. The thing had a bull head with wide stretching horns, incongruous when coupled to a human body. And around its gleaming yellow hovered a murky black cloud. This Ray recognized, without surprise, as evil, the evil inherent in the thoughts of which this beast-thing was the symbol.

Those by the altar numbered five. Two wore red robes, had shaven skulls, like the Atlantean priest he had seen on board the ship, and were servants of this foul god. A third had warrior's armor, and the fourth a rich robe and many jewels.

The latter had a small round mouth with pale lips, rather like the sucker of a devilfish. His small eyes were set deep in rolls of greasy skin. Ray knew instant hate, revulsion, as if all his emotions had been so heightened that response came quickly and in top degree.

On the lower step of the altar lay the fifth man. He had been stripped and bound, a helpless prisoner. But from him there came a kind of light that Ray read as a reflection of desperate courage. By his skin and hair, Ray guessed the captive to be Murian.

The chanting stopped, and one of the priests moved, the murky light glinting on a blade in his hand.

"Fish one!" The captive spat at the Red Robe. "Mu stands against all of you and your devil god!"

As the blade slashed down, his body arched under the blow, and then he gasped. The other priest was ready to catch the gushing blood in a waiting bowl. Hand to hand that bowl passed, and men drank from it—

Ray, sick, struggled against the will that held him there until he was released and the hall of horrors was gone. Now he stood high on a wall above a harbor choked with ships. And there he remained for some time, as if through his eyes all below was being carefully examined, though to him it meant no more than many vessels of different shapes and sizes closely crowded together.

Then the harbor in turn vanished, and he was in another hall, but this time of a palace rather than a temple. Though the walls were still of red stone, here the hall was lined with other colors, and there were tapestries of fantastic design.

The man of the jeweled robe, whom he had last seen at the altar of the bull god, sat on a throne with courtiers gathered around him. And over all that assemblage the murky cloud hovered. Ray knew it for an effluvium of spirit, and he did not question his ability to see it. Before the Poseidon—for this man could be no other—was a group of prisoners, heavily chained Murians.

Faint and far away, as if from some great distance, Ray heard the words of the ruler. Sight was far sharper than sound for him.

"You stand alone. Your motherland has left you to us. Even tonight the blood of your captain has satisfied the thirst of Ba-Al. Mu is now as a pinch of dust upon the hem of our cloak, which we shall shake off, to be scattered by the wind. You would do well to see this—"

One of the captives flung back his head, trying to clear his face of his loose, tangled hair. "Evil worshiper, Mu lives forever! Her arms are about us always. If it be her will that we die for the good of others, than we die. You spawn out of the pit of the Dark. Do you believe any son of Mu would work wickedness at your command?"

The Poseidon smiled cruelly. "So"—his voice was now so soft and far away that Ray could hardly separate one word from the next—"you still speak stiffnecked and with arrogance in your mouth, defiance on your tongues. Nay, I shall kill no more of you now. You shall I keep that your feet may sear as you are forced to run across the coals of what was once Mu."

"The motherland does not fall so easily, not while one of our race yet breathes. If you reckon so, you are the greater fool!" was the captive's prompt reply.

Now the fat, oily cheeks of the Poseidon darkened, seeming to swell with anger. "Out with them to the slime pits—out!"

The will summoned Ray again as he caught a last glimpse of the captives being dragged away. This time he found himself in the shop of a merchant, like unto those he had visited in the marketplace of the Murian city.

"Not much longer must we stand aside for the traders of Mu." There was satisfaction in the voice of the man who lifted a tankard to his lips, drank, and touched a square of linen delicately to his lips thereafter.

"The motherland has great powers—" There was a tone of doubt in that answer from one of his companions.

"Bah!" The merchant drank again and licked his lips appreciatively. "Have not the priests of Ba-Al learning also?"

Then Ray was in the upper chamber of a tower, or high building, for from a window nearby there was a hazy glimpse of lights far below. For the first time since he had stepped through time's gate, he was surrounded by objects that had kinship with his own world. Strange as some were, the tubing, and much else named it a laboratory. And at a table in the far corner were two red-robed Atlanteans.

"We must have a man to feed it again," one declaimed. And once more, though Ray stood close to the pair, their voices were dim and far away.

"There is one waiting, a Murian prisoner. Let him welcome the embraces of the Loving One, as will his kin hereafter!" The priest's vulpine face was alight with an eagerness that was like hunger, and the murk of evil was very dark over his head.

But his fellow looked down at his own hands, where

101

they lay upon the table, and there was doubt plain in his dark face.

"Do we open gates we cannot close again? Sometimes I fear we leap too far, too soon—"

"Does not the Shadow lord stand to protect his own? The day of the Flame is now at sunset."

What evil they then wrought Ray did not remember. If the will watched it through his eyes, it was, mercifully, wiped from his mind before he stood again at the dark curtain. Once more he passed through an agony of fire as he felt its fabric balled within his fists. And then, weak and ill, he opened his eyes to the tower room in Mu, its opaque wall openings like great blind eyes.

The Re Mu faced him, but the former serenity was missing from his face. And the Naacals were also men looking upon an ultimate doom with naught to defend them. Ray's fatigue was a heavy burden, a kind of sickness.

"So, that is what they do—unlock the gates that no human should lay hand to—" the Re Mu half whispered. "Do they not know that such as they have invoked always turns upon its would-be masters in the end? It can be brought forth, but to send it hence again is another matter. Peace be on those they have sent Sunward. And you"—he spoke now to Ray, reaching out to pull the robe closer about the American's shoulders—"to your our debt is beyond measure, for not to have known what they do would be our disaster."

"What happened in that laboratory?"

"Be thankful you cannot remember. We must go—to prepare our answer. But it shall rest heavily upon our minds until we lie at peace in our grave-niches. They have committed a sin for which there is no pardon, and payment shall be exacted in kind. U-Cha—bring the water of life—"

The elder Naacal handed the Emperor a cup of the sparkling water. Slipping his arm behind Ray's shoulders, the Murian ruler supported him until he had drunk all of the liquid. As it ran down his throat, Ray felt new life and energy come into him.

"You must rest. And these shall watch so that your sleep shall be dreamless. Then we will send you home—"

Already the weight of sleep pressed on Ray's eyelids. He was hardly conscious of the fact that the Naacals had produced a mat they smoothed out on the floor, that the Re Mu, with his own hands, assisted them in lowering the American to it. Yet, in spite of his desire to sleep, he shivered when memories he did not summon of what he had seen, or thought he had seen, in Atlantis returned unbidden. Then a hand touched his forehead, and words were spoken in a language he did not understand. Memory vanished, and there was only sleep.

Whe he awoke, there was a soft glow about him. Those ovals, which were not windows, held a light of their own, bathing the room, him— Someone stirred, and he turned his head slowly. Even that small movement required a vast amount of will and determination. The Lady Aiee smiled at him.

"They have told me of what you have done, and I have come that you may be tended by one of your own courtyard."

Ray's eyes closed despite his desire. "One of your own courtyard." But what had any Murian courtyard to do with him? This was not his world, nor his time, and he was the alien—

Trees, tall, tall as the towers of Mu, rising up from the soil. And between them flowed shadows that made a bewildering maze of the ground. Somewhere among them—farther—farther—he must go—farther—

"Ray! Ray!"

Faintly, like the voices of the Atlantean dreams, so came that call, but it was imperative, so demanding that he had to listen—to listen and then to stop running between the trees toward the unknown goal.

"Ray!"

His hands were caught. He tried to break the grip that held them and could not.

103

"Return!"

Not faint that call but as loud as a thunderclap heralding a storm, with such power in it that he cowered, fearing the coming of a lightning afterstroke.

"Return!" Again that command was delivered, as if there could be no question of disobedience.

Ray opened his eyes. Beside him knelt the Lady Aiee. It was her hands that held his. And behind her stood the elder Naacal, his fingers upon the lady's shoulders, as if they must be linked so.

"Stay!" It was the Naacal who commanded that. Now he loosed his grip on the Lady Aiee to bend over Ray. Between his hands appeared, as if from thin air, the crystal globe. And light from the wall panels seemed to speed into it, to reissue as a luminous cloud, bathing the American.

Once more he closed his eyes. But now there were no trees, no need to seek—nothing but healing sleep.

9

A LONG-LEGGED bird ran along the curving line in the sand that marked the high tide, searching for victims of the sea. It had already feasted on a small devilfish and was anticipating other rich finds. Rounding a rock, it squawked and flashed in retreat.

Ray, disturbed by that screech of fright, raised his head from his arms and looked about the pocket-sized cove. A butterfly with wings of metallic blue danced above his head, only to flutter away. The beach was his alone. He wanted it so. In one sense he was always alone. In spite of the warm acceptance of the Murians, there was ever in his mind a barrier between them, the feeling that this was not real, at least for him.

What had happened eventually to this land and people? Some world-wide catastrophe must have changed the whole face of the planet, to reshape it into the divisions of land and sea known in his time. Had remnants of the Murian nation escaped to more stable lands, been caught on islands that were mountain tops raised from Mu's rolling plains? Civilization must have died quickly in such chaos. The survivors would descend into savagery, and all but legend would vanish. Her kings would be the half-remembered gods of degenerate races.

Was this now the last days of Mu or her prime?

The Barren Lands, they were his own—if anything here could be linked to him, or he to it. Some day—some day he would go back there.

There was a pattering as the greedy bird, deceived and heartened by Ray's silence, ventured back. After watching the American for a long moment, the bird scuttled on to round another rock on the other side of the cove.

It shot back, again squawking wildly, and Ray heard splashing, as if someone or something moved through shallow wave wash. He hoped they would not come on, and they did not. But their voices carried easily, by some trick of the echoing rocks. A single word aroused the American to strict attention.

"—Ba-Al's temple on the night of the midyear feast. Risk our necks for Mu? If they believe that, they are fools. I say—free ourselves as Atlantis did. Expel the Sun-born. If they won't go—why, then let them meet Ba-Al. He has a use for such, I understand." The speaker laughed.

"Then you sail east?" asked another voice.

"On the third day from this, or sooner if we can clear. These Murian fools did not question my sailing authority—why should they? I am only a grain trader from Uighur, bound for the outposts of Mayax, and have taken the same route two years now. They know me when I wear that cloak. There is but one small thing. There is one of those accursed Sun-born—the Lady Ayna—in this city now, and she knows my face. I visited her courtyard before the matter of the hide ships, when I was proclaimed a five-year outlaw. If she sees me here in forbidden territory, she will report it. The Sun-born to Ba-Al, that is what I say!"

"How will you pass the eastern guards to reach our friends?"

"That is my secret. Give me what knowledge you have gained, and I shall take it safely, never fear. This is not my first trip to carry such. And your brothers in the Shadow will welcome me."

"I dare not seek too much. There are sections of the temple that are forbidden and protected. They have ways of reading more than a man's surface thoughts, these Flame-tutored priests. It is much that I have been accepted, even as a novice."

"You will get what is asked of us." There was a threat in the first voice now. "We know that in some way, recently, they have been able to penetrate the curtain of darkness. And they discovered the Loving One; so much have linked minds relayed. You must discover how they did this thing and any defense they plan—that is vital. Now, get you back before they question why one who goes to the bedside of an ailing father is seen at the seashore in talk with a merchant captain from Uighur."

"Seen?" There was sharp panic in that cry. "But you said that this was a place of safety, where we could meet without any fear of discovery."

"There is no place that is completely safe, you fool! The element of risk is always present in our business. If you do not believe that, then you are worse than a fool. Never cease to be aware that you walk a cord over a pit of fire in spite of your safeguard talisman. Now—go!"

Ray crept across the sand to the rock at the end of the cove. But he was too late to see more than that one wore the white robe of a Naacal, the other a leather tunic once stained blue, now faded and bleached by salt spray. A plain, crestless helmet hid the latter's hair, and from the rear he might be any captain of a small trader.

As they vanished up a path on the cliff wall, Ray got to his feet, brushing sand from his tunic. He tried to remember where lay the nearest guard station along the road. Surely he had passed one coming here.

When he had scrambled up to the road, there was no one in sight resembling the two he wanted to trail. A couple of elephants rocked by, throwing up a cloud of dust, their back burdens tightly lashed. And a horseman with the royal couriers' horn slung from his shoulder spurred to overtake the ponderous march of the beasts.

All travelers halted at the outer gate of the city, to be passed by a guard. An ancient custom, long abandoned, had been recently revived and was now a source of much complaint and grumbling by those who could see no reason for such delays.

"Name and rank?" a soldier asked Ray with a weary voice of one who had done this fifty times before this hour and would do it doubtlessly fifty times again the next.

"The Sun-born Ray, of the courtyard of the Lady Aiee."

"Pass." But the soldier stared in open surprise. To see one of the Sun-born on foot and alone was so out of the ordinary as to alert suspicion.

Ray hurried into the street beyond, unaware that he was already a matter of report between the sentry and his superior. The citadel—he must get there as soon as he could. Again he named himself to a sentry at the outer wall of the palace.

"The Sun-born Ray, with a message of importance for the Re Mu!"

He came into the courtyard of the fountain and, after a wait, was brought into the audience chamber of the Emperor. The Re Mu was attended now not only by the Naacals, but also by warriors who looked at the American in surprise. But the Re Mu beckoned him forward.

"One who comes in such haste must bear a matter of some import."

Ray glanced at the officers, and the Murian ruler raised his hand so those others fell back some distance. "You may speak—"

Swiftly the American told his story, and as he spoke, the Re Mu's face became a mask of authority.

"You have done well to seek us quickly with this. Can you describe these men—their faces—?"

"No, Great One. Beyond the fact that one wore a Naacal's robe and the other was a sea officer from Uighur, I have no other identification. I think that I would know their voices were I to hear them again."

"According to his own words the Lady Ayna knows the seaman. That is one aid. But the novice—"

One of the Naacals beside the Re Mu stirred, and there was cold fury in his voice.

"Be sure we shall find the traitor and also what arts he has employed that the safeguards of the Flame did not uncover him. What we learn from his lips shall be speedily yours, Lord of the Flame."

"Which leaves the seaman for us. Hold yourself in

readiness, Sun-born, to return hither and help to identify him. You have our leave to go—"

Ray returned to the courtyard of the Lady Aiee. He was tempted to visit the docks and look there for a Uighur seaman in a stained blue jerkin. But it was close to twilight, and his common sense told him that the forces the law would set in motion would be far more effective than any amateur effort on his part.

"Ray! Where have you been?" Cho strode along the garden path. "We have been seeking you—"

"I went to the seashore." Ray hesitated. Should he tell Cho the rest? Why not? There had been no promise extracted from him not to. He mounted to the terrace and found the mistress of the household already seated at the table.

"I am sorry," he said hurriedly. "I had not thought the hour so late."

"But, I think"—her expression changed—"You have a better excuse for us than mere lapse of memory. Is that not so?"

"This—" For the second time he told his story. "Then I reported it to the Re Mu."

"By the Flame! Traitors within the city!" Cho exclaimed.

"Within the temple! But how could evil cloak itself so well as to enter there undetected?" The Lady Aiee sounded shaken, uncertain, as Ray had never heard her before.

"The Naacal said they would search him out." Her distress was such that Ray was uneasy in turn. Somehow during the past days he had come to look upon her as one so sure of herself that she remained a secure support in all difficulties.

"Those who cross the Naacals," Cho replied, "do not find life so pleasant that they desire to cling to it long. One could almost pity such a one."

"No!" His mother's voice was sharp. "There is no pity for one who deliberately twists the things of light to serve the Dark. For this one knows good and, of his own will, serves evil. He is a chooser of the Shadow—

even as those of Atlantis. Pity is for the weak of spirit, not the weak of heart—"

"I think now we move one, perhaps two, steps closer to the day when the fleet goes forth to the east." Cho sounded as if he found that a satisfying thought.

Ray remembered his dream journey, or had it been a dream? To Cho, battle might be a matter of black and white, evil vanquished by good. So had the Murian always spoken of this struggle, in the rare times he mentioned the future. But there was that laboratory in the Atlantean tower and what had been blanked from Ray's memory. Now he wished he could recall it, for what might be fact can be worsened by imagination, and when he allowed himself to remember, more than one horror vividly came to life for him.

"They may have new weapons," he said now, "strange ones—"

Cho glanced at him. "I cannot ask questions, but you speak as one who knows."

Though he had not been told to keep his dream journey a secret, Ray had, instinctively, never spoken of it since the visit to the tower. And this was the first time Cho had ever approached the subject even obliquely.

"I am not sure of what I know, if I know anything at all," Ray said now. And though he spoke the truth, he was sure that the Murian took it as an evasion.

Cho shrugged. "No matter. We live under orders."

Ray hesitated. He had so little in this world to cling to—Cho, by reason of chance and then through honest liking, the Lady Aiee— Suppose he lost even such little as he had? But before he could speak, the servants brought the evening meal, and they talked of the small surface things of the day.

The American ate what was set before him, not very much aware of taste or flavor, merely that he was hungry and this satisfied his need. But he noted after a while that the Lady Aiee scarcely touched the contents of the dishes offered her. At last she arose and went to the edge of the terrace, looking beyond the garden wall to the lights of the city.

"How long will this last?" she asked. Her words were low, but they carried."We shall survive this war—that the casting of the temple lots told us. But the end comes in time. Perhaps not during our own years or in the time lived by our sons' sons. Still the darkness of the future shall swallow us up. And you tell me, Ray, in your time we are unknown. Atlantis falls and man remembers dimly; Mu goes and even legend is lost. The sea covers both of us, and new lands arise, with new races who know not the law, perhaps any law. And it all begins again. Nations form from savage bands, new cities, new learning, new struggles—but no end to pain and war and evil. Is that not also so?"

Ray nodded. "It is so."

"You say in your time men land on the moon, reach for the other planets. But if they cannot conquer the war within them, then they only carry it out and out—perhaps some day to the stars. And what will be the good of that?"

"No good," Ray agreed. "Yet—"

"Yet"—she caught the thought from him—"it is the nature of our species to be so, at war within, as well as without. And until we can conquer ourselves, we carry the touch of evil with us wherever we go. So perhaps we shall set black and bloody fingers even upon the brightness of the stars. But these are the thoughts the Shadow casts upon our minds to make us believe all struggle is for naught, so surrender comes the easier. We go up against Atlantis, lest in this time and place the Shadow does envelope the earth—our earth. Mu is old; Mayax, Uighur grow old. Atlantis is rotted by evil. What of the Barren Lands, Ray?"

"Great plains, and a forest—" He fell silent, thinking of that forest. "Trees—"

"Trees?" Cho repeated, rousing Ray to the fact that he must have said that aloud.

"Such trees as were not known in my day," he explained. "At least not in that part of the land. It is a

111

country that, I think, does not welcome men." And he realized that he had unraveled a small part of the mystery. It was true that the forest did not welcome man, that it resisted, tried to expel the intruder.

"Yet, it is your country," said the Lady Aiee.

"It will be. Now it is for no man unless he would battle it."

"Which in time he shall." That was a promise from her.

Lissa, the Lady Aiee's maid, came through the beginning dusk.

"A messenger from the citadel. The Sun-born lords are to report at once."

"Go in peace." The Lady Aiee held out her hands, one to each. "Though I think we have but little of that left to us—so treasure what we have."

No litters this time but a file of guards. And the clink of sword against body armor was sharp in the quiet side street, though lost in the hum of the main highway.

The Re Mu was enthroned in the audience chamber, but his only courtiers were two Naacals and a company of warriors. The escort with Ray and Cho saluted with bared swords, and the sullen rasp of metal against metal caused a man standing before the throne to glance malevolently at them.

"A bench for the Sun-born." The Re Mu acknowledged their reverences. Two of the warriors pulled forward a narrow seat for them to share.

The Murian ruler turned his attention to the man before him.

"Your clearances state that you sail with grain to supply the eastern outposts of Mayax."

"It is as those state, Great One."

Ray started with surprise. This was the traitor from Uighur. He would swear to it.

"Your home port is Chan-Chal?"

"That is so, Great One."

He was a younger man than Ray had expected. And there was a kind of assurance about him that was either a very well-maintained cover for a man skilled in meeting danger or else a reckless determination to defy his enemies to the end.

"How many years did you sail with the fleet?"

"The five of custom, Great One. I am no Sun-born to walk the decks for only three—"

No cover, Ray was sure. This man knew he was finished, but he would go down fighting. His defiance was now open.

"Have you heard of one Sydyk?"

"Aye. He was an officer of the fleet, outlawed for stealing public revenues."

"Sentenced to five years' outlawry. Yet now he walks the streets here. Have you seen him?"

"Why set riddles, Great One?" One of the guards stirred as if to correct the prisoner's insolence. But a slight gesture from the Emperor kept him in his place. The dark blue eyes of the Re Mu glittered in the masked calm of his face.

"No riddle. You have been identified by the Sun-born Lady Ayna, one who has reason to know Sydyk well, as that man."

"She is right. Who am I to argue with one of the Sun-born? I have broken outlawry, as have others before. Sell me in the open market according to the law."

Ray wondered—was that why the man from Uighur was so bold? Did he believe that he was merely accused of breaking outlawry and did not suspect that they knew more of him? But would the Re Mu sit in judgment on such a minor case? Had Sydyk no suspicions because he had been brought here?

"Lord Ray!"

The American started, then got to his feet to answer the Emperor's beckoning hand.

"You have heard the voice of this man before?"

"Yes, Great One. This is he of whom I spoke."

"You are willing to so swear?"

"I am."

At the Re Mu's nod Ray returned to his seat. If Sydyk

113

suspected the worst now, he was tough enough or well enough trained to give no outward sign.

"Traitor!"

The force of that broke through Sydyk's well-maintained front. He paled under the dark of his sea tan.

"Your accomplice has betrayed all your plans. And now he has gone to the reward found fitting by those who serve the Flame he tried to befoul by his very presence in its temple. We know why you have come here. You pitiful fool, will Ba-Al now come to your aid? Will even his deluded followers raise a single sword in your behalf? Speak freely and mayhap compassion may temper justice—"

Sydyk might have been staggered a moment earlier, but he was again behind his shield of confidence or desperation.

"If I die, I die. But little will be learned from me—"

"No?" The Re Mu smiled, a very small and fleeting smile. Ray, seeing that, shivered. Never would he want to be so smiled upon—

"You shall go with the Naacals."

A shade passed over the face of the man from Uighur, then was gone again.

"To the Naacals do I go then. But while I can, I shall keep a still tongue."

"Evil are you, and the willing servant of evil. Yet courage is yours if in an ill cause. But this is a time when some men must suffer for the good of many. The Sun of Mu decrees"—the Re Mu's voice took on the formal tone of ceremony—"let it be so."

They took Sydyk out, but as they passed Ray, the man from Uighur stared at the American.

"Remember me in days to come, Sun-born." He made of that title words of contempt. "For Ba-Al shall show by whose aid his true servant dies. And his temple shall see you yet. I know this as we are sometimes given true sight before death approaches!" He laughed shrilly as the soldiers dragged him on.

Cho was on his feet, staring after. "He saw—he saw

you in the Red temple. A man close to death sometimes speaks true of the future. May the one above grant that it be as an invading warrior and not a prisoner you walk so!"

"We have grown too complacent through the years." The Re Mu's voice cut across Cho's. "Another day and these traitors might have been beyond our reach. Perhaps we can learn more from Sydyk, since the novice was more timid and but lately recruited to their service."

He seemed to be musing upon his thoughts and to have forgotten them. Ray expected some dismissal, now that his part had been played, but it did not come. Long minutes dragged by, and there was silence in the chamber, except for now and then a faint scrape as some guard shifted position. What were they waiting for? Ray wriggled on the bench. He wished he dared attract attention and so be released from that attendance without purpose. It seemed to him that even in this white-walled hall there were shadows that darkened and crept upon them and the throne, as if night drew in not in a natural way but as a threat.

The curtain at the doorway parted, and a guard came, saluting the Emperor and passing to his hand a writing tablet. The Re Mu read and then looked up.

"Sydyk was unknown in person to those he served. And tonight, before he was taken, they forbade him to risk further communication with them. Lord Ray, what was it that he said to you as they took him forth?"

"That he foresaw me in the temple of Ba-Al."

"The temple of Ba-Al. But not *how* you came there. Pray to such gods as you acknowledge that he saw only a portion of the truth."

Cho stepped forward. "Great One, this Sydyk was unknown to his masters in the east, and they will not seek him for a space. Cannot one of us take his place, to enter the heart of the enemies' land?"

"Those who send spies will be prepared against them in perhaps a far more expedient manner than we have been. What think you, U-Cha? Shall we consider this?"

"It is written so in the stars."

"Then"—Cho was almost breathless—"let me offer myself for that service!"

Slowly the Re Mu shook his head. "We make no hasty decisions. We shall see, we shall see—"

"Great One—" The senior of the Naacals spoke, his voice falling to such a murmur that they could not hear. Ray saw the Emperor nod.

"Lord Cho, it is our will that you search out upon the charts of the Barren Lands such harbors as might give good hiding to any scout from the fleet."

"Yes, Great One!"

"And you, Lord Ray, will go with Ah-Kam to set into the records all of Sydyk that you heard."

The younger Naacal stepped away from the throne and waited for Ray to join him.

They went through the second doorway, into a corridor which was less public. Ray thought, perhaps a private way for the Re Mu. He looked inquiringly at his guide and saw the gleam of crystal in the other's hand. Then from it shot a dazzling beam, blinding his eyes.

10

"—SYDYK of Uighur, of the courtyard of the Lady Ma-Lin, being son to her marshal, one U-Val. In your fifteenth year you departed for fleet training, serving under—"

Names, a roll of names, ringing through Ray's head. The voice droned on and on with details from the life of one Sydyk, and though Ray tried to shut his ears, or his mind, to them, he found that he could not. He was held in thrall by that voice, and what it conveyed to his mind could not be erased either, making him conscious of all the minutiae of Sydyk's life. At the same time, though he could not open his eyes to see, he was aware of hands on his body, sensations on his skin of wet and cold, strange odors.

"You were taken by Murian guards, but you managed to win free, putting the onus of treachery upon the novice Ru-Gen, saying that he had approached you for passage out of Mu and that you had refused him. The crew of the *Cleave Wave* will also be mind-set in this story. You will follow these orders. Two hours after you drop anchor off the frontier post of U-Ma-Chal, you must contrive to come to shore alone—follow the curve of the beach north until you reach two pointed rocks standing very tall. There you await the coming of a small boat. He who commands it will say, 'The east rises,' and you will reply, 'The west falls.' You will enter the boat and do what must be done."

What—why? He was caught in a net, vainly trying to fight to freedom.

"For a month you will watch and do what has been set upon you. Then, for a space of three days, a ship of the fleet, disguised as a fruit carrier from the south, will be off the harbor of the Five Walled City. She will fly a plague flag to keep off boarders. You must, if you

117

can, reach her before the fourth day. Do you understand?"

Though he did not, Ray felt his head move in an answering nod.

"You are Sydyk out of Uighur!"

Ray opened his eyes. He was looking into the reflective surface of a mirror at a man with a brown-yellow skin and black hair falling in greasy locks about a face that, by some art, was older and coarser than his own.

"Your clothing—"

A hand appeared at one side of the mirror and indicated a bundle of stuffs waiting on a stool. He put on the rough cloth undertunic and a leather jerkin and kilt, dyed blue but stained with salt and smelling of sweat and the sea. Instead of sandals, there were sea boots of hide with a small fringe of natural hair left about their tops. His fingernails were rough and had heavy deposits of black under them. Grime lines were deep-etched in the skin of his hands. Where that small tattoo was on his wrist, a broad band of copper braceleted the skin. There was a plain sword belt of black leather and a bronze helmet without a crest.

"It is done, as well as we may," said a voice behind him, though he saw no face in the mirror over his shoulder. "Remember to slouch as you walk; you are from the far frontier, with no manners. What are you doing?" The voice was sharp, alert. Ray ran a hand along his right arm and then the other along the left. What he searched for he could not quite remember. Black, yes, it was black! And he should wear it here—and it was highly important to him!

He tried again to fight off the mist that imprisoned his mind.

"Black—" In the mirror he saw his lips frame the word. "Black armlet—mine!"

Suddenly he could see it as clearly in his mind as he saw this strange reflection in the mirror. The black armlet was his. He would not stir from this place until they gave it to him! And he fixed upon that with strange stubbornness, as if it offered some safety now.

There was movement behind him, although he could see nothing in the mirror. But now he was able to turn, as if it were a difficult business to get his reluctant body to obey him in even so small and ordinary a thing.

There were three of them. The first an officer by his dress; then one in a serving man's tunic, who was now busy with a box of small pots and bottles, over whose shoulder hung a towel stained yellow-brown like the new color of Ray's skin; and, lastly, a Naacal. It was in the priest's hands that Ray saw what he sought—a black armlet of serpents with diamond eyes. He reached for it.

"It would betray him to the first Atlantean who saw it. No trader would wear such a treasure—" The officer moved to intercept him.

But the Naacal looked at Ray. "I do not know. That he wishes it so strongly now, this is not to be lightly dismissed. Why would you have this, my son?"

To Ray that black band was a smoldering, living thing. He needed it; he must have it—it was his and they could not take it!

"Mine!" His voice was close to a snarl; his hand went to the dagger at his belt. The world, the room, narrowed to the armlet and his need for it.

But it seemed that he would not have to fight for it after all, for the Naacal, still regarding him with that deep, probing gaze, now held it out to him, his other hand waving back the officer.

"There is a reason, even if he, nor we, know it not for now. But do not wear that openly, my son."

Ray fondled the coolness of the band. No, to wear it would be dangerous; he must keep it out of sight—to be safe, very safe. He put it inside his tunic with satisfaction.

"Listen now." There was such authority in the priest's voice that Ray looked at him squarely. "You will perhaps come to believe that what we have done this night is an evil thing for you. But time and fate left us no other choice in our hour of need. No man of the motherland could put on the semblance of Sydyk and thus

119

open closed gates for our eyes. We knew that the Shadow could not bar you when you went before into its lurking place. Therefore, we must put hand again to the weapon you give us. There is this: under the power of the Flame we read the sparks and the stars. Although death shall be as a cloud over you, a cloak about your shoulders during the days before you, still, by our reading, it will claim you not. Rather will it be that what you carry in naked hands is more potent than any sword. We use you now without consent because we are driven to such measures. And you may hate us for that. Yet still—" He paused. "Go in peace with the blessing, the nine times' blessing of the Flame." His hands moved in a gesture, as if he drew some unseen substance out of the air, filled his palms with it, and then held them up to shower what he had so invisibly gathered upon the American.

The officer moved forward. "Your ship sails at daybreak. Within ten days you should be at the meeting place. During the passage of the canal stay below deck, saying you are fevered. Your mate will act as captain. Now—we shall go—"

It must have been early morning as he came out of the palace on the heels of the officer, with a couple of guardsmen trailing him. But he knew that he could not escape. Whatever compulsion they had set upon him in the citadel kept him marching, would move him, as a chessman is moved, until he accomplished what they wished of him. For the moment his mind was numb and dull, having sunk into a fog once his small battle for the armlet was won. He no longer possessed a spark of rebellion.

They came to the docks, to a grain ship. A man challenged them from its shadowed deck. Ray blinked in lantern light.

"Captain—" the seaman greeted him. "All is in readiness—"

"This is the mate, Ra-Pan." Some inner portion of the American's mind supplied a name.

"We sail at dawn." Ray returned.

120

"Aye, sir."

The officer from the citadel and the guards did not linger. When they had gone with no farewells, Ray stood by the rail. Above the harbor lay the city. Lights gleamed here and there, but only a few. The city still slept. Ray stirred restlessly. Back there—he frowned—it was so hard to think. Sydyk out of Uighur, he was Sydyk out of Uighur. He must not, he dared not, now try to think beyond that.

Dawn was here now. Ra-Pan moved across the deck. Ray turned to him with words already on his tongue as if prepared for him to say.

"I do not feel well. Do you take command for me."

And the mate appeared to find nothing amiss in that. Ray went below to a small, dark cabin. Uncurtained alcoves opened from it. He threw himself on a bunk in the one that was Sydyk's. Though he tried to sleep, over and over in his mind tumbled thoughts and memories that were Sydyk's and that made him indeed feel feverish and ill. So he got up to drink stale water from a jug. But finally sleep came, and it was dreamless.

Ray awoke shivering, chilled. A wooden trencher, with two corn-flour cakes and a strip of meat, awaited him on the table in the outer cabin. He choked down the bread, but the smell of the meat made him queasy, and he left it, going out on deck. There was a strong wind blowing, and they were on the open sea. Ra-Pan was by the wheelman. Parts of Sydyk's knowledge of the ship and its workings were Ray's to call upon, and he had been assured that the crew had been conditioned by some means to accept him as their rightful commander. But it would be very easy to make some error and awaken suspicion. He looked eastward. There, half the world away, lay Atlantis. And he did not even know what he was to do there when he arrived—if he arrived. Yet he was also certain that he could not make a single move that would not lead him to Atlantis.

They passed the canal, needing to wait their turn, so Ray spent three days below in the stale-smelling cabin. Then they were in the Inner Sea.

121

"We stop at Manoa." Ra-Pan made one of his infrequent observations one evening.

It was not a suggestion but a statement. Ray's warning sense instantly awoke. This had not been planned. And self-preservation, he had come to believe, would follow only the obeying of those orders laid upon him.

"That is not so. We go on to U-Ma-Chal."

Ra-Pan frowned. "This is not as always."

Were the controls the Naacals had set on the crewmen beginning to break? If so, the whole ship's company might mutiny.

"That does not matter." Ray tried to turn upon the Uighurian the same compelling stare the priests used. He had to convince Ra-Pan that this was proper or else they would account for him before the mission was well begun.

"Do you refuse my orders?" he demanded sharply.

It was as if the mate tried to look away but could not. He wet his lips with his tongue.

"Always it has been Manoa."

Was there or was there not an uncertain note in that? Ray hoped there was. But from now on he must be alert that Ra-Pan or some other did not question him more.

"But now it is U-Ma-Chal!" he said with emphasis. Ra-Pan nodded, the dull look once more in his eyes.

So the American watched the crew. He ate only of food he saw the mate taste, slept with a sword ready to hand, and tried to rest as little as possible.

Seven days more and they were at the eastern entrance of the sea. The open weather appeared also to be at an end; the night sky was cloudy. Ray stood close to the rail, trying to see the beacon light of the town. Within his tunic something sharp pressed into his chest. His fingers closed upon the armlet. In all the world there was but one other like it—

Who had said that? When? A white band—belonging to someone he had known long ago. He drew out the armlet and turned it around in his hand, fighting to recapture memory. The diamond eyes flashed sparks.

"Ah—"

Ray closed his fist upon the band. Ra-Pan stood there. The dullness was gone from his eyes. He stared at Ray's closed fingers as if he could see through flesh and bone.

"What do you want?" the American demanded. "You should be at the wheel."

"I came to ask if we make port this night—" But still he stared at the hand rather than looked to Ray's face.

"Have I not already said so? Get to your post!"

In spite of the American's fears, the mate tramped away. Ray shivered once more. He was very near to this part of the venture, and he did not want to know what the next would be.

"The fort signals, Captain!" the lookout called at a flash from shore. "They wish to know our mission."

"Ra-Pan"—Ray saw in this his chance, or thought he did—"go you to answer them."

He half expected the mate to object, but the Uighurian obeyed, rowed ashore by two of the crew. Ray made his own preparations in haste. He got a dinghy overboard and, alone at the oars, pulled along, using the nearby shoreline as his guide. A murmur of voices from the shore, carrying over the waves, startled him.

"Worth six months' wages, and he carries it under his tunic. Who will ever know? Kill him, or pluck him and leave him for the priests of Ba-Al. They might even pay us for him."

A lower answering mutter and then a sharp rebuttal. "Sydyk? No, they have done some of their cursed thought-meddling. That is not Sydyk, I tell you. They have set one of their own men in his place. And that bit of news is worth a fat reward from the east!"

Ray stopped rowing. So, the conditioning no longer held with the mate. And to leave the man behind him—no. He could see them now, shadows against a patch of white sand where they stood arguing. One thrust of the oars ought to take him in far enough, and there were only two—

He gave that last push, putting into it all the strength

123

he could muster. Dropping the oars, Ray leaped to the wave-washed sand. He saw those shadows swing around, and one skidded a little, but a sword glinted in the other's hand.

"I think you will make no sales to Ba-Al this night!" Ray cried. Stooping, he scooped up sand and hurled it as a cloud into the swordsman's face. Then he was on the other, striking with the side of his hand, kicking upward in the style of fighting for which this enemy was unprepared.

There was a cut-off gasp, and the other fell. Ray, half by instinct, ducked and pivoted, ready to tackle the other assailant. He bore him back with a rush until they both crashed, and then he heard a sickening crack of skull against rock and got to his feet again unharmed, but breathing hard. One of the seamen lay in a heap against a rock, very still, and the other was stretched upon the sand.

Ray went to him. There was no pulse under the American's seeking fingers. He pulled at the inert body, dragging it to lie beside the other, and set about shoveling sand over them. Whether they had any confederates he did not know, but at least he had gained some time.

It was not until he left that strip of beach, having taken the further precaution of setting his boat to drift bottom up, that reaction struck. Long ago he had learned the tricks of such warfare, but he could not remember that ever before had he dealt death with his hands. He plowed on through the sand, seeking some trace of the rocks that marked his meeting place. Inside him the cold grew, yet there was no turning from this path, nor any return to the person he sensed he had once been before Sydyk of Uighur had been sent to invade his mind.

The cold grew, and he had left his cloak in the boat, tangled about one of the seats, a mute answer, he hoped, to any suspicion that Captain Sydyk had not met with disaster. The air had frost in it, and Ray swung his arms vigorously for warmth.

Then he rounded a point of land, and before him, so massive and unmistakable as to be easily sighted, even on this cloudy night, were two pointed rocks. Certainly this was the meeting place. But if so, he was early; there was no one waiting.

Ray set his back to the nearest rock and looked out to sea. Tonight he had killed with his hands. He discovered that he was flexing his fingers, then rubbing them up and down against him, as if to brush off more than sand. They would have killed him, perhaps not at this hour and here, but in a much less merciful way, by revealing him to the Atlanteans. Ray had a dim memory of a man lying on an altar in a red-walled temple waiting a death blow. That would have been his portion, if not worse. Still— He continued to rub his hands.

Then he started away from the rock. Sounds came from across the water, the faint grate of what might be oar in oarlock on some would-be silent boat. Ray moved to the water's edge. A skiff came in through the surf, two muffled figures aboard her.

"The east rises." The voice was guttural, deep in the throat.

"The west falls." Ray made answer in a half-whisper.

"Let us be gone. The rats of Mu keep watch, and we are too near the fort for comfort."

Ray waded out to the skiff.

"It is well you are prompt," commented the Atlantean. "They patrol often nowadays, and we dare not linger long. You came alone?"

Did that seem suspicious? But the Naacal had not warned him—

"I was betrayed—"

"By whom? And—were you followed?"

"By Ra-Pan, my mate. The Murians got to him," Ray improvised. "But he is dead."

"So? Well done."

The oarsman sent them on with swift, sure strokes. They were now beyond the protection of the headlands, and the sea air was even colder. Ray could not control his shivers, though he tried hard. Out of the dark arose a hull, a peaked cabin roof against the sky. They bumped the side of a vessel, and a rope ladder was guided into Ray's hands. He climbed to the deck. No lights, not even a shielded deck lantern. They must indeed be afraid of being sighted. Then one of the men from the skiff caught him by the arm and steered him on.

"Below with you. We must get under way."

They went down a steep ladder and pushed between the flaps of a leather curtain into the main cabin. Red-painted walls, hung with an amazing collection of weapons, boxed about them. The floor was a checkerboard of black and white, marred and stained with grime. There was the odor of spilled wine, unwashed humans, and even more unpleasant reminders that the commander of this ship was not dainty in his habits.

But also there was a jumble of what might have been loot, as could be seen in a ship that had been raiding. There were metal plates as well as crude earthenware ones on the table. Silken hangings, rent and fouled, lay on the benches. The table itself was a thing of beauty, dark wood inlaid with designs of silver and ivory, though much scarred and scratched.

Ray's Atlantean guide dropped his cloak on a bench and poured wine from a begemmed flagon into a battered goblet.

"Down this. It is a chill night. A man needs a little fire to run in his veins."

Had his shudders been so apparent, Ray wondered? He could only hope they were attributed to the cold wind. He drank and choked, but turned that into a cough. Over the goblet rim he studied his host. The Atlantean was shorter by an inch or two than himself, thick of upper arm and shoulder, the width of which was somewhat balanced by a sizable paunch. His long arms ended in huge hairy paws of hands.

Unlike the Murians, who were always smooth of face, a black beard grew in a thick mat to his cheekbones. A liberal application of grease had been used to shape that growth into a point touching his upper chest. Out of this his lips showed startlingly thick and red, so brightly red that one could almost believe he had applied some coloring to them.

Though he sported so full a beard, he showed, as he now put aside a crestless bronze helmet, that his skull had been shaven except for a single thick lock at the crown. Also greased, this was wreathed about the dome of his brown skull.

He grinned, showing yellow teeth, and patted the midsection of a silken tunic stained with food droppings. His golden belt, Ray thought, had never been fashioned to contain that paunch. It was closed by a loop of chain that added several inches to its length.

"Welcome to the *Black Hawk*, brother. I am Captain Taut. Those of Mu have no reason to look upon me with favor, though the pickings are lean these days when all their merchantmen sulk protected in the Inner Sea."

Ray put down his goblet and waved aside the gesture of refilling it. "I am Sydyk out of Uighur."

"Ho—but you are a seaman. Broken officer from the fleet? They join us now and again. How does the motherland these days?"

Ray forced a laugh. "You seem to be a reader of pasts, Captain. Mu—they begin there to wake at last. I got free only in time."

Captain Taut nodded. "Well, I have always said that the Murians are far too trusting, but they cannot be thought utterly blind. Now, you seem to have had something of a wetting, Sydyk—off with those wet rags." He went to rummage in a chest, returning with new clothing.

"Good stuff. Got them off a ship we took in the North Sea before they signaled them in. Belonged to some officer. He met Ba-Al, or so I heard."

Reluctantly but not daring to show his dislike, Ray put on the dead man's clothing. Stealthily he transferred the jet armlet into new hiding.

"Turn in if you wish." Captain Taut pointed to one of the alcoves. "We do not raise land until tomorrow."

127

He went out, leaving Ray alone. Choosing a bunk that seemed less odorous than the rest, he stretched out wearily. He had come so far—but what waited beyond the next hour, the next day?

11

RAY did not dream of trees that night, but he ran and walked through scenes that flowed curiously one into another, so that he was both an onlooker and a participant in action. He was Sydyk of Uighur, reliving past years. Yet he was also another, standing apart, watching Sydyk because there was a desperate need to learn and remember all that Sydyk had done and been.

It was a cry of "Land ho!" that awoke Ray at last. He lay for a moment or two, feeling heavy and unrefreshed. There was the sound of feet crossing the deck, a muffled calling of orders. Taut had said land on the morrow. He must have slept long, sunken in those dreams.

Slowly he sat up. On a neighboring stool lay the salt crystaled clothing of Sydyk, dry now but wrinkled and yet further discolored by the wetting of the night before. Still he would rather wear that than the plundered garments. As he went on deck, he was still buckling on his sword belt.

"Holla!" Captain Taut was by the wheelman. "You must have been greatly wearied, friend, to sleep so deeply through the hours. So, you wish to see the first of the Red Land? We have been favored by Ba-Al. A following wind is behind us. I have laid a wager of five silver pieces we shall raise harbor well before night. And this time I shall be glad to anchor there. The rats of Mu grow keener-sighted, and their teeth are sharp—" He grinned and strode a step or two nearer the rail, to spit into the sea. "It is lean picking when the merchantmen come not into the North Sea. But the Poseidon's service promises more than just hard knocks and no loot, though they had better come true soon, those golden promises. And, friend, I care not if you repeat those words to Chronos's—the Poseidon's—ugly face. We wolves of the north are no sworn liege men of his, if we do choose to ally with him upon occasion. We want more than just fair promises. Now, what say you to loaf bread and other good fill for the belly—none of that black stuff that tastes of dust and black beetles, such as you find on Chronos's own ships—"

He led Ray back to the cabin. And the food, though it was dished up in a strange collection of mismatched plates, was better than any Ray had eaten since he left Mu. It would seem that such fare was one of Captain Taut's self-indulgences and something upon which he prided himself.

"I thought"—Ray waved away another dish the captain urged upon him—"that you were of the Atlantean fleet—"

"Of the fleet!" Captain Taut stared. "Me—Taut? Not so—I am a free captain. There are ten like men who harbor now at the Five Walled City. But only for now, mind you, only for now. There were no pickings elsewhere—and the Poseidon has big plans. But we own no man master; our quarrel lies with full-bellied merchantmen and the Murians who hold swords between us and that we would take. However, had they spoken up as loud and clear as Chronos, talked of our looting the Red Land, we would have chosen to stand with Mu. They keep their promises. But Mu will have none of us. Now when we must take sides, we harbor at Atlantis. There, too, is our free town of Sanpar. Chronos sent his emissary to speak us straightly—as straightly as he can speak. We know well that a man watches before him, to each side, and turns often to look across his shoulder when he comes to the Red Land. But Chronos has need of us, so we raise his banner—always making sure that there is no shadow reaching toward us from the shore. We have no love for Chronos. He is overfree with ordering this and that. One learns early the need for a slight deafness in that direction. And he sends men to Ba-Al, or to that new devil come at the Red Robes' call—the Loving One.

"It is with us like strange wolves meeting in the forests of the Barren Lands. Both growl, sniff, show fangs, but do not strike lest they provoke their own

130

deaths. Fear and hate can be evenly matched to one's fortune. So we wait and watch, fangs ready for some day when he thinks he has the greater power—"

"Ten ships of you?"

"Ten ships, and a berth on this one for you, friend, if you will it. We can use seamen who are not pledged to the Red Land. I do not think, and this I say in warning, Sydyk, that such a one as you will discover Chronos so generous a master that you will remain long in his service. When you have had enough of the smell of fear in his fine palace, come to the sea wolves. I warn you that though a man sweats blood in his service, the day comes when he will cast you forth without a piece of silver to your betterment, if he does not send you to Ba-Al. When he needed a ship to send for you, he named mine because I have some weight among the free captains, and if the Murians took me, he would smile, not pour any sop of wine to ease the thirst of my hungry ghost.

"We return; thus he has lost a small part of his gamble. The news you bear had better, for your sake, be worth such disappointment to him. But, remember, come to us if you need refuge."

"Why do you offer this? You know nothing of me," puzzled Ray.

The captain's heavy shoulders rose and fell in an exaggerated shrug. "Why? I know not. Perhaps because you are young and a seaman like unto us. I have no liking for Ba-Al, nor for the red-robed crows who croak in his temples. Or perhaps it is because I would frustrate Chronos, if only by so little. Hark—" They heard a new stir from the deck. "Come aloft. It would seem that I have won my wager, and we come now to harbor."

Ray was eager to see the main port of Atlantis. It was set on a wide bay with a narrow entrance. Beyond lay the city, not as brightly gleaming as the Murian capital but far more somber with its dark walls.

"Chronos's hold. They say it cannot be stormed because of its five walls and three canals. But"—Taut grinned again—"that has never yet been tested. Give me a hundred swords of the proper sort and a small smile or two from fortune—then—then we might just prove that belief false."

Ray glanced at the wolfish crew in the waist of the vessel. It seemed to him that their united stare at the shoreline reflected a fierce hunger.

"I believe you," he returned.

Taut laughed. "Chronos would not. Remember, if you have need, come to us."

The raider worked its way in through a mass of shipping and anchored a little beyond the docks, where merchantmen were tied up. A small boat was lowered, and two of the seamen climbed down to it. Ray nodded to the captain.

"May the Sun—" He stopped short, aware that some trick of memory had played him false. His hand went to sword hilt, though he had no chance of defense.

But the raider captain only gave him a sharp look. "Guard your tongue better, Sydyk. You have been too long in Murian lands. Here they may strike first and ask questions afterward, if they hear such a greeting. Get you gone! But remember, we lie here—"

Ray climbed over the rail, bewildered. Down in the boat he sat quietly, his eyes on the dock toward which they rowed but his thoughts occupied with Captain Taut. That unusual insistence that Ray seek him out if he got into trouble—why? Judging by his background, the raider would be far more likely to sell him out as soon as he gained a hint that Sydyk was more—or less—than he seemed. Suspicion was the necessary shield for Ray now; trust was too expensive to hold to—

A man wearing plain body armor stood on the dock as Ray disembarked.

"Whence come you, stranger?" There was a kind of insolent contempt in his demand.

"Uighur," Ray answered shortly.

"And your name might be Sydyk—?"

"It might."

"If it is, you come with me," returned the soldier. "If

132

it is not, you will discover that it is not safe to play childish games—not with those who now await you."

The Atlantean set off through the crowd, and Ray matched strides to his. A wall of red stone arose high over their heads a small distance from the dockside. They skirted this until a gate, overhung with the pointed teeth of a portcullis, opened. The soldier spoke to the guard, and they were passed to a narrow bridge over a canal where dark water swirled and rippled.

This bridge ended in another gate, this time in a gray-white wall. And then a second sweep of water with a bridge across to a black wall and a third canal. The Atlantean spoke.

"See you the guards of Atlantis? They have been well designed. If any enemy dares to come to test us, those gates will be barred and the bridges all withdrawn. There is no army that can win past such safeguards as these—"

Ray thought of Captain Taut's boast that with the right sort of followers, he could give the city dwellers something to think about. To Ray these defenses appeared too formidable, if the enemy came armed only with such weapons as he had already seen in use.

Two more walls had to be passed after the last canal before they were in the city. The buildings were of three colors, red, black, and gray-white. Those, too, looked as if they had been erected with an eye to their possible future use as fortifications.

There was a different race walking the streets. They did not have the fair skins or the height of the Murians, and there were many more armed men among them. They spoke their guttural tongue as if they did not want to be overheard, even by their close neighbors. The city of Chronos had a smell to it, one that had nothing to do with the normal odors born of many people living close together. No, this was the smell of fear. Ray wondered how he knew that, but he was sure it was true.

His guide brought him to a large square. Directly facing them was what had once been a majestic temple

133

of white marble. But now it looked as if it had been deliberately defaced and despoiled. Ray noted that the Atlanteans made a business of avoiding any close approach to it. Before the wide steps leading to what had been the temple platform were two pillars draped in dull crimson cloth, now tattered and dusty.

The soldier laughed and pointed. "See the temple of the Flame, built by those from Mu? Our fathers of Ba-Al handled it somewhat roughly on the day when our Dark One came into his own."

"Why are the pillars veiled?" Ray asked.

"It is forbidden to speak of those." The soldier glanced sharply from left to right. "Come—" He quickened his pace across the square. But still they must pass close to the defaced temple, and as they did so, the Atlantean again pointed—to a chipped and broken line running along one wall, about the height of a man's breast. Rusty brown stains were in the stone there.

"That was where we stood the Sun-born, and those who served them, when we made a final end. They did not cry out, even when death took them. They are stubborn, those Sun-born. Their children were given to Ba-Al, and it is said not even the youngest cried. They have courage—but that is all. And courage will not cloak or shield them against the will of Ba-Al. Now they have gone, save for a few in the slime pits and those given to the priests for experiments—"

"What will happen to those in the slime pits?" Ray did not look again at that wall. He fought against the picture that his imagination, aroused by the guide's words, had painted for him.

"They are brought forth sometimes and questioned. The Poseidon keeps them for some purpose. Come, it grows late."

"Tell me," he said a moment later. "You have seen Mu, man from Uighur. Is the motherland as rich as stories say?"

"It seemed so to me."

"And the Sun-born, there are many of them?"

Ray thought he saw a chance to plant a small seed of

134

doubt. "Very many—and they have strong powers there. It is their ancient homeland."

"Chronos has promised us their women when the men are sent to the altars of Ba-Al. We shall fall upon Mu, and their powers will not aid them. Then all the riches shall also be ours, and those not of the Sun-born will be our slaves. So does Ba-Al promise!" There was complete confidence in the Atlantean's voice.

Ray's fingers curled, as if about to reach for the soldier. Memory was not too dim any more. Things were breaking through the overlaid crust of Sydyk since he walked this city. To think of the Lady Aiee—the Lady Ayna so used—

"It may not be so easy. I have seen the Murians. They are good warriors—not just children to be swept easily from one's path."

"Ah—but they have no Loving One," observed the other. "Now, down there is the temple of Ba-Al."

A huge building of red stone squatted at the end of a wide avenue. But Ray caught no more than a hasty glimpse of it before they turned into another street and so came to the Poseidon's palace. Here the Atlantean left him with an officer of the guard.

Through long dark corridors, for any windows were set far apart and high, hardly more than slits in the thick stone, up narrow and winding stairs, they went. There was a damp chill, in this place of many shadows, to set one shivering. It was far more a sullen fortress than a palace, bearing no resemblance to that of the Re Mu. At last they came to a small archway that gave on a court lying open under the sky.

The officer announced Ray. "The man from Uighur."

He advanced a step or two, very much aware that this was the real test of the part he played and that the least fraction of a mistake, such as the one he had made before Taut, would mean his death. He was Sydyk, and must be only Sydyk. There was no other safety for him.

"Well, where is he, where is he?" someone demanded querulously. "Bid him step out to be seen, Magos."

"Come hither, man out of Uighur," was the order. Ray came into the light, which was that of sunset.

"You are late," complained the first voice.

"There were delays, Dread Lord," replied Ray with caution.

"Come! Come here!"

Ray approached a gold couch and went quickly to his knees, his head bowed, hoping he looked the perfect humbled and awed servant.

"Look up, look up! Let me see what manner of man you are, Sydyk of Uighur!"

This was Chronos, Poseidon of Atlantis—as he had seen him once in a dream. No, it was danger to remember that, now and here, in this company.

Small eyes in a bloated, fat cheeked face under a fringe of perfumed and elaborately curled hair; fat hands postured back and forth in studied gestures, now and then lifting to the pouting lips some dainty from a heaped plate standing on a small side table at the ruler's elbow. Beside him, but standing, was a red-robed priest, shaven of skull, very bright of eyes. Ray thought that he was more to be feared than the Poseidon he professed to serve.

"Will the Dread One be pleased to hear the words of this his slave?" Ray followed the formula that had been drilled into him.

"Shall he speak fully now, Magos?" Chronos asked the priest.

"Perhaps it would be well, saving time, Dread One. Then, if you believe it necessary, he may repeat his report before the council later."

"Speak then, man from Uighur."

"Following the orders given your slave, I journeyed to Mu," began Ray. The words came so easily that they must have been planted in his mind to be released by the asking of just such a question.

The Poseidon squirmed about among his cushions. "Yes, yes!" He was impatient. "But what of their defenses?"

Again the words came to Ray. "All the coastal forts

136

have been reinforced, with the reserves called up. And the fleet has been recalled to receive further men and new ships, and to cruise in the western seas—"

"All that is already known to us, you fool! Have you nothing of greater importance for our ears? What of the matters you were told especially to ferret out?"

"Your slave bribed a young novice of the temple—he knew of something—"

"And that—that? Know they of the Loving One?"

"Yes. The Naacals pierced the curtain of darkness and saw the Loving One—" Still the words spilled out of Ray, and he knew that they were not of his thinking but had been set in him for the answering of just such questions—though the purpose of his revelations he did not know.

Chronos balled a flat fist and dug it deeply into one of the cushions that supported his weight. "So—" He looked petulantly at the priest. "You told me that the curtain could not be penetrated, and it has been. Are the Naacals then so much more powerful than—"

"Dread One!" The Red Robe's hand made a warning gesture, indicating Ray. But if the priest did not wish such matters discussed here and now, his royal master was in no mood to be silenced.

"Do these Naacals have greater powers then?" he repeated, his voice rising shrill and sharp.

"As I have told you, Dread One"—in return the priest's tone was even and reasonable—"no mind born of Mu could have reached us. But we sensed something. If they did penetrate the temple—"

"If!" Chronos interrupted him. "They must have done so. You—do they plan any defense against the Loving One? What said this cub priest of that?"

"They work upon one, Dread Lord. But of that he could discover only that it was a ray of black light." Where *did* these words come from? Ray wanted to put his hands to his lips, smother his own voice. But it was no longer his; it was being used by a brain outside him—and in him this awoke a new kind of fear. "The novice was detected and taken before he learned more.

137

Your slave had only a small warning in time to flee—"

"A ray of black light," Magos repeated thoughtfully.

"You have heard of such? What is it?" Chronos demanded.

"I must search the records." The priest was evasive. "What else do you have to tell us?" It was as if he greatly wished to switch Chronos's attention from that particular subject.

"That Uighur wavers, Dread One," Ray heard himself reporting. "She is not the loyal daughter, ready to leap to defense of the motherland, as Mu believes—"

"Good! Good!" Chronos made a whistling sound of satisfaction.

"You see." He turned again to the priest. "Already the seed so carefully sown by our agents begins to sprout, and will speedily bear fruit. On the appointed day Mu shall call for allies, and there will be none to answer. Then she shall stand alone, ripe to our plucking."

"Tell me"—the priest now asked a question—"heard you, while in Mu, any story of a stranger lately come to high favor with the Re Mu? One who is not of Mu, but from afar, one having some strange powers?"

"There is such a tale." Ray was still only the tool of that will which had sent him here. "To its veracity your slave cannot bear witness. The commoners say that the Re Mu and the Naacals have summoned to their need a power from outside—outside—" he repeated.

Chronos sat up abruptly and cushions cascaded to the floor.

"Can this thing be true?" Again he turned upon the Red Robe for his answer.

"Who can tell, Dread One? Rumor reports many things, but few such are founded in any scrap of truth. However, this much is logic—we have our aid, and it came not from the world we know. Mayhap the Naacals have also called in the same manner. That would account for the piercing of the curtain—they could use their called one in such a way."

"Could such a summoned one prevail upon us?" persisted Chronos.

"We summon from the Dark; they from other forces—if that *is* what has happened. What man can say which is the stronger until they meet in some open battle? No matter what comes to stand under the banner of Mu, we have the Loving One and its kin strong for Atlantis. Know you no more of this matter?" he asked Ray.

"No, son of Ba-Al. Whispers in a city—and as you say, such whispers may not even be the thinnest shadow of truth."

"But they are enough to prepare us. Man from Uighur, you have done well in our cause. Is that not so, Dread One?" Magos asked of the Poseidon.

He appeared to jar the ruler out of some depth of thought.

"Oh—oh, yes, yes. You are free to go. The officer without will show you the quarters prepared for you."

Ray inched backward, still on his knees, not rising until he was at the door. When he glanced up, he saw that Poseidon and priest were whispering together, and he thought Magos was engaged in soothing his royal master.

12

RAY leaned across the wide sill of the window. In this upper story of the palace, the windows were more than the narrow slits of the lower rooms. Through the night outside, lights shone in the harbor, for he was high enough here to see beyond the walls to the docks.

Down there somewhere was the raider that had brought him here. He mused on Captain Taut's pressing and unexpected suggestion that he might find refuge on board if there were need. Why had the captain gone out of his way to speak of that, not once but several times?

The room behind him was bare, poorly furnished. The Poseidon did not treat his faithful servants from the outposts too well, it appeared. Four red walls, a dusty floor, a battered couch, and a bench— Even Ray's clothing had been taken from him, and he wore the black metal-on-leather armor of a petty officer in Atlantean service. At least they had not locked him in, as he more than half expected that they would. Taking up his black crestless helmet, he went out into the silent corridor. In fact, the hall wore so deserted a look that Ray suspected this was a not-too-much-frequented portion of the sprawling palace, which suited him well.

Now he went down into a better lighted and busier lower corridor. Soldiers and petty officers lounged on benches at its far end. He could hear the drone of their talk, with now and then a laugh. But he had no desire to join their company. Then a few words caught his attention.

"—Murians. Yes, tonight. Rare sport within the audience chamber before the hour is spent."

Murian prisoners! He must see them. This—this was another manifestation of the will which had taken over during his meeting with Chronos. There was no struggling against it.

A gong boomed hollowly, and the Atlanteans by the door snapped to attention, marched in answer. Recklessly Ray hurried to join the tail of the squad.

Here was the red hall he had seen during the dream journey, and once more Chronos occupied the gold throne. Ray lingered behind one of the pillars, assuming a guard's stiff posture, trusting thus to pass unnoted. The Poseidon raised his scepter, that symbol of authority which had been granted by Mu to the first Atlantean lord ruling here in the east, a bronze trident. The murmur of sound died.

"Let the Twelve of the Law Giving stand forth!" Chronos's voice was small and shrill in the mighty proportions of the hall, lacking the dignity he undoubtedly strove for. Twelve men moved out to take their places, six on either side of the throne.

"Hark you, men of Atlantis. This be the will of the Poseidon, the beloved of Ba-Al. On the third day of the month of slaying winds, twenty days from now, the fleet of Atlantis shall set sail toward the falsely termed 'motherland.' Mu, the oppressor, shall lie open to our fire and swords. So is it spoke, so let it be recorded—"

The twelve raised their hands.

"Is this also your will, mouthpieces of the provinces?" asked Chronos.

"Dread One, it is," they answered as one.

"Then it is so. And the word of the law may not be changed."

All in the hall chanted in answer, "This be the law, and the word of the law may not be changed."

Chronos leaned forward a little. His pale tongue caressed his pouting lips, as if he prepared to savor some new and delightful dainty.

"Bring out the Murian rats whom we have already caught in our nets!"

Ray watched a file of soldiers enter from the other side of the hall, ten men loaded with chains between them. The prisoners kept their feet with difficulty. They were spotted and befouled with smears of green slime, and they tottered, helping one another along.

141

But when they were brought to face Chronos, they gave him no salute and held their heads as proudly high as they could.

"It seems that you still have spirit. Perhaps our hospitality has been too generous!" Chronos tittered.

One of the prisoners answered rustily, as if hardships had sapped the vigor of his voice. "What do you want of us, false king?"

"Perhaps you are now ready to say your 'false' is true, to change allegiance—"

Ray knew that was no real offer, merely a cruel teasing. Already the Murian spokesman shook his head.

"We offer freedom and honor to any who join us." Chronos continued to smile.

"Honor!" The Murian's reply had whip-cut sharpness.

The Poseidon's jowls went pasty white. "So." And the evil in his voice was plain. He was silent for a long moment. Magos reached up to pluck at his sleeve. And Chronos nodded to the Red Robe.

"Ah, Magos. Yes, yes, I remember. You need more men for your laboratories, do you not?"

Ray heard a quickly stifled gasp that must have broken from one of the prisoners. But all else was silence.

"Magos and Ba-Al need men, strong men. You may have these, Magos. It would seem they are strong, since they now have the will to stand before us so. Perhaps I shall come to watch your use of them. I have been told it is strangely diverting."

Ray knew now why he had been sent here by that ruling will. But he—what could he—one man alone—do? For the present—watch and wait, be ready to seize any opportunity fortune might send. Was that his own thought or one sent by the will? To depend upon fortune was too risky—

Now! They were coming this way. He stood statue straight in the shadow of the pillar and watched the guards and the prisoners pass. Then he took a chance and flitted in their wake. After all, would any of these

142

around suspect him? They would watch for a break from those they guarded, not for outside help for their captives in the heart of Chronos's own palace.

Up the stairs—yes—this way led to the wing of the palace wherein lay his own chamber. He climbed swiftly, reached that room, and crouched behind a partly open door, a vantage point from which he could watch the party now at the far end of the corridor. There—they were putting the prisoners inside—posting a sentry—

Ray snatched up the cover from his couch and waited for the tramp of returning feet. Then he slipped out from his own door to the recess that held the next. From his belt pouch he took two of the square metal coins they had supplied him with and tossed them along the floor. They struck the stone with a jangle that sounded very loud indeed, and the sentry moved forward to look at them.

The American sprang and struck with the edge of his hand at a point where neither helm nor armor protected the sentry's throat. He caught the Atlantean before he fell and lowered him to the floor with a minimum of sound. Around the inert body went the covering, and then he dragged the bundle back to his own room and bolted the unconscious man within.

He sped back to the door the sentry had guarded and sprang its outer bolt. The Murian spokesman from the audience chamber stared across a narrow room at him.

"What do you—who are—you—?"

"Come!" Ray was busy with their chains, using the key pulled from the sentry's belt. But the spokesman jerked away from him.

"False hope—a new torture. Do not yield, comrades—"

"I am freeing you—" Ray was exasperated. They must be quick; this was no time for arguments.

"Who are you?"

"One from Mu."

"Which is easy to say but not easy to prove."

"Will you chance trust in me? Or do you want to await the pleasures of Magos?" Ray demanded. "Time waits for no second thoughts here—"

"He is right," cut in one of the others. "At least with free hands and out of this room, we can make sure that they retake only dead men. Which is a good enough hope for me!"

"And our only one. Even if we reach the harbor, there is no ship. And to strike inland is greater folly—"

Ray thought of Taut. Such a thin hope, but all he had. "There may even be a ship. But come!"

They were out in the corridor. The Murian leader stooped and caught up the sword the sentry had dropped.

"Do any of you know the inner ways of this place?" asked Ray. "I came here only this day—"

One stepped forward. "I was sent here before, but Magos did not use me." He could not control the shudder that shook his skeleton body. "I can take us as far as the outer gate."

"Then let us go!"

But they went at a crawling pace, listening, scouting. Their guide did not descend the stair Ray had used earlier but led them into a side hall and then down a narrower flight, halting suddenly before a door.

"The watchroom of the guard that serves Magos," he whispered. "Within—perhaps arms—"

Ray pushed past the Murians. In appearance he was one of the palace guard and so might pass unchallenged. He opened the door. Three men within looked up in surprise.

"You!" Ray tried to get the rasp of an order into his voice. "Up with you! The Murian prisoners have escaped!"

Two of the guards gaped at him. The third was on his feet.

"How?"

Ray was impatient. "How should I know? The order is to go out and hunt them down."

But the ready guard was eying him narrowly. "There has been no alarm gong—"

"No time to sound it yet. And—should we warn them into faster flight? Come—"

The two who had raised no question obediently headed

for the door; the other turned and reached for a small stick lying beside a gong. But Ray struck first, sharp and true, as he had in the upper hall. He did not watch his victim go down but whirled and kicked out at the nearest man, knocking him off balance to the floor, at the same time catching a glimpse of the Murian with the sword using that weapon on the guard who had reached the doorway. A second or so later the Murians were in the chamber, starting to strip the guards of their armor and weapons. There was other body armor stacked there, perhaps belonging to men off watch, and more than half of the former prisoners were soon wearing Atlantean uniforms.

When they were ready, Ray spoke. "Now, we must play a part. I am the dator in command of this cohort. We are going to deliver slaves to a ship of the fleet in the harbor. But there we have also another mission, to arrest Captain Taut of a North Sea raider, who is suspected of treason. So, as we march hence, you"—he nodded to those for whom there was no armor—"are prisoners. Do you stand ready to try this?"

"Lord, we do!" There was a fierce determination in that answer that promised ill for any who dared question them this night. Ray jerked the alarm gong from its stand and took it with him. The two unconscious guards were tied, thrust back under a table, and the dead man wedged behind the door where he could not easily be seen.

They formed up in the hall. Ray was amazed. These men did not resemble Chronos's warriors; suddenly they were those warriors! They had coiled their long hair under the helms, their rags were now uniforms, and in the half light their features could not be clearly distinguished. They moved as drilled troops.

With renewed confidence he gave the order to march. Between them wavered four prisoners, their arms apparently bound behind them. The party came into the courtyard and there, for the first time, saw sentries. Be confident, or at least have the appearance of it, Ray counseled himself.

"Who goes?" demanded the gate guard as Ray marched the squad to that portal. This was not the main entrance to the palace but a lesser one his Murian guide had suggested.

"The Dator Sydyk, on the word of the Poseidon," replied Ray. His mouth was so dry that it was hard to get those words out, and they sounded low and harsh—so perhaps natural to the Atlanteans, though he half thought the pounding of his heart could be heard as well.

"That being—?"

"Business in the harbor. Do I shout my orders to the wind?" He permitted himself a small blaze of anger, almost sure that fortune had favored them as far as she would—that they might end here in a fight. But the man waved them through.

They tramped along briskly. Ray wanted to break into a run. He expected any moment to hear a shout or a gong beat from behind. The gong he had brought from the guard room under his cloak he thrust into a bush just outside the gate.

These were the city streets, and the night was so far advanced that they were empty. But before them still were the five walls and the three canals to cross. To expect their amazing luck to hold was sheer folly, and he said as much to the Murians.

"There is this," their leader commented. "They expect ill to come from without, not from within, and unless there is an alarm from the palace— Ah, well"—he shrugged—"we can but do the best we can."

On they marched, past the ruined temple of the Flame into the lower streets, coming finally to the first of the wall gates. Ray advanced to the sentries there.

"Who goes?"

With every sense alert, he was sure they did not seem too surprised to see the squad.

"Dator Sydyk, on orders of the Poseidon."

"And your purpose, Dator?" Still no sign of alarm, no sign that this was not routine as far as the guards were concerned.

146

"To deliver oar slaves to the harbor. Also to arrest a raider captain—" He used his bluff, poor as it now seemed to him.

"You have a tablet of authority, Dator?"

Now—this was it! Ray took a step closer. "Just so, Dator. Would you look upon it? Here—" He stepped forward as if to seek the light beneath the gate and held out his hand. The officer came to meet him. Ray's other hand chopped, and he caught the slumping man against him, swinging his body around. The long dagger from his belt was now set across the bare throat of the Atlantean.

"You—" he began to the other sentries.

"Now!" He heard a soft call from the Murian commander. Men from the squad rushed the remaining guards. And those were swept away, with only one choked cry, quickly smothered, to mark the change of guard. The Murian gave an order, and the fallen men were dragged out of sight. He came back to Ray.

"You have a use for this one?"

"He is perhaps our key out."

The Murian pushed back the captive's lolling head. "He is senseless—"

"But can be roused again," Ray answered. "But let us get on—"

They passed through, closing the gate and wedging it so behind them. Ray slapped the face of his prisoner, and one of the Murians came from the small guard room in the wall to splash water onto the Atlantean. He gasped, and his eyes opened, widened. Ray clapped his hand over the mouth that had also begun to open. Again his dagger pricked the other's throat.

"You will march," he said slowly, intent upon making the other understand every word, "and you will do as we say. Thus you will live. Do otherwise—and it will not matter to you what happens to us, for you shall not see it. Understand?"

The man's head moved in a jerky nod.

"Now." Ray dropped his gagging hand and swung the Atlantean around, so they stood arm in arm, but

147

behind the prisoner the Murian leader moved up, his dagger to the other's back.

"We march," Ray ordered.

March they did to the second gate, and on the way Ray spoke in a half whisper, giving orders to their captive. Whether he could or would obey, that they must wait to see. But that the Atlantean was assured that he dealt with men who intended to carry out their threats, Ray did not doubt.

"Who goes?" It was the challenge of the second gate.

The prisoner cleared his throat and then answered.

"Dator Vu-Han. It is orders—pass this dator and his squad to the harbor."

For a moment there was silence, and Ray heard a tiny gasp from Vu-Han and felt his small movement as if the Murian-held dagger had pricked the deeper.

If the sentry had doubts, he did not voice them. Perhaps Vu-Han *would* be a key even as they hoped. But as they marched through the second gate, Ray knew that he would not breathe really free again until they reached the docks.

The third gate, the first bridge, always the Murians marching in order, Vu-Han playing the part they had set him. Fourth gate, another bridge. Too good, going too good. Something inside Ray hammered a warning. Who could expect to get away with this?

Last bridge—and beyond—the last gate. Still no alarm, free passage under Vu-Han's guidance. But it was well they had not come to depend too much upon fortune, for the Atlantean, in mid-point of that narrow way above the murky canal, suddenly swung his weight against Ray, at the same time crying out. The American had only an instant of warning, and that only because they were so close he had felt the tensing of the other's body. He threw himself forward, and the Atlantean, instead of pushing him into the flood below, sprawled across Ray's body, to fall, with a second cry, into the water. Ray was aware of the Murian officer hurdling his legs, pounding on the gate ahead, of a cry from behind, and of the trembling of the bridge under

148

him. The sentries at the gate behind would raise the bridge, would crush the fugitives between its bulk and the descending portcullis.

He scrambled forward on his hands and knees, not wasting time to get to his feet. Then his shoulder was caught, and he was pulled up to join in the Murians' flight to the already raising end of the span.

At least half their party had reached that point of safety and were fighting at the gate, and it was only because they did clear the way that the rest made the chancy leap from the quivering end to the small portion of safety beyond. Since the bridges had been designed to keep out attackers, rather than bottle in would-be escapers, that margin of footage on the other end, where the bridge embedded during use, did exist.

They fought their way through the gate and at last heard an alarm gong boom out. Coming free into the dock road, they began to run.

"Where to?" called the Murian leader.

"Can you all swim?"

Laughter rippled out of the dark. "Are we not of the fleet?"

"Then we take to the water."

They ran, still hugging shadows, winding a path among bales and boxes on the wharves. Ray paused once to get his bearings, to look for the landmark of a ship of the fleet that he had fastened on earlier as a way to reach Taut's anchorage.

"Guards!"

He did not need that warning, for he heard the thud of running feet and the shouting.

"To the water—"

They stripped off the armor, those who had posed as galley slaves already diving and paddling around waiting for the others. The sea here was cold; Ray gasped as he felt it close about him. Then he began to swim, knowing the Murians were following him. But he was stiff and chilled by the time he reached for the dangling rope ladder on the side of the ship. For a moment he paused, both because he was so stiff that any effort

149

was difficult and because he hoped for a sign from any deck watchman. But waiting was too long and dangerous. He would have to brave this as he had all else this night. So he climbed, slipping cautiously over the rail to the deck.

"Stand steady, my fine fellow!" Lantern light glinted on a naked blade and the hulk of a black shadow that held it.

Ray knew that voice. "Captain Taut!"

"Snake of deep water! Sydyk, said to be out of Uighur—" came the answer, but the blade did not waver from its readiness to slash out.

"Come in answer to your invitation, Captain—"

"With a goodly pack behind you," snorted Taut. "And what more—?"

They could hear the clamor on the docks even this far across the open water.

"What sort of serpent's egg have you hatched, man from Uighur, and why should it matter to me?"

"Why it should matter, I do not know," Ray returned as crisply. "Save that you offered me refuge. You can send us—or a portion of us—back into the hands of Chronos's guard. But I warn you that will not be easy. Or"—he paused before making his shot in the dark—"you can live longer, to lead your men into Poseidon's palace, their steel open in their hands."

"So. You have a scheme afoot and wish the raiders to do the dirty end of it. You—who are you who make free to tramp my deck without let or heed?" he growled as the Murians continued to climb over the rail and muster behind Ray, each carrying a sword he had not abandoned with the rest on the docks.

"The dirty work as you call it, Captain, has been largely done. Take service with me, and you will have a powerful ally—"

"Mu." That was statement, no question. "And what will Mu offer—with the need of going halfway around the world to collect?"

"Enrollment in her forces, pardon for past offenses, a chance to loot in Atlantis—"

150

"Your authority for all this?" Taut interrupted.

Ray pulled the jet armlet from beneath his undertunic. "Take this, and these men—to Mayax. You will find then what I have promised."

"You are very sure of yourself—"

"And of you!" returned Ray boldly. This was such an hour when even the wildest chance must be played because there was nothing else to do.

He saw the flash of lantern on blade, but that came as the captain sheathed his sword. And then the American heard Taut laugh.

"By the iron claws of Ba-Al, if you have brought ten Murians out of the city this night, then I can try to get them from the harbor. And, sea god willing, your men will speak for me in Mayax before I am blown out of the water by those who have been non-friends."

"They will speak for you."

"They—what of you?"

Ray had put his hand to his head and rubbed his fingers back and forth across his forehead. It was not really an ache there, behind flesh and bone, that he felt. It was knowledge cold and set—that he could not be a part of Taut's dash for freedom. That will which had set him on the path to Atlantis was not done with him yet.

"I have not finished what I came here to do," he said slowly, knowing he spoke the truth.

"But to return is to face certain death," protested the Murian officer.

"I have no choice." Ray's voice was bleak. "When you come, if you come, again to the motherland, tell them they have indeed fashioned a tool to their service."

"If you must stay," Taut broke in, "go you to the maker of sails in the shop by the drinking den at the end of the third wharf. Say to him my name. It may gain you a measure of safety."

"We shall return with you—" began one of the Murians.

Ray shook his head. "Mu has need of ten blades, and

151

the men to wield them, and also of what knowledge you have gained here of the city and its defenses."

"That is true, even though it be hard saying," agreed the officer. "But, remember this. When you come again into the Sun, you have ten liege men waiting to back your banner, my lord. And may the brightness of the Flame light any path you take!"

Ray returned to the ladder, eager to be away, though this time he might be going straight into the arms of Ba-Al.

13

RAY clung to one of the piles under the wharf. He could hear voices, though they were too muffled to make out words clearly. He already knew that the hunters were out. From this hiding place he could not see the raider. Would Taut be able to get out to sea, perhaps running a gauntlet of the fleet? Or would he even try? The captain's conversion to Mu was so easy that it made Ray suspicious. Perhaps he had only waited for the American to leave before he signaled the Poseidon's men to collect the escaped Murians. But if that was his plan—why let Ray go? He would be an even bigger prize.

Unless they believed that he could lead them to more Murian contacts in the city and would trail him— Yet Taut himself had given him a contact. Though, of course, the sailmaker might have the guard waiting—

He wedged himself tighter into his small crevice, but he could not stop shivering, and not only from the chill of his soaked undertunic. Why had he come back—or been sent? Somehow they had planted orders in his brain during that time they had been making him into Sydyk. And he did not understand those orders—

The movement overhead ceased. They must have gone on to search elsewhere. He had been careful not to swim to a quay near where they had taken off but one some distance to the west. But where to go now? To try to get back into the city was as good as marching up to the nearest guard with his hands in the air. And he was so tired that he wanted nothing so much as a dark corner into which he could crawl and perhaps sleep a little.

His present position was too cramped. Ray doubted whether he could make any sort of getaway if they came upon him suddenly. Better move into the open, where perhaps he had a thin chance. Clumsily he edged along one of the under support beams, transferred to another, working his way to land, while under him the water washed sluggishly. He often halted to listen for noise aloft or the sound of oars in the harbor.

He hesitated for a long moment before he swung up and managed to reach the upper side of the wharf. There were bales heaped there, and he scurried to them as one might dart for shelter, worming his way through a crack between two into a kind of cave. Although these were a barrier against the wind, still Ray shivered. He must have dozed without knowing it, for now it was gray instead of dusky in the cracks and crevices between the piled bales, and he heard the tramp of feet outside. Morning? The dock workers coming?

Ray pulled out of his hiding place on the water side, ready for a dive into the oily wash of water below if the need came. For the first time he looked down at his body, trying to judge what sort of appearance he would make in the open.

When they had taken to the water, he had left on the dockside the kilt, helm, and corselet of the guard. What covered him now was an undertunic, and it was so stained by contact with the none-too-clean waters of the harbor that it resembled a laborer's tunic. His boots—he frowned at those—but he could not discard them. Perhaps they did not look too much as if they had been part of a uniform.

For weapons he had only a dagger and his two hands. He held those out, regarding them appraisingly. In a country that knew nothing of the kind of infighting training given in his own world, they were proving to be better weapons of defense than any steel. He rubbed them up and down the front of his clammy tunic.

He was hungry; there was a pinch in his middle. Ray licked the salt taste from his lips and tried not to think of food.

"Put your back to it—jellyfish! Think you can move these by looking and wishing?"

The shout was underlined by a cracking snap. Ray

154

started, ready to slip into the scummy water. Then, instead, he wriggled to the end bale to peer around. There was a work crew moving onto the wharf under a whip-swinging overseer. Slaves probably, Ray thought. But save that they wore rope sandals and he boots, there was little outward difference between those slouching, sullen laborers and himself.

Suppose he were to join such a crew—could he pass unnoticed? But it might well be that the overseers kept too close a watch on their charges, that they would be as quick to note one too many as one too few. Better not try it.

He swung over the end of the wharf and found another place from which to climb to the quay. There were boxes there being unloaded from a cart, and a waiting line of men to take them up. Ray waited in the shadows for a chance to move on. Then he saw that other, a thin man with a face more than half masked in a bush of ragged beard. He wore a tattered tunic, and he was also keeping out of sight of the overseer, his glance flitting back and forth between the boxes and the man in charge of their unloading. Then, with a quick dart, he joined the tail end of the line of workers, coming up just in time to receive one of the boxes. Instead of following the man before him, he shot to one side and began to run, the box in his arms.

Ray seized the opportunity the other's audacious act had given him.

"Thief—stop, thief!" Whether that was the regulation cry in such circumstances, the American had no way of telling. But it brought an answering cry from the overseer. Several men dropped their burdens and broke out of line to follow the runner. Ray joined with these, playing the part of a hound after the man who dodged in and out among carts and burden bearers. Then the American saw a welcoming doorway and darted into its shadow. The portal gave slightly under the hand he put out to steady himself, and, daringly, he entered, letting it swing to behind him.

The dusk here was darker than the early morning

outside. There were many foul smells, but some odors of food made Ray's stomach knot. He walked softly, waiting a second or two outside each curtained doorway. There were small sounds from some, a grunt, a scrape, enough to let him know the building had its inhabitants. But he reached the end of the hall without seeing any of them. There was another door there, and it had an inner latch, which he eased out of its bar with infinite care.

Beyond lay a narrow alley littered with rubbish. Ray glanced from right to left along it. Mankind did not change through the centuries. This could be a back way through any slum. Some of the smells were a little more exotic than those of his own age—that was all.

There were windows in plenty looking down upon this way. But whether anyone looking through them might take an interest in him— It could well be that in such a district as this one minded one's own concerns, saw nothing, heard nothing that was not of one's private business.

He picked a way through the mess of garbage and rubbish and was drawing near to one of the side outlets when he froze. A groan? Certainly that had been a groan? And it came from behind a rotting basket piled high with refuse. Ray edged closer to the wall and kicked at a noisome heap of decaying matter.

There was only a second or two in which to regret his folly. From behind the basket a wild figure leaped at him, and the knife in one hand was as bright as the sun. Well trained in fighting tactics, Ray made a counter move to that confident attack. His hand closed about a wrist, and the knifer was hurled against the wall, but not quite in time.

Ray pressed his hand against his side. Not in his heart, but only because of luck. He could feel the warm blood ooze through the stuff of the tunic. Just now he dared not explore the amount of damage. No pain, though—not yet.

He stooped and caught up the knife the other had dropped, keeping it ready in his hand as, with his boot, he pushed at the flaccid body. His attacker must have struck his head against the wall—

As the body rolled, the head moved queerly, too loose upon the shoulders. Ray caught his breath. Dead, he thought—neck broken. The Atlantean was young, hardly more than a boy, and he was very thin, his bones showing clearly under a yellow skin that was also marked with purplish eruptions. His tunic was better than those Ray had seen on the dockside workers, and he had a belt with silver studs, a purse hanging from it.

There were two rings on his forefingers and a hoop earring in one ear. Thief—and probably a successful one. Perhaps this trick had worked well for him in the past. To groan as if he were the victim of an attack, to draw the attention of someone who did *not* mind his own business—then walk off with the profit from the would-be investigator's curiosity or folly.

Ray pressed his hand harder to his side. The wound was beginning to sting now. And he dared not let even a small hurt go untended. Leaning back against the wall, he explored the cut. It was, he believed, very shallow, more nuisance than real trouble. But he must not lose any blood to weaken him or attract attention by stains such as were already dark on his tunic.

Which left him no choice. He set to work.

A short time later he strode from the far end of the alley with more confidence then when he had entered. The boots and the leather tunic that might have betrayed him were gone. He wore the brown garment of the dead thief and, beneath it, a strip of undertunic tied tightly over the cut. The other's moccasin-like footgear was a little large on his feet, but that was better than too small. And he had a purse with silver pieces in it. There was nothing left to connect him with Sydyk the Uighurian.

The tramp of feet from behind—Ray noted that those in the street glanced up, and a few dodged into doorways. He thought it prudent to follow their example, though he did not make the mistake of looking over his shoulder to see what sent them into hiding.

Fortune and his nose had brought him to a tavern of sorts. There was the stench of sour wine and cooking. Once Ray might have found that mixture of strong odors stomach-turning; now he only wanted some food. The front of the room was open to the street. Along it marched a cohort of the Poseidon's guard. They came to a halt at the entrance to the tavern, and Ray knew that this time fortune had deserted him, and he would have to face inspection by the enemy. He glanced about the room.

There were three tables with benches on either side. And there was a door that led to another room or rooms from which came the cooking smell. Two other customers were present.

One looked as if he might well hae spent the night here. He sprawled over the end of one of the tables, his head pillows on his arms. From him came a steady series of gurgles and snorts that suggested he was still deep in a slumber that could have begun by the emptying of too many of the same kind of tankard as one lying beside him. The fingers of one of his hands were still clasped laxly about it.

The other man sat at another table facing Ray. He wore much the same sea-stained jerkin as Ray had been given to play the part of Sydyk, and he was eating with industry, first a spoonful of gravy dipped from a bowl, then a mouthful of bread from a piece he kept in his left hand. But Ray saw the single quick glance he shot at the soldiers without, and the American thought that the diner was less interested in the food than he wished to appear .

A woman shuffled out of the inner room. Her hair had been braided with leather thongs and then pulled into an erect pile on her head in a grotesque copy of the elaborate style Ray had seen on the ladies of the Poseidon's court. She had a sleeveless robe laced down the front to the waist, bagging about a bony frame, hacked off short at mid-calf. It had once been a bright orange but was now faded in streaks and stained with long drip marks here and there.

Her face was puffy fat in contrast to her lean frame, so that she presented the distinctly odd appearance of a mismated body and head. Around both arms just below the shoulders she had broad bands of copper, and a stud of gilt was set in the over-abundant curve of one nostril.

She set both fists on the table before Ray and leaned toward him a little to demand, "What'll it be?" Her voice was a whine, and he had almost to guess at her words, they were so slurred.

"Food—wine—" He was handicapped by not knowing what specific dishes one would order in such a place. Then he took a chance and pointed to the other diner. "Some of that—if it is ready."

Her grunt might be either agreement or denial. However, she turned away toward the inner room. But before she reached the door, there was a sharp sound, and they all swung around to view the entrance.

The dator of the guard stood there, two of his squad to back him. He had some of the bullying arrogance of a man who knew he need expect no opposition. Now he slammed his sheathed sword down again on the nearest table in an attention-demanding rap.

Here it comes, thought Ray. He measured the distance between him and the door to the inner room, but the woman was in the way. Also, how could he be sure there was another exit beyond? He might dash there only to find himself bottled in a trap.

The woman wiped the back of her hand across her lips. Then she smiled, or leered.

"Wine for the lords?"

"Not your rot gut," returned the dator. "You, there—" He pointed to the seaman. "Who are you and from where?"

The man swallowed what was in his mouth. "Rissak, mate on the *Sea Horse*. What of it? I've been in and out of this port more years than you've been growing hair on that chin of yours—"

"For too quick tongues there is an answer—a knife blade across them," the dator retorted, but he did not

159

push the matter further. "You then—" He had already turned to Ray.

"Ran-Sin," Ray improvised, "from the north."

"Stand up!" the dator commanded.

Ray got to his feet. Suppose he rounded the table or overturned it—could he get out to the street? Hardly, not with the rest of the cohort waiting there, doubtless ready and waiting to stop any suspicious characters their commander might flush.

But to his surprise the dator did not order his men to move in upon a prisoner. Rather did he survey the American with a long head-to-foot stare, which was repeated back from foot to head again. Perhaps— perhaps the search parties had been provided with a description, and his change of clothing with the dead thief was now to his advantage.

"Him?" One of the squad pointed to the snoring sleeper.

The dator shook his head impatiently. "Nothing like—"

So—Ray thought—he was right. They had a description of sorts. And it would also seem that the dator was one who depended only on the details as issued from official sources. But how could they know, Ray wondered as they left, that there was anyone now to be hunted? If Captain Taut had carried out his part of the bargain, should they not believe all had escaped, or at least were on the raider trying to reach the North Sea?

On the other hand, the captain could have played him false, which had a very good chance of being the truth. Or else Taut had failed, his ship had been taken, and questioning of the prisoners had uncovered the fact that Ray was still loose in the quay district. He had better believe that the worst had happened.

But what was left here to do? As yet no further order had come from the will. Why had that unseen, unheard monitor, apparently so deep set in him that he could not fight it, brought him back? For something more than to play hide and seek with Poseidon's men along the docks—of that he could be certain.

160

The woman had gone into the kitchen, and now she returned with a tray. There was a bowl of stew, a hunk of bread, and a tankard of evil-smelling liquid, which probably passed for wine in this establishment.

Ray took a coin from the thief's pouch and saw her eyes widen a fraction as she beheld it. Too much, he told himself. He did not slide it across the table, as he had first intended, but kept it between two fingers so she saw only its edge.

She smiled, with some of the same attempt to ingratiate that had been in the look she had turned upon the dator.

"You want something else, my lord?"

"A room—where a man can rest privately—" he said.

"Rest," she repeated. "Oh, perhaps we could find you such." Her eyes flickered from him to that visible edge of coin, then back to his face. Then she pointed with her chin.

"Through there," she said, indicating the entrance to the back room, "and up the stair. Take the chamber with the blue curtain."

Ray spun the coin. Her palm flattened it to the board and swept it into hiding somewhere about her person. He picked up the tray and took it with him, trying not to move with such haste as to arouse her suspicions any more.

The room with the blue door curtain was the second from the top of a breakneck flight of stairs. There had been two in the kitchen to watch him cross the end of that room—another woman, older, even less prepossessing than the hag-waitress, and a man with a bowed back who had been cutting up some stalked vegetables, so bent over his work that his chin was hard threatened by the sweep of his own knife.

Behind the blue curtain was a cell-like cubbyhole. No chair or table existed, only a bed, which was no more than a pallet raised on a frame of four legs from the dirty floor, and a shelf on the wall on which stood a jug. But there was a window with shutters, now barred. Ray set the tray on the shelf and went to open the

161

window. It resisted his efforts, but some prying with his dagger point finally freed it, and he pushed open the slats of wood.

A few feet away was a blank stone wall, probably that of a neighboring building. Ray looked down. A narrow runway between walls was there, more than half choked with refuse, full of traps for the feet of anyone who tried to use it as a way of quick escape. But at least he felt a fraction easier with that window open and close to hand.

He sat down on the edge of the unwholesome looking and smelling pallet and began to eat. The stuff tasted strange, hot and peppery—probably overspiced to induce the buying of more drink. But it satisfied his hunger, and he ate it to the last drop, wiping the bowl with a crust of bread.

Then he leaned back against the wall to think. In his interview with Chronos, that implanted will had certainly taken over and dictated what he said. He had been keenly aware of that during the process. Also, he was more than certain that the rescue of the Murians had been directed, even if the details of the action along the way had been his alone. Therefore, both incidents had been part of the reason for his being here. But what else remained for him to do?

And how long must he sulk about waiting to be nudged into accomplishing whatever duty was his? His resentment of such management was no longer quick and hot, but it was a dull and lasting fire in him. Yet until such a time as he could face those who had sent him here, he must stifle that. A man could be blinded by anger and thus easily make a mistake.

Ray stared very hard out of the window at the wall. "All right." His lips shaped the words he did not say aloud. "Here I am—just waiting. If I wait too long, perhaps I am finished, and whatever you want of me goes undone. Come through wherever you are and give me a hint. What do you want of me?"

He tried to think that, to make it a silent cry, as if he could reach across three oceans to the mind of a

Naacal—or the Re Mu, or whoever had planted the compulsion in him.

It seemed that the stones in that wall darkened—trees! Ray shut his eyes, then opened them again slowly. This was like looking through the wrong end of a pair of field glasses. Trees, row upon row of them—all tiny. Yet his mind told him that they were really tall—towering—

No! That was not the answer—not the trees! He screwed his eyelids together in an intensity of effort. The trees had no part of this. He would not look at them, think of them—

"Come in." He thought of that will now as if it were a broadcast sent on interrupted frequencies, one he could only pick up now and then. He put his head down to rest on balled fists, his eyes still tightly closed. Come in, he begged, let me know what I am to do. Before it is too late, just let me know!

Fordham held the small strip of perforated paper in his hand. So Burton believed this was the answer, did he?

" 'Do not spindle, bend, or tear,' " Hargraves quoted. "I suppose we should be used to any sort of black, white, red, green, or blue magic by now, but somehow I refuse to accept that a man can be reduced to that! Frankly I don't want to believe it. It's—it's obscene!"

"Not a man—no—" corrected Burton. "We asked for an equation that might fit a certain mind pattern so we could set up what would amount to a homing device. Your own computer gave us that. Just as it provided you earlier with your equation for Atlantis."

"Which might not have been correct at all!" flared Hargreaves. "All we saw, recorded, was a forest of trees, remember? I'll believe in Atlantis when I see a little more definite proof."

"All right, no one insisted upon its really being Atlantis," returned Fordham. "But Dr. Burton is right. We fed in the data; we got an equation; we used that equation and got—what you saw for yourself, what we

163

filmed. And we lost a man in there. It's logical to believe that he hasn't stayed right on that spot where he went to all this time. And if this will work—"

"If it will work," stressed Hargreaves.

Fordham passed his hand over his face. He was tired, so tired that it was an effort to make the smallest move. When had he really slept? He could not remember now.

"It's not all we should have," Burton cut in. "You must understand that. We have the facts from his army record, reports from people who knew him, data from his last physical, and the like. I must set the odds very high against its working. But it is the best we can do. To have a better chance, we ought to have his behavior pattern charted, other reports, reaching back at least two years—"

"Since we don't have those"—Fordham's words slurred into each other wearily—"we'll try this. Miracles have happened—"

Hargreaves shrugged. "I'm beginning to believe that General Colfax is right. Send in a search party—"

"And maybe lose them, too?" Fordham asked. "Not until we must." He looked again at the strip of paper that, the computer reported, added up to a man—a living, breathing, walking, talking, thinking, hating, loving man. Or did it? They would never be sure, unless their long shot succeeded and Ray Osborne came out of a forest of giant trees to face them and his own world again in answer to this experimental broadcast.

14

DANGER? Ray raised his head, listening intently. But there was no sound from the hall outside. He stood up and stepped softly to look out of the window, down into that slit. No one stood there. Yet in him now there was such a feeling of being under close scrutiny that it was almost as if he could turn his head and see a figure in the other corner of the room.

Accompanying that sensation of being spied upon came a driving desire to be in the open, one he could not withstand any longer. The walls about him might be moving in to cut off air needed by his laboring lungs. Over all hung such an aura of menace as he had known before only in nightmares. Though he held onto remnants of caution, Ray knew that he could not stay in this temporary hiding place, that he was being tipped out of it as he himself might tip over a basket to set some small terrified animal on the run again.

This had no kinship with the compulsion that had kept him in the Atlantean port—this, he was sure, was of the enemy. But it was also something he could not easily fight.

All right—he would get out of here. Or else—Ray licked his lips—if the pressure continued to build, he would simply stand there shrieking his identity aloud to these four walls until his enemies appeared to collect him.

Move in obedience to that order—by yielding so much, he might still retain something of his own will. And as long as he had even a fraction of that, he would keep fighting, dodging, running! If he only knew why he had been left here, then he might have both a purpose and a reason to stand firm.

The sailmaker's shop Captain Taut had mentioned, should he head for that? He had no reason at all to believe in the good will of the raider captain. Still it was all he had—a shadow of help.

He turned suddenly, and his hand went to his side. The wound there was tender enough to make him wince. He had inspected it again in the privacy of this room. It had crusted over, and if it were clean, healing had already begun.

Ray went to the window again and studied the runway one story below. When he leaned out as far as he dared without overbalancing, he could see that to his left, at the front of the tavern, there was no opening to the outer street, only a high boarding making a dead end. The other way—yes, there was perhaps an exit there. Quickly he stripped the top cover—and the only one, he discovered—from the bed, making its end fast to the leg of the supporting frame. It did not give a very long rope, but enough to provide him with a safer landing. Then he was through the window, swinging over the debris. Ray let go and fell as he had been taught to tumble to save himself from hurt. Only such lessons had never been practiced with a view to landing in a dump.

Crashing through a top layer of refuse, the American struck less fragile material with bruising force. For a moment or two he lay in the mess, pain shooting along his side, fearing almost to move lest he discover a broken bone.

Finally, because that feeling of being hunted was so strong, Ray clawed his way up and out of the debris. With one hand against the wall for support over the entrapping footing, he began a careful journey toward the rear of the tavern. If the crash of his landing had alarmed any inhabitant of the other upper rooms, apparently it had not led them to investigate.

The narrow slit reached the end of the building, but still a high fence of rotting boards walled him in on the right. To the left the windowless wall of the other structure continued. The wood of the fence was dry and powdery, and Ray thought he could kick a way through

166

it, but there was no need for such drastic methods of escape as yet.

He struggled on through the noisome swamp of the refuse and finally came to a right angle of the fence meant to bottle up the slit. As he went, the need for freedom, for space in which to run, had so worked in him that, as he fronted that barrier, caution was burned away and he kicked and tore at the disintegrating wood, breaking his way out into an alley much the same as that in which he had met the thief.

Shaking off as much as he could of the filth left by his trip down the slit, Ray looked right and left, uncertain as to which might promise a small measure of safety, if any safety was to be found in this maze of dockside warrens.

If he had not totally lost his sense of direction, then the sail shop lay to the left. Well ahead a figure was busied, poking through the refuse, turning over nasty piles of litter with a long stick, now and then pouncing upon some bit it transferred to a bag it dragged behind. All Ray could see was stick-thin bare arms protruding from a huddle of rags so old and grimed that they had lost all color. The closer he approached the scavenger, the less human it seemed. But when he was perhaps the length of its search stick away, it moved with a speed he would not have thought possible for such a walking skeleton, swinging that same stick around to trip him up, while from the swathing of rags hooding its head came a shrill cackling.

Again trained reflexes saved Ray as he dodged that tripping stick. And the scavenger, apparently overbalanced when his weapon did not connect with Ray's shins as planned, went tottering on a step or two, pulled by the very force of the intended blow.

"Yahhhh!" First failure was not deterring the assailant from another try. But Ray could not bring himself to close with the creature. This was not as human as the thief, rather something that had slid so far down from the human that it was loathsome.

He kicked the bag it had been using to store its

167

harvest and dodged again. Swinging the stick, it tottered on, tripping upon the bag, and fell with a shrill wail. Ray ran.

His breath was coming in sharp gasps when he reached the end of the alley. The way was narrow, hardly wider than his outstretched arms, and it gave upon a street that was much in use. Heavy wagons moved there, going to the dock laden, returning empty. Men in uniform drove those wagons, and some had guards riding on them as well. Ray leaned against the wall, in what he hoped was inconspicuous shadow, to watch, at first incuriously, as he got back his wind, then with some attention.

War supplies was his guess, being loaded on the ships of the fleet. Preparations for an all-out attempt against either Mayax or Mu. Surely they would have to deal with Mayax before they took—or tried to take—Mu. But how did Chronos hope to engage all the rest of the world in open war unless there was a way of reaching Mu by sailing east instead of west? He had never seen a complete map of this world. What about Africa? Did that continent exist in this age, and if so, who held it? Too bad he knew so little that was helpful.

But possible geographical changes slipped from his mind. He might have left the tavern room, escaped the attack of the scavenger, but he had not lost that sense of being under surveillance, and it acted now as a spur to keep him moving.

Any extraordinary behavior here would certainly alert the guards on the drays. Ray began to walk along, hugging the walls of the buildings to his left, heading back to the harbor. If—if whatever will kept him here wanted him back in the city, perhaps these wagons might be the answer to such a return. He tried to examine them without betraying too much interest, searching for any way of hiding on one of the returning ones.

According to his cursory inspection, there was no chance of that—not in broad daylight, anyway. Ray reached the end of the cross street and faced the wide thoroughfare forming the spine from which the docks made one-sided ribs. He crossed the line of carts as they drew up for a wait, making himself walk at an even pace, fighting against hunching his shoulders under the eyes of the drivers and guards, expecting any moment to hear a cry raised, feel steel bite at him.

His trip through the alley had brought him well along the harbor. Now he was near the western end and began to watch for the sailmaker's shop or the wine booth that would identify it.

"Stop!" It was an instant or two before Ray realized that command had not been heard by his ear but rang in his head. And with it came a pressure for obedience.

"Come!" He had stopped, yes. The sheer surprise had brought him to a halt, so suddenly that a man ran into him and turned with a snarl to demand, in argot Ray could barely understand, what he thought he was doing.

"Come!" Again that calm assumption that he would obey, that he had no recourse, but to answer that call.

He turned away from the scowling Atlantean. There was no help; he had to answer that imperious summons. But it was not from the will that had kept him here. And as he obeyed it against all his desires, he knew that that other shrank, dwindled—as if the two pressures could not exist together within him.

"Come!"

Come where? His conscious mind might not know that, but whatever now controlled his body seemed to be sure. He walked east, not at any hurried pace but steadily as he had done before. And he could not break the hold that kept him going one step after another.

The docks were crowded, and Ray threaded a way among men, wagons, beasts of burden. He passed the tavern from which he had fled only a little while ago, went on and on—

There was a flow of brilliant color here—the tunics of men, the bright blankets and panniers of the animals —but Ray became aware of a spot of red that seemed to glow with some inner fire. And it waited—for him. He

169

was imprisoned in a cell of flesh and bone that moved to the command of what also animated that red pillar there— No, not a pillar, but a robe—a robe of a deep blood shade, and wearing it, someone who was more than a mere man.

Fear lives with all men from their birth to their dying. There are many small fears, and sometimes terrors that are not small from which a man may cower in the dust or run shrieking to escape. Fear can be a prod to action, an enemy to battle, or a blanket that saps sane life. Ray thought he had known fear many times before he marched toward it on the harbor road of Atlantis. But such fear as this—never!

"Come!"

He was coming. There was no choice left him, no trick learned in his own world that he could call to his aid. He was mesmerized by that terrible aura of fear, drawn to it—

They were only a few feet apart now, he and that Red Robe with the closed face upon which there was no triumph, no lust of battle. The priest's will was all centered on one thing, to hold and then to draw, even as he was doing.

Ray stared into that lean face, with its beaked nose, its point of chin, finding it familiar. Then the priest raised his hand, and about his wrist was a shining band that caught Ray's eyes for a moment. Watch band reported one small portion of his brain. Watch band—watch—here— His! His watch—which had been taken from him on the Atlantean ship at the beginning of this whole wild adventure. And this—this was the Red Robe from that ship.

The hand holding that watch gestured. Pain burst in Ray's head, and he dropped under the blow aimed by the warrior who had moved in behind him.

Ray lay in the dark, and under him was a hard surface, so chill that its cold and damp made his bones ache. He moved his hand to the pulsing agony of his head and heard metal scrape, felt the jerk at his wrist preventing him from completing that movement.

"Do you wake at last, comrade?" Words out of the dark. It seemed to take a long time for them to register any meaning in his mind. "I had come to think but your empty husk lay there and that you had escaped—"

"Who—who are you?" Ray looked in the direction of that voice, but the dark was too complete to see anything.

"One like yourself, a prisoner waiting the pleasure of Chronos! May his bones rot before his flesh and his spirit wail on the winds, homeless forever!"

"Are you Murian?" Ray tried to pull himself up a little, then fell back, for the pain in his head was worse.

The other made a sound that might have been laughter, except in this place there was no laughter. "No. I am Atlantean born, though no friend to Chronos and his liegemen. And you?"

Ray hesitated. What was he? A spy he might say. "I came from Mu." That much he could answer, giving away no more than they already knew.

"What mean you?" the other demanded eagerly. "Is there a landing—war?"

"Not yet."

"But perhaps soon? That is good hearing to one who has been here for five years—"

"Here?" Ray could not believe that. This hole—how could anyone measure time or even keep his sanity?

"No. In this cell only a short time. You do not count days in the dark when there is only the black of night. But they have brought food eight times. However, before they dragged me here, I was captive above where there is day in the cells and sometimes even sun. But of what passes outside these walls, I do not know."

"Atlantis moves against Mu."

"It took them long enough to nerve themselves to that. For a hundred years the priests of Ba-Al have wrought what manner of magic they could to this end. Five years ago when I tried to ship out, they were approaching some summit of their evil. Men whispered of that—"

"How is it that you still live?"

171

Again that sound which was almost laughter. "Brave as Chronos would like to think himself, he dares not go against ancient prophecies. There is some blood he cannot shed until he is truly master of the world—which will be a long time coming. And he will not kill the true holder of the Trident, since it was vowed long ago that that would bring the wrath of the sea in upon the land."

"What do you mean?"

"The line of the true Poseidons was supposed to have ended a hundred years ago, but in truth it did not, for the last Poseidon's daughter, rather than accept as her consort the man chosen by the priests of Ba-Al, fled into the mountains, letting it be thought she died. There she exchanged bracelets with the captain of her guard, a Sun-born true to her. And I am a direct descendant of that union, as Chronos knows. He has slain all the Sun-born he can lay hands on, destroyed the temple of the Flame, but he dares not yet put knife to me—for it is written in the stars, to be read even by the priests of the Shadow, that Atlantis will endure only as long as does the true blood. He keeps me safe under his hand, but he does not kill."

"But you are loyal to Mu?"

"How could it be otherwise?" asked the other simply. "I am of the house of the Sun in Atlantis; the son may not turn against his mother. Chronos is not of the Sun-born; that is one reason his hate for them is so black and bitter. But now I say, comrade, may the Sun speed the ships of Mu, for I cannot believe they are waiting for the Shadow's sons to attack first—"

"I hope that they come," Ray answered. But, he thought, what was he doing in the middle of this quarrel which was none of his? He could hope for some miracle to save him from whatever fate those of Atlantis prepared for him, but to count much on such a hope was folly.

"Now, comrade, what of you? Just a short time ago they brought you here. You say you are from Mu, yet in

172

their torchlight you had not the look of the motherland—"

"My name is Ray and I am from the Barren Lands—"

"The Barren Lands? Have they then established a
colony there?"

"I am not of Mu, save that the Re Mu has granted me
that courtesy," Ray said slowly. Granted him? No,
lulled his suspicions that he might prove to be a
weapon—or whatever he meant to the will that ruled
him here. Will—Ray suddenly became conscious that
that was gone from him. Either it had been banished
by the force that Red Robe had used to draw him
tamely into captivity, or else it had withdrawn because
he was no longer of use.

"The Barren Lands," the other repeated. "Wait—
they come!"

A sharp click and an oblong of light appeared in the
wall. Ray tried to shield his eyes as two soldiers bearing rods that gave off yellow light stepped within.

"Welcome, hounds of Chronos!" cried his cellmate.
"How goes it with you? Have those of Mu come down
upon you yet, or do you still brew some foul Shadow
magic hoping thus to make yourselves new walls against
Murian steel?"

Ray turned his head. Fastened to the wall near him
was a young man, emaciated, the cheerfulness of his
voice belied by deep lines about his well-cut mouth.
And silver frosted his long black hair.

One of the warriors grunted as he set a gourd of
water and some hunks of dark bread on the floor. His
companions thrust one light rod through an iron ring
in the wall before they left together.

"Now I wonder what is the meaning of that?" The
Atlantean prisoner pointed to the light. "They plan
some trickery. In this prison one comes in time to
question the very stones of the walls. Chronos does
nothing without purpose. He learned that much from
Magos."

He reached for the nearest hunk of bread and passed
it to Ray. "Best eat while you may, comrade. Chronos

173

has a fondness for experiments, and he might wish to see how long we can live without even crumbs. You have named yourself—let me do likewise. I am Uranos."

"Eat but half," Uranos advised as Ray chewed the tasteless stuff. "It is better to have less today than none tomorrow. Chronos hatches some plan beneath his misshapen skull that holds nothing but ill for us. Me he fears, not for what I, a prisoner, can do, but because I am who I am. And you must also threaten him in some fashion, or he would not hold us together. The promise made by the stars may not save me—"

"I met a man, the captain of a raider, who swore he could take this city if he led the proper men. In spite of all the walls and canals," Ray said slowly, not knowing why that came into his mind now.

Uranos frowned. "It could well be done. There are secrets within Chronos's walls, which he has manned so securely, that are secrets even to him."

"You mean?"

"Rooms and passages underground where the foot of man has not stirred dust these hundred years. I have heard tales of such, and perhaps your captain has also, or knows even more than tales. If he has found such a way, the core of the city might lie open to him. But this captain is loyal to the Shadow, is he not?"

"No longer, or so I hope. He sailed with escaped Murian prisoners on board—"

"Then"—Uranos smiled—"perhaps in the future Chronos may have some unsought visitors. Would that I could look upon his face if and when that happens. Also I think he shall lie uneasy tonight—"

"Why?"

"I suspect we have been overheard, and a report of our words will be speedily carried to Chronos!"

"Someone listening?" Ray stared at the walls.

"Years of such hospitality have given me keen ears. It is not the first time this has happened. Now there will be a mighty scurrying, hunting underground ways. Whisper a warning into a coward's ear and he will straightway feel a knife pricking his throat. But there

174

are hundreds of passages, mostly long sealed, and he will never find them all. So will he sweat and fear—"

"But what if he finds the right passage and sets an ambush there?" It seemed to Ray that his cellmate was entirely too optimistic.

"That is as fortune decrees, but somehow I think it will not happen. What man may change the lines written on his forehead at birth, or the future the stars foretell? I believe that I shall live to reign here—"

In spite of himself Ray was moved by the Atlantean's confidence. Could these men really see the future, or a portion of it? What had the Lady Ayna once said—that they saw *a* future but that some decision of their own could change it.

"How can you be so sure?"

Uranos looked at him, and now that glance steadied into a hard, measuring stare.

"If you have passed the First Mysteries, as by your age you must have, how can you ask that? What manner of man are you? Of the Barren Lands you said, Murian by the Re Mu's favor—but no colonist. What *are* you?"

"No man of this time—"

"You mean?"

"I was born into the world of the far future. I came through time to here. How and why I do not know."

Uranos was silent for a long moment. If the same story had been told him, Ray wondered, would he have believed it?

"So—then did the Naacals send forth a summons also? One that you answered by your coming?"

"No, I came by accident." He told the story in a few sentences.

"And if you can never return?"

"That I do not know. Nor even if I have any future beyond this hour, or this day. Judging by our present circumstances, probably not."

Uranos shook his head. "It is well to be prepared for ill, but do not yet toss away the future, my friend. Let us forget a little and give those who listen something to be heard. Tell me of your world—no, let me first show you mine—"

And he talked of his boyhood in the mountain valleys and of how he had hunted horses in the plains.

"Comrade, nowhere in the world is there aught to equal the beauty of a horse finishing a race, his mane long on the wind, his hoofs pounding as war drums. The sailors speak of ships, the huntsmen of the elk at bay—but the horse fills my heart. And did I not ride Flamebreather to victory five times over!" Passionate longing broke through his voice.

"Tell me—" he began after a pause, and then made a sharp gesture toward the door. "They come again," he said in a half whisper.

And it seemed to Ray that a kind of evil shadow came first, dimming the light rod, hanging about them.

15

ACCOMPANYING the guards this time was one of the Red Robes.

"All hail, brother of the Shadow," Uranos addressed him as their guards released their chains from rings in the wall. "Why does the servant of Ba-Al come to disturb us?"

The priest looked from Ray to Uranos and then centered his stare on the Sun-born. The American thought that he had never seen so cold and measuring a regard. He did not answer Uranos but spoke to the guards.

"Bring them forth."

They found it hard to get to their feet. The short chains had so held them that the muscles of their backs and thighs were cramped. But pushes from the guards sent them stumbling out into a narrow hall.

"They count us mighty heroes," Uranos observed. "See, brother, they must send eight warriors and a priest to have us out!"

But if he were trying to bait the Atlanteans into some move, none of their escort arose to his needling. Instead, the soldiers closed upon them, urging them on at a fast pace after the hurrying priest. They went on up and down dark passages, and Ray thought how like this was to a giant spider web, with Chronos, like a bloated insect, in its midst. Then they came to a wider and better lighted hall and halted before a door curtain of metal, not fabric.

Their guards shifted uneasily, keeping their attention riveted upon the curtain. It was, Ray decided, as if they were unhappy at being sent here. Then the priest placed his right hand on the screen, and it opened at what could have been only a light touch. With an audible sigh of relief, the warrior nearest Ray thrust the American on the heels of the Red Robe, with Uranos, similarly urged, beside him.

Two Red Robes waited and caught at their chains as if this was a matter in which they had long practice. Ray had no chance to struggle before his arms were locked firmly behind him.

"On!" commanded the third priest who had led them.

They crossed a bare room and went through a second door into a chamber with walls the rusty brown of dried blood. There was a single large chair there, carved from one block of black stone, which looked none too comfortable. But its occupant appeared as much at his ease as Chronos lolling among cushions. Magos brooded. There was a satiated, yet anticipatory look about him, such as might have been worn by a vulture perched above a slaughter yard.

He was smiling, if the rictus that twisted his thin lips could be given such a definition, leaning forward slightly to hear the better some tale now being whispered into his ear by another priest. But when his eyes rested upon the prisoners, it became a wide and evil smirk.

"So, my lord Sun-born, Poseidon-who-has-no-hope-of-being, you have come to me at last," he said to Uranos. "Do you hold in memory now a past meeting when I spoke to you of the will of the Dark master and you refused to listen? You cut yourself from the future that day, Uranos. Do you regret that?"

Uranos held his head high. "Magos, you claim to be the son of Ba-Al upon earth. Does the Shadow agree to that, I wonder? But I can well believe you aspire to play the role as fittingly as something born of flesh and blood can, since such evil otherwise would not come into any sane mind. If you propose to entreat me again—"

"Entreat you—*you!*" The high priest laughed, a chill, thin sound that might have issued from the bony jaws of a skull. "Magos does not ask a second time. Nor have you any value now. This time you will serve another purpose."

178

"That shall be as the Sun decides. The future lies within the temple—"

"Ba-Al's shrine."

"I think not. There still stands another temple in this city."

Magos's smile was gone. His eyes burned as Ray had never seen a human's burn before.

"The Flame is long quenched. You pay a debt—"

"And I say to you, Magos, that in the end the paying shall come from you. And it shall be such a paying as this world has never seen."

There was such conviction in Uranos's voice that one could believe he looked into the future, reading there enough to make that not a threat but a prophecy.

"Dare you believe that, you who are an insect upon which the servant of Ba-Al can set a sandal and not realize that he has crushed aught at all? Dare you speak to me—me, the ruler of the world under the shadow?"

"Has Chronos heard such words, Magos? He sees himself the ruler of the world."

The smile returned to the priest's vulturine face. "Chronos? Who—what is Chronos? A man uses a tool to aid in a task. Once done, that tool may be thrown away, perhaps broken. When I choose, I shall brush Chronos into nothingness. Think not to appeal to Chronos—"

It was Uranos's turn to laugh. "And again I say, Magos, Chronos might not agree with your words. I think, were they to be reported to him, there might be a visitor to your sleeping chamber with the night, one carrying steel and knowing how to use it silently—"

But Magos continued to smile. "That is of no importance, certainly no concern of yours."

"Then why have you sent for us, son of the pit?"

"Like other men, Uranos, at times I wish amusement. And games of chance interest me. My friend, Conth"—he nodded to the priest who had been whispering to him—"has wagered me a curious ring out of Uighur, a ring that is said to give its holder some odd

179

powers, that I cannot keep a man alive for seven days in the laboratories while he undergoes some changes. Now I am proud of the skill of my workmen, and I desire that ring with its attractive history. So I thought of all the prisoners within these walls who could be spared, and I summoned you—"

Uranos might not be broken, but he had been shaken enough to say, "Devil!"

"So have others called me before they passed through that door." The high priest pointed to an opening at the far end of the room. "And yet later they blessed me when I granted them death—much, much later. You are strong, Uranos; so does this other one look also. I think I shall win my wager."

He arose, and the icy claws of the priest behind Ray fastened on the American's shoulders, propelling him forward. Magos had taken two steps before he turned and came back.

"Now I am a true son of the Shadow. It has come to me that perhaps Ba-Al should have a voice in this. Therefore, you twain shall choose between black and white stones. He to whom my lord sends the black shall save my wager, and he who gains the white shall wait for a while. Yes, that is fit and proper."

The other priests echoed his laughter. Ray watched Conth bring a bowl and ostentatiously drop two stones, one white, one black, into it. Then once more Magos held up a hand.

"Put in two of the white. If both draw, then I know that Ba-Al wishes them for himself. The will of the Shadow is our full desire. Conth shall draw for Uranos, and Path-tan for this stranger. Draw, Conth—"

Magos took the bowl and held it well above the eye level of the lesser priest. Conth's hand moved and opened to show a white stone on his palm.

Path-tan came forward and dipped his fingers in turn. Then he tossed his prize to the floor, where it rolled to touch Ray's foot. It was also white.

"Our lord has spoken." Magos broke the silence. "By his will be it so."

The other priests echoed his words. But Ray wondered—had it been only a trick? Why did Magos want to threaten and then reprieve? Or indeed had chance selected the stones and Magos been superstitious enough to allow himself to be balked, believing Ba-Al had guided the priest's groping fingers?

"Uranos." The high priest came a step closer. "What do you expect—the altar and the knife—or"—he paused—"the embrace of the Loving One?"

"What matters it how a Sun-born warrior faces death as long as he does so under the Flame? The body dies, but not that which is the true man. And in death do I conquer, as well you know, who have chosen to turn down the path of the Shadow. The altar of this devil you speak of—the Loving One—"

"The devil I speak of?" Magos replied. "You should not utter words about things you do not know so lightly, Uranos. The Loving One it shall be, and you will call upon your Flame in that hour, and it will not leap to your calling. Then you will beg for death—but it shall come in its own time and by its own desire. And for you—likewise!" For the first time since they had entered that room the high priest looked straight at Ray. "Take them to the temple so that they may be ready at hand when the hour strikes—"

Once more they traveled through dark passages, some of them so dusky that they might be moving through an endless night. Once Ray saw trickles of oily moisture on the walls and slimy tracks left by nameless dwellers in these underground ways.

They came to steps climbing up and up, passing at least two other levels of floors, then out into a red-walled corridor with rods of light set at regular intervals along it, and finally into the hall of murals, which Ray had seen during that dream journey.

"We are in the temple of Ba-Al." Uranos spoke for the first time since they had left Magos. "See you, brother, how the Lord of the Shadow would keep his foul amusements ever before his worshipers' eyes?"

Ray gave those obscene pictures but a glance and then averted his gaze.

"Be silent!" One of their escort slapped Uranos across the mouth vicously. "Time for speech, yes, and for wailing and calling upon a long-quenched Flame will come. They say that the Sun-born do not know how to beg for mercy. But then the Sun-born have not yet met the Loving One. I warrant you will squeal as loudly at the last as did the last Murian who went into the embrace of That Which Crawls!"

They were put in a small side chamber, their chains again snapped to rings in the walls, and then the priests left them. "What was Magos's purpose?" Ray asked when they were alone. "Did he play a game with those stones? Or did he really believe Ba-Al made the choice?"

"Who knows?" the other returned. "If he played a game, it was not wholly aimed at us, I think. This Loving One—I wish I knew more."

He did not agree, Ray decided. He leaned his head against the wall as his older problem came back full force. Why had the will kept him here in the heart of the enemy's country? What had been the task he had not completed? Since he had been summoned by the Red Robe on the quay, that void which the will had filled had been empty in him. Had it fled or been driven out by the power of the Atlantean priest?

Why was he here?

The stones at his back were chill and cold; he was lost. Not this time in a forest of giant trees but in a place he could not describe, where not his body, but another part of him, drifted without purpose—beyond his control. Lost, yes, as he never thought anyone or anything could be lost—

Then—that which he had become—that drifting wisp of near nothingness was caught—held—drawn in another direction—and by the will!

Ray was in his body, and there was a tingling in his flesh, a warmth under his skin, which had once come from the sparkling water in the Murian citadel. In him again the will was firmly seated—waiting—though for what he did not know.

"Brother!"

Ray turned his head and looked to the other. Uranos had pulled to the end of his chains and was trying to touch Ray with one outstretched hand. His face mirrored amazement and concern.

"How is it with you?" he asked as Ray's gaze met his.

"Well—now," the American answered and knew that was the truth. With the will had come confidence. Yet do not depend upon it, caution urged.

"You—it was as if you went from your body—" half whispered Uranos.

"But I have returned," Ray said. "And also—" He hesitated.

"Yes—?" Uranos asked.

"I think—listen!" His head still rested against the wall, and it seemed to him that through the stone came sound, very dim and far away.

The Atlantean turned his head and laid his right ear also to the wall.

"Like sea surf," he said after a long moment. "What is it?"

They were not given long to speculate. The priests returned to unhook their chains. As they came into the great hall of the temple, that sound was clearer, sharper, as if some acoustic property of the building picked up and amplified it. It was now indeed a roaring. Uranos kept turning his head.

"That—this is battle!" he cried out suddenly.

"Mu!" But how? Ray questioned his own answer. There surely had not been time enough for the motherland to gather an army, to strike thus at the very heartland of the enemy. But could he be sure of that either?

It may well be." Uranos looked to the priest holding his chains. "Look well to the wings of your Shadow now, brother of the pit. When the Flame dances, all darkness fails. And when the motherland comes to cleanse the land, naught will remain to give your Dark god cover—"

The priest struck him. "Ba-Al is not blown as a feather on the breeze. The Loving One will make you forget all but itself—and soon!"

Uranos spat blood from a cut lip. "Look about you. So gather now the spirits of the murdered dead! Think you they shall not guide their avengers, call through your streets for an end to Ba-Al's rule? I say to you, the Five Walled City shall vanish from the earth, and even its name will be lost to the memory of man. Ba-Al must seek again the pit from which he crawled, and those who serve him will be left to face the light they fear more than any sword. That which you have called up shall be master, not servant, before it is also sent once more into its own place!"

He spoke not as one voicing threats but with such assurance that he might have been a prophet who believed implicitly in his vision of a future shortly to come.

Again the priest raised his hand to strike, but he did not complete that blow. The roaring had faded somewhat, and now they heard a pounding, as if someone ran through the halls. A priest, who wore a brazen corselet over his robe and carried a helm within the crook of his arm, came hastily from behind a row of pillars.

"The Murians—" he panted. "They have sunk ships across the mouth of the harbor after loosing two fire galleys to ram in among the fleet. They landed other forces to the north, and the herdsmen of the plains have revolted to join them. Magos bids you bring these carrion forth to the pyramid above the walls that he may show them what power we can send out to eat them up!"

This—this was what he had been sent to do, said the will within Ray. This was a part of the battle in which he would be the weapon.

The first sharp consciousness of that ebbed as the priests hurried him on with Uranos. Men who were

184

dressed half as priests and half as mailed warriors closed about them and brought them out of the temple.

They could hear the roar better, see the glare of fire beyond the walls and canals, spreading from the docks. There was a tenseness to be felt in the city, its streets crowded with soldiers so that the party from the temple was slowed. Shock was a part of it, Ray sensed. The Atlanteans had not expected this blow—not so soon—and not here. How *had* the Murian forces managed to move so fast and with such secrecy that they appeared to have caught their enemies unaware—bottled the Atlanteans in their city?

It must be past dawn, but the sky was murky with darkening clouds. And to those one of their guard called their attention.

"See, your Sun is veiled. So does Ba-Al draw his protective curtains over us this day!"

Uranos was jostled against Ray, and the American noticed the other was breathing deeply, drawing the air, tainted though it was with all the pollution of the city, into his lungs eagerly. Then he remembered that his fellow prisoner had been a long time captive, and to him this air was fresh with a kind of freedom.

"They take us to the west wall. See—there is the pyramid," Uranos observed.

There was an erection of alternate red and black blocks, very dark under the lowering sky. Its top was a square platform reaching perhaps some ten feet higher than the adjacent wall. Up there a small group stood awaiting them.

The flight of stairs leading aloft was very steep, its treads narrow. Twice Ray stumbled, to be finally pulled and hauled along by the guards.

Magos was there. And beside him, still in a gold court robe, with no martial trappings of helm or body armor, Chronos. But the latter did not turn to look as the prisoners were half boosted onto the platform. He was biting the nails on his stubby fingers, staring out, not at the smoke and flame above the harbor, but at the distant clouds, so low-lying. An officer came up the steps of the pyramid at breakneck speed.

"Dread One," he reported, "those who entered the city from the ruined temple have been driven back again—"

Chronos turned his head. There were flecks of white at the corners of his fleshy lips. His eyes were wild and did not seem to really see outward but rather inward. And Ray knew that this would-be ruler of the world was now filled with fear.

"Kill! Kill!" he screeched. "Let there be blood and burning. Let not one escape! Return not unless you bring also their heads—each and every head!"

The officer passed Ray in his going. And the American noted that his face was drawn and haggard, as if the news he had brought was not good but ill and that he had reported defeat instead of part-victory.

It was Magos who gave the next order. Chronos stared once more at the clouds from which came the sound that had been like a distant murmur of ugly, angry surf within the temple and that was not the raging of a sea gone mad but the clamor of a major battle.

"Place them at the pillars—lash them fast," Magos commanded his priests.

The platform on which they stood was ringed with pillars. They were strong, firmly rooted, and several feet taller than Ray and Uranos who were now bound to them. Uranos nodded across to Ray as Magos came to inspect their bonds narrowly. Then the high priest called to Chronos.

"All is in readiness, Dread One. Shall it be done?"

His manner was outwardly subservient, but malice lurked beneath the lip service he gave the Poseidon. Almost reluctantly Chronos came away from his view of the battle.

His fingers, bloody where he had bitten the nail quicks, were pressed to his wobbling paunch as if some inner pain thrust there. But he summoned the energy to laugh at Uranos.

186

"Ha—true blood dies—Atlantis falls—is that not what they said all those years agone? Well, those who mouthed that did not know the Loving One!" He looked then to Ray.

"Sydyk out of Uighur—more or less than that, Magos tells me— If you are he—or that—which the Naacals called from another world, then now is the time we shall see whose calling has summoned a greater power. And I think that you are the less—since Phedor was able to summon you when he wrought magic with what was once against your flesh. Such magic moves lesser men, and when you answered to it, then you proved that you were not of the Outer Ones, the terrible ones we have dealings with. So shall you be food for the greater and aid it in bringing forth more of its kind—"

Some of that made sense, but not all. It was apparent that the Atlanteans knew or guessed his identity, thought that he might be some focus of unknown power—but, was that true? Ray sought to reach the will within him. It lay there still, but to his appeal there came no answer.

"Can those beyond"—Chronos waved his hand—"can they see clearly?"

"Yes. They have far-seeing glasses that will be trained upon us."

"Then begin, begin! What do you wait for? Or is there danger for us?" The Poseidon gave back a step or two, edging for the stair head.

"Never, Dread One. The Loving One will not turn against its masters. Prepare them for the embrace—"

Guards were on Ray, slashing at his worn tunic, ripping it down so that he stood bare to the waist. One drew his dagger and cut twice across the American's breast, leaving a shallow cross-shaped wound that welled blood. There was no harm in the cuts, and the reason for them Ray could not guess. Uranos, he saw, had been similarly marked.

"Go!" As Magos gave permission, the priestly guards departed with the speed of those leaving an ill-omened place. And Chronos withdrew to the very edge of the platform. It was plain that for all Magos's reassurance, he did not want to front too closely this ultimate weapon.

Magos held a brown bowl of such rough fashioning that he might have patted it together moments earlier from the mud of some riverbank. In this he dropped dully glowing bits of charcoal taken from a footed brazier. Setting it equidistant from the pillars and the prisoners, he puffed the coals into glowing life and then tossed a handful of black powder on them.

Curling brown smoke followed and with it such a stench as made Ray cough, while it irritated his eyes until tears ran down his cheeks. It was as if all the unclean things in the city had been reduced to the handful of powder and set afire.

The smoke cleared, but the nauseating odor still hung there. Chronos had now retreated one step down the stairway. But Magos was smiling, and all the rest of his life—if he had much more of life, Ray thought—he would remember that smile.

"Has your evil failed to answer your call?" asked Uranos. "You have produced smoke and a mighty smell. But what else follows, Magos?"

"Look before you, Uranos. Even now That Which Crawls comes to claim our offerings, that it may wax strong enough to open wide a door for all its blood-kin!" answered the priest.

Ray stared at the stone to which the priest pointed. There was an odd-looking shadow there. And it was growing! Under his gaze it gathered form, as if it drew substance from the very material on which it rested. And as it grew in girth, so did it gain in solidarity. No longer was it shadow.

16

FOR Ray the whole world narrowed to that shadow which was no longer shadow. Bloated sides swelled yet larger; a head pushed up and out, a blind head with no mark of eyes. Yet the head wove back and forth as if it quested by either sight or sound. Then green-black horns snapped into being, to break the wormlike outline of the head.

It had no legs but, beneath, a gaping mouth that puckered and relaxed rhythmically, wavered, thickened, grew in extension; two tentacles, and on these were ulcer pits of suckers. In color it was basically black, yet splotched here and there with a dull and loathsome green, and from it came an odor to make a man retch. A giant snail lacking any shell, a slug— Comparisons arose in Ray's mind, but none were as stomach-turning as the thing itself.

Magos came forward, and, at either the sound or the vibration of his step, the monster's head whipped around. Its long neck stretched; the horns waved vigorously.

"Seek your prey, dweller in the Outer Darkness," commanded the priest. "The blood drips to beckon you—seek your prey!"

The thing raised its head high. Ray wanted to close his eyes, but he could not. A moment or two and then the cuts in his flesh or Uranos's would guide it.

Those horns continued to weave jointlessly, as if testing the air. Then suddenly it lowered the worm head and humped its back as might a slug in movement. As smoothly as a flow of polluted water, it glided toward the prisoners.

It had chosen, Ray saw. His horror at that moment was so great that it paralyzed him—for he was the choice. After it moved a short distance, it gathered its bulk together in a crouch. Again the horn-waving head arose as if to verify the scent. The stench from it was a

189

gas. Ray wanted the thing to spring now—to finish this. But instead it waited, as if it savored—like a refinement of the promised feast—the disgust and fear of its victim, deliberately prolonging the advance as though to suck in his repugnance.

Then it flowed again—nearer. And from this there was no escape. No escape—or was there? Was it Ray Osborne or was it the will which had brought him here that stirred then? Suppose— What he supposed he did not know but only grasped wildly—as a man caught in the sucking maw of quicksand would catch at any branch overhanging that spot—for something within him with which to do battle.

Black—black—the creeping thing of the Dark—the blackness. What fought black? White—light! The white of the temple walls of Mu; the white of a Naacal's robe; the white of—of Flame! But fire was red—yellow— Not so! The Flame was white—white with a dazzling purity. White! The will within him, all within him that dreaded death, as mankind dreaded extinction, stiffened into defense. A white Flame—

And this thing from the pit—it dreaded that Flame. Ray felt it check, felt the small flash of uneasiness that lay behind that check. Its head jerked faster from side to side. Now it was no longer silent. A low, whining note hurt his ears. Or was that sound at all?

Flame—a shooting Flame—a Flame that moved and made a wall before that thing. It was there—he could actually see it now—white Flame that might have seared his eyes with its force and yet did not. And in him that will swelled and flowered but—only through him. So this was the why and wherefore—he was the instrument through which— Then the will blotted out his own thoughts; it must have the whole of him in this struggle.

Again the thing gave a little ground, and its keening whine grew the shriller. Fear—its fear grew! He must use that fear as the handler of a savage beast uses a lash to ward off attack. And like a whip he cracked his thought:

"Back, nameless evil, back into the world wherein you were set to dwell! Cross not into this! Back to the foulness that is rightfully yours!"

But the thing retreated no farther, only lay there, its head darting from side to side as if it butted against a wall. Then Ray knew Magos was holding it, using his counter powers to drive it on. He, too, drew upon some inner will or force. Ray faltered. The Loving One humped forward. Flame—the Flame was there—

Again the slug's advance was stayed; the angry whine arose. Under Magos's urging it rocked back and forth, its baffled cry growing louder. But this time Ray held. How long could he do so?

They were locked in silent battle. Magos and his creature of the Dark striving to find some weakness, Ray the channel for the will that drew heavily upon his strength. He was weakening. The thing flowed—stopped, flowed again.

"Brother, give it my body!" Faint and far away was that call. "Give it me and gain time—"

"No!" Ray rallied. His body was trembling; he felt as if only the chains that bound him to the pillar kept him on his feet. Forward crept the Loving One—

"On!" commanded Magos.

"Back!" ordered Ray and the will.

Noise—shouting—

Ray's concentration broke. The Loving One leaped. Too late the American tried to set the barrier again. A tentacle slapped across his body; the suckers fastened greedily on the bloody cuts. He shrank and yet could not move from the contamination of that embrace.

Flame—Flame—but there was no Flame that would touch the thing now mad with blood hunger. Only he was not yet done! It was as if deep within him he now fronted that will and demanded of it as it had demanded of him.

Ray's head raised. Come, he told that will—be with me now! And if it had made of him a servant and a weapon, so now in the depths of extremity he reversed that. Into him flowed, after a second or two of amazed

191

resistance, a kind of power such as he had never felt before.

The loathsome flesh pressed to him quivered. Slowly, with the added torture of physical pain, the tentacles loosened as, reluctantly, fighting, the monster drew back. Magos had released his pressure. Too late he saw what was happening.

"Flame!" Ray thought he shouted that aloud. It was an order, to his own strength, to the will he had seized. "Flame!"

Again it was there, the leaping, dazzling Flame.

"Hold—those of Mu climb the stair!" Words—without meaning. All that existed in the world was that Flame created out of thought, which must be held, and held, and held—

The Loving One twisted and turned, hissing, but it retreated from the Flame. There was a cry from the stairs.

"Hold!" shouted Uranos again. "Hold but a little longer, brother!"

Magos was desperate. Ray felt the loosing of the Red priest's power. He was strong—maybe too strong. But if he won, he must first face a fight, a real fight—

The high priest strode back and forth across the platform, his thoughts sharp and swift, like thunderbolts, prodding the thing. The Loving One reared, writhed, twisted, crept forward—

And the Flame dwindled. It was not Ray's spirit but his body that weakened. And again the tentacles closed about him.

"Ray! Ray!" A call. He tried to draw upon the will, but there was nothing left—

White fire—the Flame again? Ray raised his head.

No, just a ray, touching the horns of the Loving One. It writhed against him. But the tentacles dropped, tearing his flesh. There was a roaring in his head, he saw distortedly, as through a watery mist.

Clash of steel against steel. Then he was falling, free, of the pillar. Someone caught him, steadied his limp body, lowered him gently. He saw a face wavering in and out of focus. Cho—from far away and very long ago—Cho—

"The—Loving—One—" He tried to warn and thought that perhaps his words were not even a whisper. But those ice-blue eyes understood; lips curved in a smile as frost-filled as a winter storm.

"Watch, brother."

The Murian raised his hand. Cupped in the palm was a crystal, flashing rainbow lights. And from its center rayed a shaft of white light. Again Cho played that upon the horns of the thing and so drove the crawler back, for it could not escape the beam he turned upon it.

Magos stood beyond, his face contorted into a mask that had only a faint humanity in it. And the power in him—Ray could feel it aimed at them—at the Loving One. Yet the monster was out of his control.

"Devil!" Magos screamed.

"Drinker of blood," Cho returned. "Listen now to this beast of yours. I think it hungers. And is not true that when it comes to your call, it must be fed, one way or another? Behold—the reckoning!"

The Loving One, as if goaded beyond endurance, sprang—not at the Murians but at the priest. Its tentacles closed about Magos with the grim grip of a trap. The priest tore one arm free and thrust at the obscene roundness of the slug body. His dagger sank into the black hide, but when it was withdrawn again, there was no trace of a wound on the sleek skin. And all the while the Loving One fed.

Ray's head fell back on Cho's arm. He had been too close to that himself to watch now. But the Murian did not look away, and when the monster would have turned at last, Cho held it with the beam.

There was one scream. Cho's arm tightened about the American. Then the Murian raised the crystal for the last time.

"It is done," he said. "Now we destroy the doer."

Ray looked once more. A tattered bundle of stained rags lay upon the stone. Above that oozed the monster, and it was crooning to itself. Just as Magos's rage had earlier reached to them, so did now a horrible satisfaction.

The light became a sharp sword of radiance. At its touch the creature ceased to croon its contentment and moved uneasily. Then it whined, shrilly, its plaint hurting in one's head.

Now the beam changed color, from white to faint rose, from rose to red. Then it rippled, as if rising in ever strengthening waves from a concealed source. And in Ray's body he felt the rhythm of that rippling.

While the Loving One twisted, writhed, its whining became a vibration, too high for human ears to catch any longer. Then it started to dissolve. Its outlines blurred; a black pool oozed slowly from under it. And the stench was a sickness in the air.

Still Cho held the light steady on that writhing bulk. Once the creature seemed to make a last desperate effort to survive. Its head lifted, the body heaved as if to hurl itself at the Murian, but the light chained it fast.

So it perished, the body becoming a pool of liquid corruption, which, in turn, was consumed by the ray. Then there was a shouting on the platform, echoed from the street below.

"The city falls," Cho said. "They throw down swords and call for mercy. And now—we must see to your wounds, brother—"

Another Murian in armor went to his knees beside the American. Under that helmet, surely—Ray frowned —a face he had seen. Yes—this was he who had led the prisoners.

"You—then Taut did as he promised—"

"Surely, lord, and better—" began the other, but Cho shook his head.

"Time for talking later. This now—" He smeared a paste across Ray's breast. "Now, a cloak about you. We must get you into the hands of the Naacals as soon as we can—"

194

"Lord!" One of the Murians spoke; his hand rested on Uranos's shoulder. "What of this Atlantean?"

"Cho." Ray summoned what small strength he still possessed. "This is the real Poseidon, Uranos—their prisoner, too. Listen to him—"

"That shall be done."

Ray sank back on the cloak. The invading party here was a small one, eight Murians and four wild-looking rogues who might have come from Taut's own ship. Uranos knelt beside him.

"Warriors' high salute to you, comrade. And for your courtesy in remembering me—my thanks. Of the Atlanteans taken—I do not think that one will find any to speak for him—"

Ray looked in the direction the other pointed. Two of the Murians were tying the hands of Chronos behind his fat body.

"He was captured—"

"Yes. It was his hate and his cowardice that kept him here. He wanted to witness our ending, and he feared the battle below. So for him the game is now lost, and I do not think he will relish what will follow."

Ray listened in a dreamy detachment. The ointment Cho had used on his wounds had taken away the pain. And he felt queerly light and empty. The will was gone once more, and this time for good—or so he believed. All about him was hazy, as if the place, the men, all else save he himself, had no reality. He was alive; the Loving One—whatever that horror had been—was gone, taking Magos with it. And Chronos was a prisoner.

"It seems"—Cho returned from the head of the stairs—"that we must stay here yet a while. To travel the streets now is a matter of fighting; there are pockets of desperate men who will not surrender." He sat down on his heels by Ray and slipped from his own arm a band of black, transferring its coolness to the American's limp arm. "This was, in a way, our key to the city."

"How?" The touch of the armlet had an odd effect on

195

Ray. It steadied the world and brought it into focus again.

"Captain Taut brought it and the Murians to speak for him. And Taut knew an inner way to bring troops inside the walls."

"As I said," Uranos commented, "there were secrets of which Chronos knew nothing, which even the Red Robes had not explored."

"But—" Ray touched the armlet with his other hand, running his fingers along it. "How did Mu get here—so soon?"

"Ask the Re Mu, ask the Naacals—ask those who appeared to us to be so blind to danger and so lacking in preparedness. The legions of Uighur came in from the east, and our fleet from Mayax. But I sailed with Taut in the vanguard, claiming my right—"

"Your right?"

Cho looked surprised. "Are we not sword brothers? The Re Mu said that you were already in service within the Red Land—so thus I would come. I think we set a record—look—" He held out his palm and showed red blisters on the skin. "Even officers took their turn at the oars when there was need. Taut had the command, and I am but a first-year swordsman when compared to his experience in such raids. He knows this coast better than any warder. Once, when he was pursued by a guard ship whose commander could not be bought off, he stumbled upon a secret. It is a narrow break in the cliffs, so small a fault one cannot believe that it gives upon aught worthwhile. But there is a scrap of beach and a cave, and then a tunnel that must have been cut by men before the recording of time. The tunnel leads under the city to the lower chambers of the temple of the Flame.

"We landed there by night. And a party remained to lead in later forces from the fleet. Taut swore that the sons of the Shadow depended so much upon their rings of walls and water that they would be part vanquished already if we appeared in their midst. And I believe he had the right of that.

196

"At dawn we captured a Red Robe, and I think he mistook us for spirits of the murdered Sun-born, for he told us freely that Magos planned to summon the Loving One and feed it well. The nature of that monster was such that it would thereby be able to bring from its own pit others of its kind, loosing thus a weapon we could not stand against.

"We thought that what he drooled about would happen in the temple of Ba-Al, and we fought to reach there. It was not until later we saw what chanced here and knew of our mistake. Without the walls the legions of Uighur are in action, and with them those of Atlantis who have never taken kindly to rule by the priests of the Greater Dark. Now such resistance that remains is being hunted out, pocket by pocket, while ever more men come through the temple passage—"

"And this?" Ray pointed to the crystal.

"Of the Naacals' making, but they have only a few of them. This was sent to me just before I entered the passage. We were warned that we must be very close to that monster before it could be used. But, Ray, twice we saw that evil thing retreat, and yet you were bound and had no weapon at all!"

"He has done what I would have sworn none could do!" Uranos burst out. "He beat back that fear with his will, held the Dark at bay."

"No," said Ray, his fingers still slipping about the jet armlet, that touch which tied him to the here and now. "I did what was set upon me to do, I summoned the Flame—"

"The Flame?" questioned Cho.

"The white Flame," repeated Ray, once more slipping into that odd state of detachment.

"The undying Flame," Cho said. "But that—that is not of man, for man to look upon! Truly the shield of the motherland was raised above you on this day!"

"Once that Flame burned in the sanctuary of the altar in this city." Uranos spoke then.

"But never will it so again," answered Cho.

"What do you mean?" asked the Atlantean prince.

"The Re Mu has decreed that after the taking of this city it shall be utterly destroyed, so that its name will not be remembered by men. For what was wrought here was an opening of gates between two worlds meant never to be kin to one another, so that the Loving One and its kind were freed into space—"

Two worlds—never meant to be kin to one another. The words lingered with Ray.

"And the people?" inquired Uranos swiftly. "What of the dwellers within this city?"

"Those who are evil must face the fruits of their evil and make accounting therefor. The others will be sent inland. And the Atlantean fleet will disappear from the seas of the world—"

"The inlaid plains are rich, and peace abides there," observed Uranos. "Perhaps greatness shall come to us again."

"So they say it is written," Cho agreed soberly, "for in the passing of time the motherland shall fall. Thereafter Atlantis will take rule on land and sea, as Chronos had thought to do now—but that lies yet in the future."

"And in time that, too, shall pass—"

Cho nodded. "That, too shall pass."

"And thereafter—what comes?"

"The rise of new lands—among them yours, Ray."

"A long time," said Ray. "A long, long time—many lands, many rulers, Babylon and Crete, Egypt, Greece, Rome, and many others. Even in my time the world shall not lie under one rule and is still divided into many nations, and those sometimes at war."

"The war against Ba-Al and the Shadow ceases never." Cho arose and went to look down the stairs again.

"We can go now, I believe," he said when he returned. "To the temple—"

Ray tried to sit up, found that impossible, and at last closed his eyes while they somehow got him down that steep stair. Twice they had to beat off small attacks before they reached the ruined temple. Pain had returned to Ray. Each step of the men who carried him on an improvised litter sent a throb through his chest.

But at last they were under a broken roof, and one of the Naacals hurried to them. Ray was lifted onto a couch of piled mats and roused under the examination of the Murian priest.

"How is he?" asked Cho.

"He will do well. Now go to your duties, my son. Your sword brother is safe."

Ray gasped.

"Yes, this is painful." The priest nodded. "But such wounds, from such a source, must be well cleansed—"

"I know you," Ray said slowly. "You—you were waiting in the hall—with the light—before—before—"

"Before you came on this journey," the other finished for him. "Yes, that is the truth."

"The will—"

"Was not mine," answered the other. "Now, rest in peace. You will understand in due time. Now—sleep—" That was an order, and the finger touching Ray's forehead appeared to seal it. He slept.

"It's all set." Burton looked down a slope of snow-covered ground to the drifted hump of the mound. "This is only a patch job. We can't promise anything—you understand that, don't you?"

"You've said it often enough so we ought to," growled Hargreaves. "What's our next move?"

"We are able now to step up the entrance power and hold it steady for five intervals," Fordham answered, "beginning with the space of an hour, reducing from then on. The last time it will hold for only about five minutes. And we've scheduled the tries for a week apart. If the mind search can draw Osborne, then he'll find the door open once every seven days—for five times. After that, we'll need another period to recharge, maybe a month—if we are lucky."

"A gamble, pure and simple, a gamble," commented Hargreaves.

"A gamble, yes, but hardly a simple one. This is one of the most complex experiments we have ever tried. A moon shot is your simple gamble—a schoolroom exercise compared to this," Burton retorted.

"When do you make the first try?" General Colfax spoke for the first time.

"In exactly fourteen hours, five minutes. Then we open the gate and hold it for an hour. Dr. Burton activates the seeker according to the equation—"

"And then—we just wait." The general spoke as if to himself.

"We wait," echoed Fordham.

"And maybe," added Hargreaves, "we just go on waiting—forever."

17

RAY struggled up on one arm to look out into the main hall of the ruined temple. Part of the roof was open to the night sky, and light rods were set in the old brackets to illuminate the stone blocks now serving Murian war captains as tables and seats.

"How is it with you?"

The American looked over his shoulder at an approaching Naacal.

"Better—"

The priest smiled. "So you're weary of our tending and would be up and about? Well—" His fingers touched Ray's wrist and hunted for his pulse. "Perhaps if I do not suffer such folly, you will be out on your own anyway." He clapped his hands, and a man wearing the shorter white tunic of a temple servant brought clothing.

With help Ray slipped a soft leather tunic over the bandages that wrapped him mummy-wise from armpit to waist. Over that went a kilt reinforced with metal strips, but no breast plate. The priest waved that aside.

"You will not need it, and the weight is too much for your wounds."

"Cho—?" asked Ray.

"At present he is on duty at the western gate."

"And the city?"

"It has surrendered, save for the inner keep of the palace. When most of the guard discovered Chronos taken, they threw down their arms. Those who still fight are the Red Robes of Ba-Al and such others as have good reason to believe they deserve no mercy at our hands."

"Ray!" Cho came swiftly across the hall. He stopped a short distance off to survey the American from head to foot. "Good—warrior ready. But you have no sword. This perhaps—I took it but a short time ago from the captain of the gate—" He had in his hands a belt and sheathed sword, the hilt of which gleamed red with a pattern of rubies.

"Now—that is better. You must be ready—"

"For what? The Naacal said most of the fighting was over."

"Not for battle, no. But the Re Mu enters the city at dawn. All but the inner part of the palace is now ours."

"And Chronos?"

"Swords from the private guard at the Great One hold him safe. The Re Mu wishes to see you."

And I, thought Ray, wish to see him. There are questions—but whether he would ever get a chance to ask them, that he did not know. That sense of unreality had closed about him again. He watched and listened, but he was not a part of all this. And now no touching of the armlet reunited him with this world in which he stood, like a spectator at a vivid pageant.

He was with Cho as the Re Mu entered the Five Walled City. He saw the white war chariot of the Sun drawn by snorting stallions crunch over the debris of battle. And he even copied Cho's war salute to the Emperor and went forward with the Murian when that ruler beckoned to them.

"I see you, my lords—" The Re Mu gave the formal greeting as Ray again followed Cho's lead and touched knee to the dust of the roadway.

Cho bowed his head to give the conventional answer: "We are yours, Great One, with all loyalty and strength."

But Ray looked up into those remote blue eyes. If the Re Mu read his thoughts here and now, he knew that Ray did not echo that and that his outward show of homage was only that—show.

"Never, I think, has the Sun been so ably served, my lords—" returned the Emperor. "Come to me within the hour—"

"We hear and obey," Cho agreed, and they got to their feet as the chariot rumbled on.

Hear and obey, yes; he had heard and would obey—in this much, but not by choice. And he would have answers—Trailing Cho, the American followed the royal procession into the heart of the city. Townspeople were being herded along by Murian troops, also converging on the center of their half-destroyed capital.

Though the soldiers tried to keep some sort of order and clear lanes through the throng, the ways were choked. Cho appealed to a harassed officer.

"We are summoned by the Great One. How may we—?"

The officer threw up his hands. "Not this way, Sunborn. Take to the lesser streets, even to the roofs, but you will make no haste—"

Cho took his advice, bringing them into a side way and finally weaving an in-and-out route to reach the temple once more.

"Where is Uranos?" Ray asked as they came at last to their goal. He was panting with effort and had to lean against a wall.

"I do not know. He went to the Re Mu last night. If he is as he claims—" But Cho broke off, for they were now a part of a crowd of officers and men drawn up behind a hastily arranged throne. Blocks from the fane had been set together and draped with brilliant war cloaks. There the Re Mu had taken his seat to judge the city. About him was a glittering mass of polished and bejeweled armor, with here and there the plain white robe of a Naacal for contrast, while at the Emperor's right, on a lower block seat, the Naacal U-Cha leaned forward a little as if he were so shortsighted he had difficulty in making out with clarity the scene before him.

As Cho and Ray mingled with the warriors, there was a sharp and demanding roll of war drums, four of them together, standing waist-high to the drummers on the steps. And as that died away, so did the surflike murmur of the throng.

The Re Mu's face was expressionless, yet in some strange way it was as if he saw not just the multitude of people gathered there but each and every man or woman in it as an individual whom he was to judge.

203

Ray watched people in the nearer ranks drop their heads, look to left or right, but in the end they once more raised their eyes as if commanded to do so by a power they could not disobey.

Then the Emperor's hand lifted but an inch or two from the clasp it held, fingers locked upon the hilt of a bared sword that stood upright between his knees, and pointed to the cracked and stained stone under his feet. At that slightest of gestures, one of the warriors moved out a pace or so to his left. Under the edge of that man's helm Ray saw a face that he knew. It was Uranos.

"People of Atlantis—" The Re Mu's voice rang with the same compelling note as the drums. "Dwellers under the cloak of the Shadow—"

A ripple crossed the crowded square. They were falling to their knees, holding up their hands, some in swift abasement, others more reluctantly.

"Forgive—" A kind of sobbing wail, which grew stronger, followed that ripple.

"Some things go beyond the bounds of forgiveness. Look you, choosers of the Dark, upon the stains that stand upon these walls, think you how they came to bear such red testimony against you." The Emperor's sword swung up, and the rising sun caught fire along its blade, making it flame. It pointed to the walls where the Sun-born had had their ending.

"We did as those over us commanded, Great One. Forgive!"

"And I say unto you, men of heart would have risen and put down any who gave such commands. It becomes no man in a day of judgment to hide behind an order that was evil, saying, 'I did as I was commanded.' In each man at birth is placed the knowledge of good and evil, and each day, each hour, is he allowed choices of both. If he chooses ill out of fear or weakness or lust or greed or rage, still he has had a choice, and by that choice he shall be judged when the final day comes. When your forefathers came to this land, they were given two treasures, that they might look upon them and remember the right—" Again his sword flashed

204

and this time pointed to the pillars still covered with the dusty, tattered cloths. "Behold, those now go cloaked from sight because of shame and hate and fear, because you dare not look upon what you have so openly betrayed. Thus did you blot out the symbols of right and justice, choosing rather the cover of the Shadow, some of you following it even to the pit. So must this city be erased from the sight of men—blood cover blood. Is not that justice—the kind you understand the best, men of Atlantis?"

"Mercy—mercy—" It was a thin wail—from the women and children, Ray believed. He saw no man in that throng give tongue.

"And what mercy did you show in your day, men of Atlantis? Think upon that! No, this city shall be as if it never was—and that by nightfall. And you who have made it an abode of uncleanness, what shall be done with you?"

They were silent now, save here and there where a child or woman cried.

"Yes, an abiding place for unclean things have you made this city. Behold, this temple lies in ruins while that of Ba-Al proudly stands. Give me a reason, men of Atlantis, why you should not also suffer the fate of your city?"

"Mercy, Great One. If not for us, then for the children of our courtyards." A single voice raised that plea.

"Harken to my words. There are different justices and differing judgments. You are weak and foolish, but evil was taught unto you—the most of you. It did not spring in all of you equally. Therefore, I say unto you, go forth from this city, taking naught save what you can carry of food and clothing within your own two hands. And be forth of the gates by sundown—lest the greater judgment overtake you in the end."

Uranos moved then and went on his knees before the Emperor.

"Great One, these are my people. Suffer me to go with them, to lead them until they can build anew—"

205

"Uranos, in the past these turned their faces from your house, set aside the rule of those of your blood, to take unto themselves a leader of their own choice, another of those choices that they made freely. In the motherland, honor and a service fitted to you await your coming. In this place where the blood of your kindred still stains the wall before your eyes, do you say this? Do you wish to lead these people?"

"Great One, you have spoken much of choices in this life and the making of them, and thereafter abiding by the results of such choosing. Though I am of the Sunborn, yet am I also of this land, sharing it with these people. So do I choose to go with them, and that is a free choice. Alo, I will abide by all that comes of it."

The Re Mu's sword rose high in the air, then descended to touch Uranos lightly on the right shoulder and on the left. Finally he reversed that blade and held out the hilt, which Uranos kissed.

"Listen well, men of Atlantis," the Emperor commanded. "I set before you now such a leader as you have not had since the old days when this was a fair, clean land. He is of the Sun-born, yet also is he of Atlantis, an Atlantean of Atlanteans, and no foreign conqueror. So I say unto you, cherish him and obey him and abide by such a choice.

"Uranos, Poseidon of Atlantis, do you swear to establish once more the dwelling of the Flame, to walk with your people in the light, warring upon the Shadow and all its legions, to hold to the law and the justice, under the Sun, to be a sword and shield for the motherland in her hour of need?"

"Upon the Flame do I swear it, for me and for my people, Great One."

For the second time he kissed the hilt of the Re Mu's sword and then arose and turned to face those watching him from below. They gave him no greeting, but as he walked down the steps of the temple, they pressed forward. Some went to their knees, kissing his hands, the hem of his cloak. With them about him, he turned once more to face the throne now above him.

206

"We shall obey the commands laid upon us, and at sunset we shall be gone," he said.

The ripple spread once more across the square, and Ray thought the people were preparing to scatter. Only once more the drums rolled, and that summons held them. In the issuing silence the Re Mu spoke again.

"Men of Atlantis, you have come to judgment. Now do you also judge. What will you do with this man?"

The Murians about the throne parted, and a party of guards came through. Chronos, white, his face twitching, his head jerking from side to side, was half led, half dragged in their midst.

Sound then, such a rising snarl came from the crowd as made Ray step back a pace. He had heard, read, of mob fury, but he had never seen it in action. This was as horrible in its way as the Loving One—

"To us, Great One, to us!" The scream arose from a hundred and then thousands of throats.

"What say you, Chronos? Is this justice? Do you wish it?"

To Ray's amazement the deposed Poseidon lifted his head, stilling that crazy jerking.

"Yes," he answered. Did he have some idea that that meant escape, or was he mad?

The Re Mu nodded. "The choice is yours, so be it."

As the Murian guards stepped back, the mob licked up in a wave and Chronos was gone. No scream, no sound, save a kind of worrying—an eddy in the mob—then nothing. The throng broke, streamed away from the square, and the Re Mu rose from his improvised throne and went back into the temple, the Naacals closing in about him. An officer came to Cho and Ray.

"The Great One wishes you."

They came into that part of the temple where there was a stone much hacked and defaced with scorching, a central altar once, Ray believed. And by that now stood both the Re Mu and U-Cha. It was to Cho the Emperor first spoke.

"You asked of us the post of greatest danger, Sunborn. And you wrought well thereafter. Also by your

207

hands was that spawn of evil—that thing summoned from another world—slain. What do you claim from us in return?"

"Naught. The duty was mine."

The Re Mu smiled. "Naught—the answer of youth and courage and what lies in the morning of life. But your naught is not enough. To you the serpent, and after you those of your sons and sons' sons. Come you—"

Cho knelt at the Emperor's feet. From his own war helm the Re Mu detached a circlet of a striking serpent, fitting it on Cho's, while those about raised their bared swords.

"You—" The Re Mu looked to Ray. "Ah, yes, you have that to ask of us also. No, by rights you can demand. Since you did not surrender your will to duty, the choice was taken from you."

"Yes," Ray replied shortly.

"You were not of our blood; this was not your quarrel. In our moment of great danger, we forged of you a weapon of which we had need. If you think all this, it is the truth. I have spoken much of choices and of standing by the result of such choices. We chose to use a stranger who trusted us, and this was ill doing. But for this I have a single answer: my choice lay between the good of one man and the salvation of all my people.

"We could not reach into this land; it was too well guarded by barriers that were not only visible men and steel, walls and water, but also that which had been raised by Magos and his adepts to speedily trip any of our blood daring to venture here. I think you had a taste of their weapons when you were taken at last.

"Because you were not of us, you had certain inborn safeguards we could not hope to develop. Thus we put into you that which we had that was needful to open doors. You were the key, the only one we had."

"Even to the Loving One?" asked Ray evenly. He had not knelt as did Cho. He was gazing eye to eye with this man who ruled most of a world. And now there was no awe between them.

208

"Even to the Loving One," agreed the Re Mu. "That was only the first, the scout, if you will, of an army of its kind Magos would have loosed upon us. It, too, was a key, for each time it was summoned, and fed, it grew a stronger tie with this world. Eventually it would have brought its kind—and perhaps worse—for the place from which Magos summoned it is alien and, to us, always the stronghold of the enemy. And we do not know what other horrors that pit may hold. So you were to be the bait to bring it forth when there was still a chance to deal with it and close that gate.

"And I say that, in all our history, no man ever served the motherland as have you, a stranger. Nor has any man ever faced such evil and held it powerless for a space. It is not in my power to reward you fittingly, for to speak of rewards is to belittle what you have done. But ask whatever you desire—"

"Return to my own time and place," asked Ray.

The Re Mu stood in silence. Then he said slowly, "our knowledge, all that exists, shall be yours. Whether this can be done, I do not know. But if it cannot—?"

"I do not know. Only that I am"—it was Ray's turn to hesitate, to find it difficult to put into words his feelings—"not of this time. It may be that I cannot return, but I must try—"

"So be it!"

As Ray stepped back, Cho matched step with him. The Murian was sober-faced.

"Do—do you hate us, brother?" he asked. "Because of what they willed you to do? I did not know that this was so. But I can see how it would raise anger in a man—"

"Hate—" Ray repeated. He felt no emotion, only a kind of weary emptiness, an odd dislocation, as if he were not a part of life any more but existed in a place not meant for him. A swimmer in the ocean, looking upon all the wonders and colors of a world that was not his own and never could be, in which he was the alien visitor, might feel this way, Ray decided. Since he had been emptied of the will and seen the Loving One die,

209

he had been an onlooker only. And to be real again—

"No, not hate," he said more to himself than Cho. "Only tired—I am tired—"

"And—if you cannot return?" The Murian put out his hand but did not quite touch Ray, as if he, also, felt they were somehow separate and even a meeting of fingers upon fingers could not in any way unite them.

"I do not know—"

Cho's hand dropped to his side, but he continued to walk beside Ray, now and then glancing at him. He *was* tired, Ray thought, and now he went back to that place in the temple where he had been brought for treatment, stretching out on the couch there. Cho had thrown himself down on a neighboring pile of cloaks and was quickly asleep. But though he was so weary, the American could not sleep himself. He shut his eyes and tried to picture—yes, this time *tried* to see the trees, the silent forest.

The Re Mu had offered him whatever he wished. A ship might be the answer, a ship to the north, and then across the plain and into the dusk of the forest—to the place where he had entered this time. And what if he did come to stand once more on that very spot and nothing happened?

He heard a small movement nearby and opened his eyes. U-Cha, looking very old—old and faded in his white robe, as if that had far more substance than the frail body it covered—stood there gazing down at him.

"You were that will," Ray said.

"I was that will—in part," agreed the Naacal.

"But," he added, "the will was less than you held it to be, though you may not believe that, for the strength behind the will was more than half yours."

"But I did not want—"

"To do our bidding? Yes, that is also true. Only, think upon this—when the will had need, there were depths to draw upon such as you will not find among us. Different you are, complex to our measuring, for you have been shaped in other days by a life we know nothing of. But I think that what you are now is not what you were when you stepped from your time into ours. A smith draws molten metal from the heat and beats upon it. He chills, reheats, works. And what he has in his hands at the end of his labors is not what he held at the beginning."

Ray sat up. Under the bandages his wounds pained him a little. And somehow that pain was faintly reassuring, making him more alive instead of only a detached onlooker.

"Do you mean—that this change might keep me here?"

"It is a thought that perhaps you should hold in your mind, my son, for this much I am sure of—you are not the same man who came to us. Perhaps that change began even as you entered from your world and is of a process like unto growth. So—"

"So I should be prepared to fail. Very well, you have warned me. But will you also help me?"

"With all that we have—we know—yes."

"Not here," said Ray, "nor in Mu, but in the north—"

U-Cha looked at him in surprise. "To the north—in the Barren Lands? But we have no temple, no place of learning—"

"I only know that it is from the north I came and there I must return. Also that it must be soon, I believe, or not at all."

U-Cha's head bowed. "So be it."

Then he raised his thin hand, on the back of which the old veins made heavy blue ridges. And in the air between them he drew a sign that to Ray was not visible.

"Let your spirit rest and your mind give ease to your body, for it is not this day, nor tomorrow, nor perhaps many tomorrows, that we can aid you on that trail. Until then be at peace."

And Ray, lying back upon the couch, discovered sleep waiting, a dreamless rest in which no shadows or memories dared to move.

At sunset he stood outside the city in company with Cho and those tough raiders who had guided the Murian

211

forces into the citadel. The last of the survivors from the town were straggling through the inland gates, forming into family groups, then into companies, to trudge on and on, the mounted rebels from the plains forming the guard to keep them moving, while in the city a house-to-house search was in progress to make sure no hiders were forgotten. And it was dusk when the last of those searchers also came forth. When they, too, reached the hills, beams of light shot from the Murian ships offshore, from points inland. There was a crash as those rays met, louder than any thunder-clap, a shuddering of ground that knocked many of the watchers from their feet. And a cloud of gritty dust was caught by whirling winds, drawn up to darken the sky still more.

"The temple of Ba-Al—" Cho caught at the American's shoulder. "Look you to the temple!"

In the rubble the sullen red-walled structure still squatted, to their eyes intact. Again the beams closed, now aimed upon that one building alone, but when they were gone, still it stood.

Then from the sky itself, as if their machines of destruction had drawn some force of nature, came a jagged stroke of blinding, dazzling light. There was a sound to deafen them, and when they could see again, the temple was gone.

But in that moment Ray had a curious impression he could neither believe nor explain, nor did he ever speak of it afterwards. He thought he saw a black shadow, not unlike that of a crouching human body surmounted by a bull's head, flee into the night, drawing about it as a concealing cloak the very substance of the normal dark.

As they turned to seek their ships, a mounted man rode up from the slow-moving snake of the Atlantean refugees. Uranos leaned from the saddle to speak to Ray.

"Comrade, I have not forgotten. All mine is yours; ask it of me. Thus shall it also be with our sons and sons' sons. Should you call, and I shall come, even unto

212

have need—the ends of the earth. Now I must go with my people. But remember, brother—"

Ray's hand went to clasp his. "No debt between us." This he must make the other understand. "Go in peace, freely—"

The fingers tightened on his and then loosed, and the rider was gone. But Cho was now beside the American.

"The ships wait—and also the motherland—"

Together they started for the shore.

18

"THIS is your landing? You are sure of the place?"

Ray could almost agree to the doubt expressed by Captain Taut. There was no marker on that deserted and empty shore, and one piece of this coast was very like another, but Ray was sure.

"Right there," he repeated confidently. He turned his head; it was hard even by so little to break that cord which he had felt drawing him with an intensity that grew stronger the nearer they approached the Barren Lands.

Home to the motherland, Cho had said days earlier. But Ray had known then that such a return could not be for him, would not be. As he had told U-Cha, there was only one road to take, and that lay north. And Taut, sailing under new orders, to hunt down fugitive fragments of the Atlantean fleet scouts, had agreed to set him ashore where he wished.

The raider captain pulled his sea cloak tighter about his thick shoulders. There was a chill breeze, more like the breath of the winters Ray had known in the land this would become. Now he could see patches of white ashore, traces of snow.

"We'll cruise to the east. Light your signal fire when you want to be taken off—"

Ray nodded. That signal, he thought, would probably never be lighted. Best make Taut understand that.

"I may not return at all," he said. "I go to find my own people."

"Ask no questions, and you'll be told no fancy tales," replied the other. "Oh, aye, every man is entitled to his own secrets. There is no colony here, only wilds and things in them such as make for hard meetings, one way or another. There were Atlantean ships cruising here, and some will turn pirate now. Outlaws make their camps back there." He waved his hand to the shore. "Walk quietly, warrior, and keep your hand ever on sword hilt while you do so. We'll watch for your signal."

"And if you do not see it within five days, go about your own business and do not seek me further," repeated Ray firmly.

"Agreed. But then what do I report when I return? That I landed you in a wilderness, that you would have no escort from among us, and that I left you alone here? I think that I would have to accept sword-challenge if I said that. Especially when facing the Sun-born Cho whom you tricked when you stole away from him to come aboard my ship, bearing those orders with you."

"Tell him to ask his questions of U-Cha, the Naacal. There are those who know what I must do."

Ray was impatient. He almost wanted to dive over the side of the ship and swim. But at last Taut did not appear to wish to waste more time in argument. The captain gave orders, and Ray was rowed ashore. He jumped from the boat to the wave-washed sand and turned to catch the provision bag the steersman threw to him. But he did not wait thereafter to watch the boat return to the ship.

Wind and wave had worked upon the sand dunes, but not too far away were fire-smoked stones. Yes, his inner urging had led him aright. This was the place of the Atlantean camp where he had been a captive. Now—

Ray cached the bag of supplies behind a convenient rock. That was only an unnecessary burden and one he would probably never see again. He began to walk on as steady a course inland as if his feet followed a well-marked road, as sure of his route as if that path stretched smoothly-paved before him.

In time he came to the ravine where lay the cleaned bones of the elk. He scrambled up the rise down which they had brought him a prisoner. Before him, against the sky, was the dark line of the forest. There was no sun today. The sky was cold and drear, and winter bit more deeply here.

Dark was that forest, for, in spite of the season, there had not been a complete loss of leaves from the trees, so a dusky canopy still hung overhead. He put aside a withered vine that struck against the crest of his Murian helmet and paused to pull the hem of his cloak from the thorny grasp of a bush.

Beneath the soles of his high sea boots was a moss carpet, its green only faintly touched with brown. As he looked on down those tree aisles, he could see only murk. This was his recurring dream of the forest and what might walk there to meet him. Yet this was his road, and now he had no power to turn from it. There was no will overriding his fears and desires as there had been in Atlantis, but he felt an overwhelming need to go on and on, to reach the place where he had come through time. The need had been only an uneasiness of spirit at first, but it had grown stronger and stronger each day, pulling at him in a way he could no longer resist, even if he had wanted to.

The leather and denim he had worn then were gone. He had a tunic of hide, tanned to fabric-softness, the metal-enforced kilt of a soldier, and over his bandaged chest a corselet of metal. A sword belt weighed about his waist, the sheath rubbing against his thigh. By so much had he changed. He wondered fleetingly what they would think when they saw him, the men of his own time. His fantastic story—perhaps his clothing would give it some credence.

Heedless of scratches, Ray broke through the last of the underbrush that fringed the true forest and trotted on down the aisle before him. He had fled this way in panic. Would he be able to find again the exact spot of the breakthrough? At least that pull on him continued, and he had come to trust it as a kind of homing device.

He was running again, this time into the wood, not from it. Now—now—now—

"Something is coming in!" Burton pushed aside one earphone.

They could see the alien scene on the screen, the

giant trees, the edge of the forest glade. Hargreaves glanced around at the others gathered there. He thought—they didn't really believe it. Until now—in spite of the film, all the other shots—they didn't believe it. You can't—until you actually see it for yourself.

"A reading—give me a reading!" Burton demanded sharply of one of his three assistants.

Each repeated a series of coordinates, and Burton adjusted dials before him, frowning.

"Dalberg—repeat!"

The man to the left reread his figures. Burton's pencil dug hard into the surface of the pad at his elbow as he scribbled. His frown deepened. He added, crossed out with a vicious stroke, and set down another line of figures.

"What is it?" asked General Colfax.

Burton waved an impatient demand for quiet. "Campbell—try—" Another flood of equations was delivered to his right-hand neighbor. Fingers flicked keys; dials were turned. Burton hunched his shoulders, leaning farther forward until his nose tip was not far from that smaller viewscreen repeating the scene on the larger.

Fordham spoke for the first time. "Ten minutes to go on this hold."

Burton looked around. "That may not be enough. We have him—or someone—on the beam. You've got to hold longer—"

"If we do, we'll have to draw from the reserve. And we may blow any chance of another try very soon."

"But we have him, I tell you!"

"You said—'him or something.' " The general spoke again. "You didn't sound so sure a moment ago."

"We're doing this all on a supposition basis, on an equation built from inadequate data," Burton replied. "Naturally we must expect some variation. Well, we do have a fix on a mind now, and it's coming in, answering the beam. I don't think we could pick up anything but your man. We built our call around what we know of him—and him only."

"But you're still not sure." The general picked up a small com from the table to give his own orders.

"Small, alert your men. Pick up whoever comes through, I want him brought here on the double the minute he shows."

Fordham consulted his own dials. "Six minutes to go on this setting. How close is he now?" he asked of Burton.

"Less than a mile. You'll have to switch onto the extra time, I tell you!"

Fordham's fingers drummed on the edge of the panel. Finally he pulled a mike to him. "Let her go onto extra. Yes, I said switch onto extra when the time is up!"

Those trees on the screen, just an innocent picture now, Hargreaves thought. There were men stationed down there by the Indian mound, ready to jump on what was being pulled through, back into their time. This Ray Osborne—or someone—or *something*. It was human with a human brain or Burton's beam could not have snared it, pulled it in. But was it their man or someone whose true world included that awesome forest?

Ray's boot toe caught in a half-rotted, earth-embedded branch. He threw out his arms in an involuntary effort to keep his balance and managed to remain on his feet as he tottered forward into a glade. His hand slapped against a tree trunk, and he gripped the bark. Then—the tree—it was fading! He stumbled again and went to one knee. Shadows whirling in and out, around and about him in a giddy dance. There was a larger shadow looming—heaped earth—a mound—The Indian mound!

With an inarticulate cry Ray threw himself at that. But his hands did not touch earth, even though he could see it. He pulled himself up. There was the mound, but though he drove his fist at its solid surface— What solid surface? His hand went into— through—what his eyes assured him was frozen earth.

218

He backed away a step or two, his hands still up and out. Shadows running toward him from behind the mound, less stable than the earth he could not touch. Men—he could see faces, uniforms, but they were misty. He watched them throw out hands, try to hold him. One launched himself in a tackle aimed at Ray's knees—to go sprawling along the ground, his hands grasping the same nothingness that Ray had met in the mound.

"No—no!" Ray heard his own wild shout. This was the end of the nightmare, the end he had never met in sleep but had to face waking. He retreated again. The shadow men—one raised a gun—fired.

"No!" Ray cried again. The forest, safety in the forest. Will it to return, will the trees back again!

The shadow men and the mound which was and yet was not—no!

A wild rebellion burst in him. And that cord which had pulled him back to this insanity broke. Trees—trees— Ray closed his eyes and thought of trees. Suddenly in his mind they stood, tall, strong, alive again. *Will* it, urged that inner part of him. Remember, you held against the Loving One; you must hold now—or else be lost in a shadow world where you cannot exist. Trees!

Substance against his shoulder. Not daring to open his eyes, Ray put out his hand, and it struck the roughness of bark. He curled his fingers tight, trying to anchor himself to that. A tree!

Salt sweat trickled down his cheeks. Trees—around him trees and not a world of substanceless shadows!

He dared now to open his eyes. Yes, there were trees about him. But ahead—as if he looked through an open door or window—he saw the lift of the mound's sides, and against it men—soldiers. They were more real than shadows now—but that was because they were in their place and he in his, not trying to move across a forbidden barrier. The cord that had drawn him here was broken. Instead he looked at strangers in a strange and forbidden world.

For a long moment they stood so. Then that window —in what, time or space?—vanished. He was alone in the forest. With a gasp, Ray leaned against the tree at his side.

What had happened? He had surely half returned to his own time. The mound, the uniforms on the men, were eye-proof of that. But he had not been able to go wholly through. See but touch not—never again. He must accept that there was to be no return. But for the moment the sheer relief of escape from that half-world was all that he knew.

"What happened?" General Colfax broke the silence first.

Burton sat still, staring into the screen, his fingers gripping the edge of the board before him, a look of complete disbelief on his face. Fordham answered first.

"We're finished—for the present. The installations are burned out—completely." He tapped the surface of some of the dials before him. Their needles remained fixed and quiet.

"You saw him." Burton turned his head, looking to Hargreaves in appeal. "You *did* see him?"

"A shadow—a ghost—" Hargreaves fumbled for the proper word of description.

"He wore armor," the general supplied, "and a sword. Not your man. Or, if he was, what has he been doing— over there? But why didn't he come through?"

"He can't," Fordham answered. "If that was Osborne and we brought him back, he's no longer of our world. There were plenty of theories we studied when we set up Operation Atlantis. You know the old paradox they always cite when one discusses time travel—that a man could go back and alter his own family history and the result would be that he himself would never be born at all. We weren't attempting that type of time travel. But suppose Osborne in some way did something important to the history on that level—became involved in action that gave him roots there. Then— well—he might become fixed in that world."

The general got to his feet. "If you're right—then the same thing might happen to anyone who tried to cross over?"

Fordham nodded. The general turned his small com unit around.

"I'll make my report."

"To suspend the project," Fordham said, rather than questioned.

"To suspend. Maybe we can look through. But I'd advise no going through—not until we know more— much more—"

"And Osborne?" asked Burton.

"If that was Osborne, he seems to have found a place for himself. Unless we can learn more, he'll stay—" Fordham replied.

"I think," said Hargreaves, "that maybe he's not too badly off—always supposing we did catch Osborne in that mind-beam. He's been gone some weeks, lost in an unknown world. When he returns, or half returns, he's wearing armor, carrying a weapon. Apparently he's made a good contact with whoever inhabits that level and found so much of a place among them that he has been provided with clothing and arms. Also—if Dr. Fordham is right—perhaps he has accomplished something important over there. I wonder"—he looked at the blank screen—"I wonder what it was."

"Well"—Burton arose slowly—"we'll probably never know. He's somewhere we can't reach—in safety."

"Not somewhere"—Fordham shook his head—"but somewhen, an uncharted somewhen."

The com in General Colfax's hand crackled. He raised it to his ear. "Colfax here, come in." He listened for a moment and then turned to face the others. There was shocked amazement in his face.

"Report from the Pentagon. A new landmass in the Atlantic, another in the Pacific—not rising from the sea bottom—just suddenly *there!* Right there, as if they had always been—"

"Atlantis—" Fordham half whispered. "But how— why—?"

221

"Ask your computers for a new equation. We plant a man over there by mistake—and we get two continents in exchange. It seems we may have a somewhen on this side, too. Only it's in the here and now, and we have to deal with it. Those lands—if they have people—if they are open—they'll have to be dealt with."

"Up for grabs, unless they've arrived complete with inhabitants," commented Hargreaves. "Perhaps we had better begin wondering about that. Maybe Osborne will have the best of two possible worlds from now on."

Tall trees, but nothing alarming about them now in spite of the gloom beneath their sky-piercing branches. Ray moved easily. He only hoped that he could find his way back to the shore now that the guide that had brought him no longer operated. The sense of security that had come with the return of the trees still held. It was as if his escape from the shadowy half world was an escape from a danger threatening more than his body.

There was no going back. He accepted that now. What U-Cha had warned must be the truth. His actions here had set a barrier between him and the past. Now that he knew that and accepted it, the reality he had lost in the Five Walled City enclosed him again. This was the here and now and was all he had—or needed. After all, his own time had no more to offer—rather less than he had found here.

He was out of the forest, and now he fell into a jog trot. How long had he been ashore? It was still far from evening. Perhaps the raider still hung close enough to see his signal soon.

Now Ray was running, as he had once run from the same wood before. What had the Re Mu promised—whatever he asked for? Now, now he was beginning to know what he did want—a stake in this land. There might be those willing to settle here. But it was his own land, his last link with the past—though he must not hold to it for that reason. The Barren Lands—that name was all wrong. They were not barren—look at that forest, this plain! Good land—just waiting for man.

Overhead, the clouds parted, letting through the brightness of the sun. The dried grasses of the plains turned golden under his feet. Barren? No! Someday there would be cities here, people—

Ray was breathing hard. He slowed to a walk as he came at last to the seashore. But in spite of the pain beneath his ribs, the weariness settling on him, he began to comb the rocks for driftwood. A big pile, enough to make a pillar of smoke once some brush was added to it. Taut's lookout ought to catch sight of it soon.

He squatted on his heels to touch the fire stick from his belt pouch to that fire. He blew it into vigorous life.

Barren Lands—real lands— He thought of that window and the shadows moving beyond it. This was the here and now. What was *that*? Somewhere—no, somewhen. And it had no life for him any more. He threw on some more brush and watched the dark smoke spiral up under the sun, a warm and now comforting sun.

CLASSIC BESTSELLERS
from FAWCETT BOOKS

☐ THE WIND by Dorothy Scarborough	04579	$2.25
☐ THE FAMILY MOSKAT by Isaac Bashevis Singer	24066	$2.95
☐ THE GHOST WRITER by Philip Roth	24322	$2.75
☐ THE ICE AGE by Margaret Drabble	04300	$2.25
☐ ALL QUIET ON THE WESTERN FRONT by Erich Maria Remarque	23808	$2.50
☐ TO KILL A MOCKINGBIRD by Harper Lee	08376	$2.50
☐ SHOW BOAT by Edna Ferber	23191	$1.95
☐ THEM by Joyce Carol Oates	23944	$2.50
☐ THE FLOUNDER by Gunter Grass	24180	$2.95
☐ THE CHOSEN by Chaim Potok	24200	$2.25
☐ THE SOURCE by James A. Michener	23859	$2.95

Buy them at your local bookstore or use this handy coupon for ordering.

COLUMBIA BOOK SERVICE (a CBS Publications Co.)
32275 Mally Road, P.O. Box FB, Madison Heights, MI 48071

Please send me the books I have checked above. Orders for less than 5 books must include 75¢ for the first book and 25¢ for each additional book to cover postage and handling. Orders for 5 books or more postage is FREE. Send check or money order only.

Cost $_____	Name _____
Sales tax*_____	Address_____
Postage_____	City _____
Total $_____	State_____ Zip _____

* The government requires us to collect sales tax in all states except AK, DE, MT, NH and OR.

This offer expires 1 October 81   8117